ARFIVE

ARFIVE

A. B. Guthrie, Jr.

HOUGHTON MIFFLIN COMPANY
BOSTON

SECOND PRINTING   W

COPYRIGHT © 1970 BY A. B. GUTHRIE, JR.
ALL RIGHTS RESERVED. NO PART OF THIS WORK MAY BE RE-
PRODUCED OR TRANSMITTED IN ANY FORM BY ANY MEANS,
ELECTRONIC OR MECHANICAL, INCLUDING PHOTOCOPYING AND
RECORDING, OR BY ANY INFORMATION STORAGE OR RETRIEVAL
SYSTEM, WITHOUT PERMISSION IN WRITING FROM THE PUBLISHER.

LIBRARY OF CONGRESS CATALOG CARD NUMBER: 79-125648
PRINTED IN THE UNITED STATES OF AMERICA

To Carol, my wife, and Janie, my sister,
for their needed faith and encouragement
and, bless them, their patience.

Author's Note

If acknowledgments are appropriate, let them all go to the little Montana town in which I grew up. I have not tried for physical exactitude in this revisitation and, indeed, have taken some liberties with the place and its setting; but, save for the town, this book could not have been written.

If anyone sees in these pages a resemblance to himself or departed kinsfolk, classify him as exceedingly fanciful. It is true that I have borrowed spare bits from remembered and actual persons, and here and there, rarely, used actual happenings — but only as the slightest of aids in the creation of characters and the invention of other circumstances far removed from realities. Fiction always departs from the record. Characters develop a vitality and will of their own. Of themselves they think and do and experience and become like nobody else, alive or dead. Thus it was that my father, who alone may be vaguely recognized here, exerted his own fictional independence and, oblivious of me, grew away from the actual man of remembrance.

It follows that there never was a Nicolas Brudd, a Sarge Kraker, a Merc Marsh or others of contrasting constitutions. They flew up and away from the bushes of imagination.

Exceptions, more or less: Eva Fox indeed was a madam, known by that name, whom I glimpsed a few times in my boyhood; Fatty Adlam was a saloonkeeper in fact, one by nature glad to quit the business; Soo Son, the Chinese, my good acquaintance, did operate a restaurant and now sleeps with his ancestors.

Part One

1

BENTON COLLINGSWORTH stepped off the train, turned and helped little Mary Jess down and then gave a hand to May, who was carrying Tommie.

"Stage for Arfive's waitin', I see," the conductor said, his voice raised above Tommie's wails. He put down the hand luggage they'd brought. A trunk was somewhere in the baggage car. The rest — another trunk and a couple of crates and the china closet and the odds and ends considered worth keeping — would come later by freight.

For a long moment Collingsworth gazed around, feeling more and more as if Providence or accident or his own inadvertence had deposited them at the wrong place. He had thought that the reading of letters and journals and atlases had prepared him for Montana. He had thought observations taken at train stops and out of coach windows all along the long way from Indiana had made him ready. On this last hitch, on this mixed train destined for the coalfields of Canada, he had kept his gaze on the landscape, looking hard through the streaked pane that, pushed up, worked like an open damper for engine smoke and coal cinders always aimed for the eyes.

But he had not expected the perfection of nowhere, the culmination of nothing. To be sure, there was a slab-sided shack that called itself a post office and general mercantile. There were a livery barn and a blacksmith shop hard by it. There were a couple of slope-hipped saddle horses waiting at a rack. There was a log saloon with three or four loafers in front of it. He supposed the team and coach at the barn's hitching post constituted the conveyance to Arfive.

He blinked. There or not, these manifestations that flicked in his vision were lost, just as he and his family were lost — lost in distances the eye couldn't penetrate or, penetrating, recoiled from. They were crumbs on the limitless platter of space. The skyline was so far, yet strangely so near, that not even imagination could embrace it, and the sky so deep as to make heaven remote from a prayer. A tree or even a shrub would have helped, would have given a shred of identity to person and place. But all was nameless desert, inhabited by minute illusion.

And here was home. Here, just thirty miles to the west, would be home.

"Well! All right?" he asked.

May answered, "Just fine."

Fine. Yes. Fine and dandy. A pale, tired woman with a smudge on her cheek and a fretful baby in arms. Fine, with a girl child hanging to her wrinkled skirt. Just dandy, here in the nowhere.

"Come on," he said.

He picked up the baggage and made for the coach and placed the baggage nearby.

"I have to peepee, Father," Mary Jess said.

"Again!"

"And Tommie's hungry," May put in. "He'll have to nurse. Come on, Mary Jess. We'll go behind the barn."

"Dirt on your face," Collingsworth told her.

"Imagine that," she answered, trying, he knew, to lift him

by lightness. "There's Cosmoline in the bag, and, while I'm at it, I'll change Tommie." She picked up the satchel that contained the little necessities and, trailed by Mary Jess, made off, her head straight and brave and real in this world of nothing. He watched her out of sight.

Then he marched toward the loafers in front of the saloon. There were four of them, he made out now, besides a squatted and motionless figure half-draped in a blanket, whom he took to be an Indian even before he noticed the plaited hair. Probably a drunken Indian, if what he had read was right. It crossed his mind that the four men might have come from the same mold or, more fitting, the same barn — manure-flecked boots, abused hats, vests but no coats, faded shirts, saddle-worn trousers, hayseeds here or there. And in their eyes a sharp and watching curiosity, the sun-squinted curiosity of men accustomed to look far because there was little to see.

They saw him, he suspected, as something new on the landscape, an out-of-place man with a full suit and good hat and white shirt and tie and laced shoes. A dandy, they were thinking. Let them think then! He hadn't dressed to be conspicuous, heaven knew. This country was at fault, this new country.

He spoke abruptly to the nearest of the men. "You the coachman?"

With a bare flip of his thumb the man indicated the door. "Inside."

As Collingsworth stepped to enter, an older man came out and stopped. His garb, if little different from that of the rest, was newer and cleaner. He stood silent, waiting, and it struck Collingsworth that there was an air of confidence about him that the others lacked, a sort of emanation of authority.

"You the coachman?"

"Coachman?" When the man smiled, his whole face

5

smiled. It flashed through Collingsworth's mind that some faces did not. "We haven't worked up that far. Nope. I'm just the skinner."

"I don't understand."

One of the listening men chuckled. The man who called himself the skinner turned on him easily. "Aw, shut up, Clyde. Won't any of us live long enough to laugh at all you don't know."

The man who had chuckled chuckled again. "Right from the Bible," he said.

The skinner or whatever he was turned back to Collingsworth. "I'm the stage driver, if you savvy that."

"My family and I want to get to Arfive."

"I reckoned you all did," the driver answered. Now, beyond the locution, Collingsworth recognized a lingering southernism in the man's speech. He had heard such pronunciations sometimes in southern Indiana.

"I'm your man," the driver went on. He indicated the train, the engine of which was gently panting. "Soon as they throw off the mail and the baggage."

Collingsworth looked back of him and saw that his family had emerged from behind the barn. He called to May, "Be with you in a few minutes."

"They're fixin' to unload the stuff now," the driver said. "No other pilgrims today. Might just as well get you and your folks settled." As they walked toward the stage, the driver asked, "You want to ride outside with me?"

"Well —"

"Room inside, though. It's up to you. A man sees more from the driver's seat." He paused as if considering his words, then added, "Any man. Any seat." Again the smile wrote friendliness on all his face.

"Thanks. I will," Collingsworth answered, for it had come to him that he did want to ride in the driver's seat, free of any enclosure, where his eyes could roam and his lungs drink the air. "Drink" was the descriptive word: "drink" as in the case of cider fresh from the press. He breathed deep.

He helped his family inside the stage while the driver undid the tie rope. The driver hadn't identified himself. In the presence of May, to whom he gave a bare "Howdy, missus," a certain shyness appeared to afflict him.

With a forlorn moan of the whistle that seemed to die almost at birth, with chuffings and clankings the train started to roll. Collingsworth wondered whether he was glad to be out of it.

"It won't be long now," he said, once sure that May and the children were settled. "I'll ride up front. Call if you need me."

He climbed to his seat beside the driver. The driver asked, "All set?" At a nod he cramped the team around and made for what appeared to Collingsworth now to be a pitiful bit of possessions. It had seemed a whole lot in Indiana.

Maybe it was better so, he thought, since the stage itself was small — just a box for the shelter of passengers and a side-boarded platform in back, drawn by only two horses. A jerry-built vehicle, he would say, handcrafted some years before. He noticed a whip in the whip socket and a rifle, muzzle down, angled against the seat.

The driver whoaed his team near the baggage and mail sack and got down to load up but first wrapped the reins around a hub to make sure the team would stand. Collingsworth descended to help him.

It wasn't until they were seated again and lined out on a trail that presumably did for a road that the driver announced, "Name's Ewing. Mort Ewing."

"Benton Collingsworth."

"Uh-huh," Ewing said, shaking hands, as if somehow he already knew. "When I'm late, they call me Post Mortem

7

Ewing." His big smile broke again. "It don't happen much because I don't drive much. This morning my regular man come down with a bad case of bottle fever."

"Oh. Then you own this line?"

Ewing considered. "Or it owns me. That's the trouble with getting along in the world. You got to drag so many things with you." He made a little gesture of dismissal. "I wasn't meanin' families, Prof."

"What! I'm not a professor."

"Close enough. Got the brand on you. First principal of the first high school in the county, aren't you? Or about to be? That's Prof to me."

"I'd prefer that you call me Bent or Benton."

"Prof fits you, not to make little of you." Ewing took the whip and flicked a horse that was lagging in harness. "Benton, now, I don't call to mind anyone else with that handle."

Well, Collingsworth thought, as long as he was going to be Prof, he might as well supply some support. "Namesake of Thomas Hart Benton. My family, especially my grandfather, admired him. You might say, perhaps, he's one of the reasons I'm here. You understand the reference, I'm sure."

Ewing nodded as if he did but for a while had nothing to say. When at last he spoke, it was musingly. "Thomas Hart Benton. Huh? Senator from Missouri. Champion of the West. Father-in-law of John C. Fremont, him that thought to be President."

Collingsworth let his feelings edge his words. "All right. I'm a chump."

Ewing turned on him a look that could have been taken for honest astonishment. "Oh, no! It's just that even a jackass picks up a few things." For an instant he let the words float, then added, "The reference, you understand, is to me."

Not necessarily, Collingsworth thought with discomfort. On a foolish impulse he had tried to show off and had been shown up, been humbled, one might say. But the devil with any apology.

Squinting, he knew why the men he had seen wore the wrinkles of squint. This country was too bright for the open eye. On all the miles of it the sun glittered. Near and far the land wore a sun polish, a sun sheen; and all the sky was hard with shine. By narrowing his lids he could see that the soil was not nearly so bare as he'd thought. A low-growing grass grew on it, grass that was buffalo grass, he supposed, though not a cow grazed it. He imagined the want of water was the reason. He did not feel like asking. A big bird flushed in front of them and circled over, uttering a two-toned cry like the last of the world's protests. He wondered what it was until Ewing, as if sensing his reluctance to inquire, said, "A curlew, a gilly-galoo bird, as some call 'em."

His words broke the little tension that Collingsworth felt. "Thanks. I like to know the birds."

"We got a God's plenty of all kinds. Why, a man can shoot a mess of prairie chickens within a couple of hollers of Arfive."

"Mind telling me what the town's like?"

"It's got trees, Prof. It's not like here." One arm swept out, seeming to bring in its circle the whole bald distance ahead of them. It came to Collingsworth's mind that distance — this distance — could imprison or free a man. It could crowd or release him. It could give him wings.

"Plenty of water, too," Ewing went on. "Crick on one side, river on t'other. The town's a comer to my way of thinkin', though I hope it don't come so far as to leave itself behind. There's maybe six hundred people there, not countin' Injun drifters. And how about you and the new high school? There's many a bigger place can't say as much."

"I suppose so."

"To get down to cases, we got two general stores, a good restaurant run by a Chink name of Soo Son, a butcher shop, harness and saddle shop, blacksmith shop, Woodmen's Hall and three saloons, one of them named the Family Liquor Store. I forgot the hotel, which ain't as bedbuggy as some."

He turned his gaze on Collingsworth. His expression was — what was it? — quizzical. "Last but not least is the whorehouse that Eva Fox runs." He caught Collingsworth's look and added quickly, "They can't hear me inside."

"If that's a recommendation."

"Didn't say it was or wasn't. It's just there. But, knowin' your history, Prof, you ever hear of a civilization without whores?" Not that it proved anything, but Collingsworth had to admit that he hadn't. "It's better'n squaws, don't you reckon?"

"I wouldn't know."

The wide, easy smile creased Ewing's face. "Course you wouldn't."

"You didn't mention the school building."

"So I didn't. Figured you'd been told that much already. Grade school's right new, built of native sandstone. You'll have to make do with the Woodmen's Hall until the high school goes up. The money's been voted."

"I know."

"And you know there's a church. Methodist."

"Yes. I was reared one."

"What you don't know is we just got what you call a resident minister. Salvation was kind of hit or miss before, havin' to wait on a travelin' parson to tail it up."

Collingsworth wasn't sure what was meant. For want of anything else to say, he asked, "You've met the new man?"

"Seen him. I hear he's all prayer and grace and glory to God, and repent, O ye sinners."

In spite of himself Collingsworth laughed. A man could believe, as he did, but still appreciate a description, disrespectful though it was, that fit some men of the cloth he had known, men of empty heads and full mouths and sole possession of righteousness. He said, "Not very orthodox, are you?"

"Sure." Once more came that quizzical, that probing expression. "Straight Republican."

The team breasted a long, easy slope; and from the top of it the empty world flowed to an end, flowed to a notched and purple barricade where motion stopped as seas stopped against high and ragged shores. They weren't clouds there in the west: they were mountains, near enough to touch yet forever beyond reach. They were purple and blue and patched high with white. The shores of sleep, Collingsworth thought, and gave himself an F in description.

"The Rocky Mountains?" he asked.

"Main range. Arfive sits twenty mile this side."

A rabbit as large as a spaniel flushed from a clump of grass near the trail and leaped weightless and presently stood up, its upthrust ears bigger than papaws. The variable hare, no doubt. The jack rabbit of the high plains.

"See?" Ewing said.

A half mile farther away, in the direction of the pointing finger, brown and white moved, units of brown and white, a dozen of them, airy as wind, as tufts in a wind.

Ewing said, "Antelope. Good eating, Prof."

"Lewis and Clark called them goats."

"Yep. They got mixed up sometimes. Never did see a true mountain goat. These here's rightly called pronghorns."

Again the range of the man's knowledge astonished Collingsworth. Obviously he had read widely — and gained not a thing in his manner of speech.

As if hunching away from the purple backdrop of the mountains, a purple hill began to outline itself, its features soft at first, muted, one might say, by the farther violence. Its almost uniform sides flowed from broad base to point. Like a cone. No. Like a pyramid. Like a structure carefully planned and as carefully shaped. With a little imagination a man could tell himself that the Divine Sculptor had taken pains with it.

With his whip Ewing indicated it. "Titty Butte," he said.

"What!"

"Buttes, we call 'em. Not hills, Prof." He broke the little silence by adding, "You can see the resemblance."

"And you call it that?"

"Did. But times are changin'. Nowadays, for the good of society and the pertection of pups, there's a move on to call it Breast Butte. Breast Butte and Breast River that runs close to it. It's mostly women — them as have 'em — don't like 'em called Titty. But some of us ain't likely to change."

Ewing fell silent, musing, Collingsworth supposed, on the ways of propriety. After a moment he went on. "What's wrong with a right name, Prof? Titty, boobie, breast — what's the difference? Never could get it through my head. Always, seems like, people got to think up parlor words for words that mean the same. Me, I stick with old and simple. What's that the poet said about a rose?"

" 'A rose by any other name —' "

"Would smell as sweet or stink as bad." Ewing touched up the horses. "Get in the collar, you pelters."

They were going down a slope now, and around and in advance of them the sights were changing. Some gaunt, horned cows grazed here and there. A herder with a dog sat on a little knoll, not far from a band of sheep and the canvas-covered wagon that must house him. He raised a lonely hand and let it fall. A bird, a lark perhaps — *bird thou never wert* — sprinkled a song in the dry grass. No fences yet, though. Not a fence or a building. Ahead and down, a mile or more away, a snarled ribbon of green wound. There, Collingsworth imagined, would be the Breast River. To ask about it would be to change the subject.

"Yep," Ewing answered. "There's the Titty. In flood now."

"In flood? How so?"

"Snow in the mountains, more'n ever I saw. Then come a sudden warm streak and rains high up, one day on top of another. Snow melt and rain. That's the how-so of it."

"Dangerous crossing?"

"Never lost a passenger yet, Prof. Got bowled over just once and wished I could swim, but all that come of it was a bath. No people aboard." Ewing smiled, his eyes on that other time. "I lost the year's load of Monkey Ward catalogues, though. Bad for business and worse for us." He paused, perhaps waiting for a cue.

Collingsworth said, "Oh?"

"Our secret readin' suffered, and that's not the all of it. Head and hind end, what's a privy without a catalogue in it?"

Not much of a joke, a chestnut in western dress — no, in Ewing's dress — but Collingsworth smiled.

They began creaking down a bald hill, and the river came into sight and, this side of it, a rattletrap barn and a corral and a hitching post and an outhouse standing naked and desolate upstream from them. An old man doddered out from the barn. Ewing drew up beside it.

"Gonna change?" the old man asked.

Before he answered, Ewing faced Collingsworth. "Privy up yonder," he said, pointing.

Collingsworth let himself down and opened the stage door, hoping Mary Jess wouldn't say peepee again. It would be revealing enough, God knew, for his females to go traipsing up to the outhouse.

He got them out and spoke shortly, not wanting to risk an announcement of need. "Up there," he said with a jerk of his head. May had the satchel and the baby and, followed by Mary Jess, set off as serenely as a blackberry picker.

13

Ewing went into the barn, no doubt to relieve himself, and came out and said to the old man, "I don't guess I'll change, then. This team ain't fagged by a long shot, and it'll be steadier about crossin' over."

Not until then did Collingsworth really look at the river. It wasn't in flood as he knew floods. It had none of the slow, foul, upward creep of the White or the Wabash. Muddy rather than foul, it was a torrent. Even at the lips of its shores it raced. Creeping was for creepers, not for waters with far destinations. But waters with far destinations had little time for depth, either. The Breast, boiling over boulders, sweeping unbroken when it could, did not look deep. It didn't need to look deep to look dangerous.

Collingsworth made for the barn, seeing in passing that feed bags had been put on the team. When he came out, May and the children were waiting.

Now he could say, "How goes it, Maysie? Feel up to the rest of the trip?"

"How much longer, Father?" Mary Jess asked. The question was not a complaint. The child never complained, even now when so tired she appeared almost feverish.

"Here," Collingsworth said, "let me take Tommie."

May turned the baby over to him and answered Mary Jess. "We'll be there before you know it, sweetheart. You're going to take a nice nap. Then it won't be so far."

The baby smiled his dear and unmeaning smile. Thank the Lord, he'd quit crying. Collingsworth kissed him.

"We got along just fine," May said, "and we are up to the rest. Tommie slept most of the way. I fixed the curtains so Mary Jess and I could see out."

"Great, isn't it?" Collingsworth asked, putting a confidence into his voice that would be closer to truth once they were over the river. "I didn't know my eyes could see so far."

Mary Jess put in, "Did you see the king of the bunny rabbits? That's what Mamma said he was. The king."

"And so he is, and I saw him. Now, Maysie, don't be afraid when we ford the river. And don't you, Mary Jess. We'll be across in no time and hi-ho on our way."

Ewing came scuffing toward the stage, absently kicking from his path bits of harness and orphaned links of chain and a broken piece of corral pole that the old man had allowed to accumulate. Anticipating him, Collingsworth put his family inside and mounted to his seat.

Wordless now, Ewing drove the horses to the edge of the river and checked to let them drink, his eyes studying the restless water. After the first long draft the horses raised their heads and appeared to study it, too, before drinking more.

"All right," Ewing said, his voice harsh. "Get up now!" He spanked the team with the reins.

Both horses hesitated, then plunged ahead. The stage creaked and lurched and ground through the shore gravel and lurched harder in the boulders of the stream bed. Collingsworth found himself holding on and looked quickly back, right and left. No one thrown out yet, thank heavens — but he should be inside with his family.

The horses snorted and felt for footing and stumbled on, the muscles writhing in their haunches; and the water churned and rose hub deep and deeper. May would be trying to keep her feet up from the floorboards.

Midway, Ewing said, " 'Bout there."

It was then that the off horse fell. It struggled up and fell again and, rising a second time, stood off-balance and unmoving. Nor would the lash of the whip get it going.

Ewing said, "Christ sake!" He swiveled around and yelled back to shore, "Have to double-team! Quick!"

The old man shuffled toward the barn.

"Leg," Ewing said. "Good crucified Jesus! You hold the team."

But Collingsworth was already busy with his shoes. "You can't swim." He felt the coach inching sidewise.

"I'm the skinner."

"Skin then!" He had his shoes off. Next came his coat.

Holding on to the coach, he let himself into the water. His toes cramped and curled at its touch. Now, hanging on, he saw May, her face as anxious as at the illness and death of their firstborn. He made himself smile while the water quarreled at his side. "Help's coming. Don't worry."

As he cast off from the coach, her words reached him like an echo. "Benton! Oh, Benton!"

He flattened and stroked, fighting the current. By the Lord, water would never defeat him.

The old man was waiting to help him ashore. He didn't need any help, much less the little help the old man could give. He hadn't lost more than thirty yards to the push of the water.

"I got the team harnessed and outside," the old man said as Collingsworth lifted himself and came, dripping, to dry land. "What's left to do is just latch on to the doubletree."

"Come on!" Collingsworth hurried him to the horses that stood harnessed and tied to the rack.

The old man dragged up a doubletree and started attaching to it the tugs that led from one horse. Collingsworth stepped in to hook up the other.

Too late the old man yelled, "Watch it!"

Collingsworth hadn't seen the kick coming. It caught him in the thigh and knocked him down, and for a bare instant he lay there, thinking his leg might be broken. Something pushed into him from underneath, and he struggled to his hands and knees and saw it was the piece of corral pole. He seized it and rose and limped to the head of the horse that had kicked him and swung it. The pole broke between the horse's ears. The horse sagged in its harness, and its eyes glazed, but it didn't go down. Collingsworth crippled back and finished attaching the traces. Here was one horse that wouldn't kick for a while. He felt the old man's eyes on him.

"Short chain," the old man said, lifting the hooked end of it from the doubletree. He might have been writing a telegram. "Hook to the tongue loop. Pull enough."

Collingsworth took the chain, tucked the end once around his belt and anchored it with the hook.

Watching, the old man said, "God Almighty and Davy Jones."

"Team has to pull me there. Any better ideas?"

For an answer the old man trudged around and untied the horses. Collingsworth gathered up the reins.

He let the horses draw the doubletree to the water, the big chain that bound him to them hanging loose and heavy from his belt. His leg was going to be all right.

To pull alongside the stage and its team, he had to approach from upstream, calculating distance and drift with a nicety he doubted he had. The reins were the thing, the reins to keep the horses on course. He clasped them tight and shouted, "Get up!"

It seemed long before the team lunged, before the chain snapped taut and yanked him along with his belt cinched on his spine. He ran to the chain's pull, ran until he fell down and got up and fell and got up and couldn't run anymore. He could only lurch and go flat and fight for footing while the flood tore at him and new boulders waited unseen to trip him up, to bruise or break foot and knee. He jerked one rein hard.

It dodged crazily into his head that he was like a boy again, running so fast downhill that he couldn't hold up or keep up and so sprawled. The force of gravity, and gravity was the chain that pulled him sprawling.

Now he could find no foothold at all, and the tide washed him, strangling, out of line with the horses. It swung him around on his anchor chain almost against the side of the horse that had kicked him. He grabbed for a harness hold and caught a breath and reined the team dead upstream. Back in line, he could climb to his feet, long enough to set the horses on course again.

He had some of the hang of it now. Resist the chain. Slant backward, feet feeling in front. Snug reins for balance. Drive chariot!

He forced the team alongside the stage team and drove just ahead and pulled up. If the nigh horse hooked to the stage would just stand? He said, "Easy, boy," almost into its ear. He crooked an arm around the neck yoke to steady himself. He went to work on the chain. An infernal impediment, the reins and the short reach of that one arm. When at last he was free, he rammed the hook into the iron loop on the tongue.

He yanked his arm from the yoke then and caught the balled point of the hames with one hand. The reins, held in the other, looked even enough. He glanced back, blinking water, and saw only Ewing, bent forward for a signal. Collingsworth bobbed his head. Above the voice of the water he heard the command of the whip.

They were moving. He could tell by the strain on his arm and the heave of the horse the current forced him against. They were moving, and now he could wade easily enough, and the crunch of iron tires on gravel came to his ears, and he straightened his horses out what little they needed. Looking back, he saw May's face at the side of the coach like a picture held out. The picture was smiling.

Ewing called, "Whoa, now." He climbed down and came forward and took the reins from Collingsworth's hands, reserving his words if he had any.

Collingsworth hurried back. "May, you all right? Children all right?"

"A little wet. I am at least. Oh, Benton, you're a mess." What she meant was, he knew, thank God, he was safe.

"Great introduction to the wild and woolly," he answered. By George, it had been. "Want to get out?"

"Maybe we'll just stay here if it won't be too long. Would you believe it, the baby's asleep?"

He nodded and went to join Ewing, who was busy with horses and harness. "I'll hook up the fresh team," Ewing said, "and trail the spare horse into town, but old Shorty —"

He made a little gesture that Collingsworth followed. Old Shorty stood with one leg lifted and useless. It was bent like an elbow between knee and pastern. Slowly for a man who had seemed decisive, Ewing began stripping the gear from the cripple. "Got lodged between boulders, I reckon," he said in a flat voice. "Must have." He carried the harness to the rear of the stage and came back with a halter that he fitted on Shorty. Not until he had the thing buckled did he say, "You did what I couldn't 've, Prof."

It was his thanks, Collingsworth guessed. Whatever it was, it was hard to acknowledge. He shrugged. "Only did what I could."

When Ewing had substituted the fresh team and tied the extra horse to the tail of the stage, he came around and brought down the rifle. The injured horse stood on its three legs, its head down. Ewing went to it, holding the gun, and Collingsworth stepped closer.

"Truest horse a man ever had," Ewing said. He might have been writing an epitaph in the air. He stroked the horse's neck. "Shorty. Old Shorty."

With a show of decision, of acceptance, he turned to Collingsworth to say, "I'll coax him downriver a piece so's he won't foul the ford. Don't matter too much, long as coyotes and wolves got empty guts." Collingsworth nodded. "And, Prof, will you drive the stage on a ways? It ain't a good sight for women and children."

Collingsworth answered, "No, Mort. You take the stage. I'll take Shorty."

Ewing didn't answer immediately. His gaze crossed the river and focused, Collingsworth realized of a sudden, on the spot where he had clubbed the horse that had kicked him. So Ewing had seen.

Collingsworth had a short answer. "It won't be a pleasure." Silently, then, Ewing handed him the rifle and halter rope.

As Collingsworth started to lead away, the horse hobbling behind him, Mary Jess called from the stage. "Father! Please don't make the poor horsey walk. It hurts him."

He dropped the rope and went over to her and extended his hand and laid it on her head. Her braided hair, tied with two little bows, was lighter and finer than the finest cornsilk. "Don't you worry, honey." How should he say it? "It's just a little way to the finest pasture the horsey ever saw."

He took the rope and moved off, hearing behind him the beginning grind of wheels. Not until he had topped and descended a low knoll, going easy because of the horse, did he come to a halt. The stage was out of sight.

The horse looked at him. An old, slobbery horse with a no-good leg and the mist of pain in its eyes. Pain and perhaps hope underneath, for man was God and could do anything if he chose — stop pain, mend bones, save souls. God will take care of me. Yes. Of course. But God wished he had a blindfold for those praying eyes.

The rifle was slow in getting itself cocked and coming up. Its sights wavered away from the point of kill. When finally it fired, it shook every distance.

Shorty collapsed to the shot, not thrashing once. Only the hide moved, the whole hide, riffling small as water to the touch of a pebble. It was as if each hair had its own death to die. When they had all died, Collingsworth levered out the spent cartridge, put the rifle on half cock and removed the halter. Wolf bait was left. Just as good, better, than food for the worms. The stage couldn't be far away.

It wasn't. Ewing had pulled up when out of sight. Collingsworth tossed the halter in the back of the stage and went around to mount. No sounds came from inside. Collingsworth climbed to his seat and put the rifle in place. To the question in Ewing's eyes, he only nodded. Ewing clucked to the horses.

For miles they rode without speaking, rode silent and westward into the sun. It was, Collingsworth could fancy, as if the shot had shot down all words. He had none to ask about the little earth rats or ground squirrels that he saw.

Finally, as the sun touched the mountains, Ewing said, "I declare. I forgot."

"About what?"

"Grub — and your missus and little one. I reckon they're hungry enough to eat the heel of a boot."

"We'll manage."

"Seldom I have ladies or children aboard, or take so long gettin' home. Men, they make out. But Soo Son will be open, or I'll tail him up."

"Something very simple will do."

"You got that at the house the school board rented, pendin' your pleasure."

"What?"

"Oh, fresh milk, a settin' of eggs, bread, bacon, butter and the like of that."

"That's enough, but who in the world — ?"

"People." Ewing could smile now, and, smiling, say without overtones, "It ain't every day brains comes to our camp."

"And they don't even know me."

The sun sank, leaving a high fire over the mountains, leaving a glory; and below them spread a green valley with the softened shapes of settlement in it. The air was so quiet one could think it was walled against wind. What was it and who wrote it? A *beauteous evening, calm and free.*

Dark had fallen when they pulled up to the drugstore and post office where Ewing got out to drop the mail sack, explaining that that service came first and then he'd take them on home. Lamps glowed here and there, not bright enough to reveal very much. A few men met the stage, out of habit or curiosity about the new prof, whom they'd see wrinkled and unfit for inspection. They stood back, all of them, until Ewing returned. Then one of them stepped forward with him and offered his hand.

"I'm Jay Ross," he said, "and you're the professor." The man was heavy rather than fat. He had a broad face and an open, exploring gaze. In his free hand he held a fat cigar.

"Yes," Collingsworth answered. "But principal, not professor. I've looked forward to meeting you."

"You and Ewing get along all right?"

"Just fine."

"Figured you would." He waved his cigar in Ewing's direction. "We all do on the school board." He chuckled, as if at an absurdity. "So far."

"School board!"

"Why, sure. Didn't old Post Mortem tell you?"

So now it was plain. Now he knew why he had been invited to share the driver's seat. A sounding-out, was it? A sizing-up. A test. A trial.

Had he passed?

2

AFTER DELIVERING the Collingsworths and helping Collingsworth inside with their belongings, Ewing took his outfit to McCabe's livery stable. Because old Rank was out and probably drunk again, he had to see to the horses himself. Such was the life of a skinner, he thought while he stood outside and shaped a cigarette he really didn't want.

He rolled a pebble under the sole of his boot. Once, maybe, before the ice age that books speculated about, it had been a proud thrust of rock. Then the glaciers had taken it and through the years trundled it, and here it was now, big and proud as a pea. He shrugged against the feeling inside him. It was the loss of old Shorty that lowered his spirits. It was the absence of grub.

Down the street the oil lamps of the saloons announced business as usual. The boys at the Arfive House would be waiting for a report, one more positive than he was ready to make. He kept worrying the pebble.

Of all the damn things, Mrs. Collingsworth had asked him to stay and take supper with them! Dishes enough in one bag, she had said. Camp dishes they had taken to use on the train. And the bacon and fresh bread and good eggs that unknown friends had provided! Please stay. Jesus Christ, a worn-out woman in a strange house with two babies and the duffel not yet put away. Some women were like that, but, like potatoes, they were damn few to the hill.

After he had refused, clumsily he knew, Prof had said to the little girl, "Mary Jess, you haven't forgotten your manners?"

Mary Jess stepped to him, with a confidence unexpected, and held out her hand. "Thank you very much for a nice ride." Her eyes, meeting his, were wide and quiet and grave, too grave somehow for a little girl. "Father said your horsey was on good pasture now."

"Well —" He had to swallow in the face of that inquiring gravity. "Well, sure he is. Richest graze ever."

How old was the girl? Four or six? Make it as old as hope and smile at yourself.

He tossed away the unlighted cigarette and walked to the light that told him Soo Son was still open. The place was empty of customers, he thought as he entered. Then he heard voices and a low laugh from beyond the black curtain that closed off the rear. There, in booths reached by a side door, Eva Fox and her girls could eat. Wouldn't do to feed them in public. He reckoned the place was still open on account of their presence.

Soo Son waddled up along the counter, smiling. He was a happy Chinaman — maybe. "Stage pletty late," he said.

Ewing nodded. "Some trouble. Not much. Roast beef and potatoes if you got 'em, Soo Son."

Still smiling, Soo Son turned toward the kitchen. A happy Chinaman, huh? Picker in abandoned gold diggings, ranch and roundup cook and now restaurant owner. No more'n couple or so years ago, he had imported a Chinese bride, complete with Oriental duds and once-bound, baby-size feet. The feet made her totter. Then one day, before Ewing had the contract, she had tottered to the stage and taken off, never to show up again. Not at the time or later did Soo Son ever talk about her. Maybe he was pleased she had gone.

One thing about food put in front of a hungry man — it haltered his thought. Grub came first, meat and potatoes and gravy and bread pudding with raisins in it like good-byes from rabbits. Over coffee, then, the mind could worm around some more.

Collingsworth ought to be here. He should see how proper the place was. In bigger towns a street would divide the saved from the lost, the sinners from the nonsinners, if any. Lacking the size for such separation, Arfive — hurrah — had its curtain. Propriety plus. Used to be, in old Fort Benton, the girls would parade in the afternoon, tempting the appetites, drumming up business for themselves and, one move farther on, for the pulpit-pounders, who rejoiced at remorse. It must be discouraging that not enough were remorseful.

But Arfive had removed temptation, or anyhow screened it. The pure people could eat without contamination. If any were weak enough to want to listen, all they would hear were soft murmurs or stifled laughs, for the whores had been warned to be quiet. Yup, a great thing, that curtain. Without it some good citizen, seeing, might lose his virtue or catch a dose at long distance.

Ewing paid Soo Son and went out. The men at the Arfive house would be getting impatient.

The other members of the school board were there when he entered, even old white-whiskered Sterling McLaine who, if he drank at all, drank at home. Jay Ross looked around as the door swung to, and Merc Marsh lifted a hand. They weren't alone. Fatty Adlam, the barkeep, had his usual specimens. It flitted in Ewing's mind that to them the bar was as central as a corral to a corral-balky horse. The place had the smell, not of hay and horse manure, but of spilled booze and baths not taken.

And here, moving up as Ewing started toward Ross, was Sarge Kraker, the fool deputy sheriff, with the gun proud on his hip that his position made seemly. He had, Ewing recognized, quite a load on.

"Well, old Post Mortem," he asked, "how'd you make out with the sister?"

Ewing looked him over. Without a position, without a six-shooter, he would come down to size — a tolerated no-good who attracted a fringe of ragtags because he was brash. More than his badge, the revolver set him up in a land where common men didn't wear arms anymore, unless against wolves and coyotes and rattlesnakes.

"He didn't break any laws," Ewing replied. Then, answering to the little beat in him, he added, "What he is is no skin off your ass. Not yet." He pushed on by.

The other members followed him to a felt-covered table in the rear where men played poker or solo. It was unoccupied now. Though not private, it was separated from the bar by a narrow archway.

They sat down, not speaking. Their eyes asked enough, more than he wanted to answer. Ross chomped the end off a cigar. Old Mr. McLaine rested his arms on the table. Except that he wasn't, Merc Marsh might have been thinking of business at the Arfive Mercantile Store.

Fatty Adlam came to the table, carrying his great belly lightly, as if, like a balloon, it had nothing in it but air. Ewing ordered a beer and set about rolling a cigarette.

Finally a word came out from alongside Ross's cigar. "Well?"

"You seen him."

"Just a peek." Ross waved his smoke. "And the others didn't."

It was easiest, if least important, to describe the looks of the man. "He's square-faced, medium tall and, I would say, built for action. Not puny by a hell of a sight."

Marsh asked, "What do you mean 'action'?"

"That's what we were scared of, wasn't it — gettin' a feller who'd take low and go down?"

They nodded, their minds probably back on the nights they had spent wondering what kind of a man would teach school.

"Nevertheless," old Mr. McLaine said, "looks don't prove anything."

So they didn't. What was wanted was an untroubled judgment, clear as word from on high, exact as Merc Marsh's ledgers. All right. He was exaggerating. They only wanted assurance. That came first. But beyond it and in him was a kind of unease, a feeling, somehow, of shift all around.

He said, "If ever I saw one, he's a champeen swimmer."

Ross asked, "Now what?" For all that Ewing liked him, Ross had the face of a frog, the broad jaw, the wide mouth and eyes that demanded an answer.

He told them then about the accident and about Collingsworth's help. He told them in full, almost. Why tattletale the abuse of a horse?

"Good. Fine," Marsh said when the story was finished. In agreement the other two went down and up with their heads.

"You have told us something." Old Mr. McLaine stroked his paper-white beard. "Time will tell. But his real qualifications, Mr. Ewing? Did you perhaps catch a glimmer?"

"How in hell would I catch it? Of all of us you're the only one educated."

Mr. McLaine pulled some more at his beard. A fine, old gentleman, retired from the New York bar and come west to be with his kinsfolk, a sometime helper with deeds and contracts and legal advice, but first of all a reader with a library from which Ewing had borrowed.

Through with the combing of whiskers, Mr. McLaine observed, "I know the range of your interests."

"All I can say is I found him right interesting. My hunch says amen."

"And still, Mr. Ewing, you seem not quite comfortable."

"It's not about qualifications."

"What, then?"

"Nothing. Anyhow, I got a lesson in manners."

Ross's boring eyes were sly. "From his missus?"

"Uh-huh. And from another lady, maybe four years old, maybe six."

They didn't ask him the how of it, perhaps thinking he was just joshing — which wasn't the whole truth. "I don't reckon he's one of us or ever will be," he said, moving a hand to take in the saloon. "Not like in here. And he kind of kicked over the traces when I named Eva Fox."

Ross asked, "So you think that's against him? Like we'd asked him to keep his whistle wet and polish his pole? We hired him for class." Ross had two daughters, one ready for high school, one just about.

Ewing smiled a small smile. A big one wouldn't be right. "I know, Jay." His voice trailed off to itself. "Manners. Change."

"Sure, that's progress. But one man cuts such a swathe?"

"Not one man," Mr. McLaine put in, "not one man alone, but time and men and growing up or merely growing older. We have law and order here of sorts, a wide-open law and order which countenances drunkenness and gambling and fist-fights and brothels. And despair and tragedy, sometimes, sometimes too often." The old man shook his head. "I have seen its coming, long before now. The winds are blowing."

"To where?" Ross asked. "I want a clean town, much as anyone else. But don't tell me the winds blow to an end of saloons or a lock on Eva Fox's door." His bold eyes were incredulous. "Not the end of a friendly game now and then."

"No," Mr. McLaine answered. "Not that but a curb. A division, even an antagonism, between mannerly people and those not so mannerly. It is in the nature of things as camps grow older. First, lawlessness, then loose law and order, then churches and schools and social sanctions and, finally, a town, not a camp. The preacher and the schoolmaster are harbingers, and homesteaders will hasten the change."

Ross said, "Christ Jesus, they'll die away, those homesteaders! But all the same we can do with some manners."

Old Mr. McLaine had said it, had cut out and branded it, if not altogether. It seemed all a matter of manners. How you dressed. Where you went. Whether you partook. Whether you paid for a hump or got it for nothing and legal. Matter of manners. Matter of attitudes. Matter of a camp growing up. How-de-do, ma'am, and how are the children and I'll see you in church. Good-bye to the old free and easy. Just as well, maybe better — but it was his age that could say so.

Ross asked him, pushing back his chair, "Goin' out to the ranch?"

"No. It'll keep. Got to see if my stage driver's come sober." At the ranch he could have finished the book about a boat, *Beagle*, written by a man name of Darwin.

Before they could rise, Kraker interrupted. He came up with the swagger of a man who alone carried a gun. From behind him his heelers were watching. His voice was over hearty. "Court about to adjourn?"

For a moment they were silent, wondering like himself, Ewing knew, how to answer a jackass. It was Mr. McLaine who did. "I was not aware," he said, speaking clipped like a lawyer, "that you were a party to the proceedings."

"Can't a free American testify?"

"Only if he qualifies as a witness."

"Oh, I qualify," Kraker said, and grinned back at his retinue. "And here's my testimony. A man schoolteacher! Well, piss against the wind!"

The mannerly son of a bitch! Ewing kicked himself back and got up, shoving against Kraker for room. His voice came out low. "You leave him alone!" Now he had it. He had his report. "He's a man!"

3

"GOOD MORNIN', missus."

Mr. Ewing stood at the door. His smile was small and tentative, as if apology for his intrusion shaped and shortened it.

"Good morning," May Collingsworth answered. She put a hand to her hair, knowing it must be a sight. "Please come in."

He hesitated. "Awful early to be callin'. Is Professor around?"

"He ought to be here any time. He went to the store. Do come in."

He stepped back, saying, "Well, now," but entered as she swung the door wider.

She took him into the little parlor and motioned him to a seat. The house wasn't bad, she thought, but not fit for company yet, not in their first morning in it. It was furnished after a fashion and would look still better when their own belongings arrived. "Little skimpy," Benton had said last night, his good heartiness in contrast to his words. She wished Mr. Ewing had given her time to sort and put away the things they had brought.

"Everything all right?" His hat swung between thumb and finger.

"We're so pleased with the house."

"Where's the little lady?"

"Mary Jess? Oh, in back. She's learning to jump rope. And Tommie's taking his morning nap."

"Good," he said, as if that were the only word he could find.

She searched for something to break the half-uneasy silence. "No driving stage today?"

"My regular driver come out of a sick spell." It was in some exaggeration of ladyship, she supposed, that he didn't mention the man had been drunk, as Benton had told her. "I'm headed for the ranch," he went on, "but thought I'd drop by here first. Anything wantin', missus?"

She shook her head. "People have been so good."

He gave a flip to his hat, dismissing generosity. "I reckon other folks will be comin' by. Can't wait to see you all."

"We want to get acquainted — and soon."

"Yes, ma'am. Now any time I can help —"

"I know. We can count on you."

"Sure 'nough."

A man old but not old. Forty or thereabouts. Weatherworn was better. Weatherworn and, for no good reason, uncomfortable. Benton had called him surprising. She imagined, somehow, that he kept a good part of himself unrevealed — that part that was his alone. But, then, who didn't except man and wife?

He rose from the chair. "Be sure to tell Prof I come by."

Be sure to tell him, as if not telling him would sully honor, or might. It was to laugh, as Benton sometimes said.

She saw him to the door and watched him stride down the front path and swing on a saddle horse. He lifted a hand in good-bye.

She stood a minute after closing the door, telling herself again that the place was all right, if untidy. It was frame, with curlicues festooned along the top of the front porch. It had a yard and picket fence and an old barn in back. Hop vines shielded the walkway to the privy. There was a thing the unmet friends had forgotten — bed vessels. One could fancy, smiling, that they thought higher education erased the lower needs. She hoped Benton had unbent enough to purchase a couple.

Parlor, dining room, two bedrooms and kitchen, where dirty clothes waited, where water was heating that she'd drawn from the pump just outside and poured into a tub on top of the wood-and-coal range. Fuel, the friends hadn't forgotten.

She was putting things to soak when Benton called from the front door. "Hi-ho, Maysie." For an instant she thought he was alone. "Visitors." She dried her hands on her apron and left the apron on. It at least was fresher than the dress underneath.

With Benton was a man — wasn't he the one named Ross? — and a woman in a flowered hat who wore gloves. Benton had his arms full of parcels. "I was lucky enough to encounter them just outside," he said. "You've seen Mr. Ross, Maysie, and here's Mrs. Ross with him. Excuse me while I take these things to the kitchen."

He hitched his burdens, and it was then that a sack fell and a bed vessel rolled out of it, its granite clattering on the bare floor. He looked at May, stricken, while the blood climbed in his face.

May laughed and picked the dreadful thing up. Benton marched past her, leaving it dangling from her hand. To his back Ross said, "What's wrong, Prof? Never seen a thunder-mug in your life?"

Ross — she must remember to call him Mr. Ross — was in a black business suit and carried a derby hat.

"Please come in," she said. When she had them seated was time enough to put down the bed vessel.

Mrs. Ross had hardly smiled. Neither did she show embarrassment. She had, May thought, the air of a woman who had changed and washed many a diaper. Wind and sun or something had etched little wrinkles on her face, sad-looking wrinkles from which she gazed with sad-looking eyes. But her back was straight and her expression not fearful, and she wore her smart and no doubt expensive linen dress in quiet style. Altogether, she was impressive.

Benton came in, still grim, and caught sight of the vessel that now sat on the floor like proof of disaster. And all of a sudden he laughed his good laugh. It sometimes happened that way after little misadventures had vexed him. "Fierce, huh?" he asked. "Fierce," meaning comical or outlandish, was one of his words.

"We do hope you'll be comfortable," Mrs. Ross said.

"Oh, we are. We will be. Everyone's so friendly. Why wouldn't we be?"

"Yes. I suppose."

"Sure, you can't help but be." Mr. Ross apparently felt his wife's words needed enforcement. As if somewhat impatient, he wiped a skull on which, May remarked again, not much hair grew. "A man could look a long time and not even tie this place."

"Men do like it," Mrs. Ross added.

May asked, "But not women?"

"You may find it lonely. Some people do." Did she sigh? "Loneliness and the wind."

"Aw, stop that stuff, Frances," Mr. Ross said.

Loneliness and the wind, and a woman ranch-fettered, work-marked, weather-branded. The years receding like distance. Hope of joys forever elusive. Loneliness and the wind in a smart linen dress. And no love. That had to be it. No binding love.

Mr. Ross bit the end from a cigar, put the end in his pocket and lighted up. When May returned with a saucer to be used

34

as an ashtray, he was saying, "Now, Prof, you got two young ones."

"Mary Jess and Tommie."

"So what do you need? What first?"

"We have what we need, within limits."

"No, sir, you don't." Mr. Ross blew out a thoughtful plume of smoke, then asked, "You savvy how to juice a cow?"

"If I know —"

"Pail one, I mean?" Mr. Ross went through exaggerated movements of milking.

May thought she detected a flicker of distaste on Mrs. Ross's face.

"How to milk? Any Hoosier does."

"All right. What you goin' to milk unless she's a cow? That's first."

"In time, I suppose. I thought we could buy milk."

"Not easy. Not likely. Now and then, maybe. Not regular." He puffed again. "The barn you got here is good enough."

"But pasture."

Mr. Ross quit smoking for a minute and laughed a wheezing laugh. "Pasture? Good Lord, Prof, there's pasture all around. Just turn the cow loose. She'll find grass. And once she knows there's bran waiting for her, why, come milking time, she'll likely mosey on home." He studied the band on his cigar as if to find the right words there. "Generally, that is. But once a month or so — well, you might have to look for her. You know how cows are. Most all creation, far as that goes."

Again Mrs. Ross might have shown the shadow of aversion.

"I am not in position to buy one." Benton was shying away. "Not yet."

"Who mentioned buying? I got an extra at the ranch, half

35

Jersey. Hard enough to get the men to milk one cow, let alone two. You can borrow her. If you like her, keep her."

Not until Mary Jess entered did May know she'd left the back yard. She asked of everybody, "Are we going to have a cow?"

May said, "Mary Jess, you haven't met Mr. and Mrs. Ross."

Before the child could say as much as hello, Mr. Ross boomed, "You bet you are. A nice cow. Come over here, little sister. I been hearing about you." Mary Jess walked right to him. He lifted her to his knee. "A good milker."

"What's her name?"

Mr. Ross held his cigar away after she had knuckled her nose. "Well, now, I have girls, two of them, but bigger than you. They named her Dearie."

Mary Jess clasped her hands. The title to the cow might have been in them.

Benton put in, "But see here, Mr. Ross —"

"Jay's the name."

It wasn't that Benton didn't want or need the cow. It was the thought of involvement, of lessening the freedom which he called being his own man. A gift, she knew, seemed to him like losing a part of possession.

"Well, Jay, then — it is generous of you but not necessary. I'll buy the cow."

And what with?

"Let's let time tell, huh?"

She had made up her mind about Mr. Ross, calling him a boor and what not, and yet he had understood and said the right thing.

"I'll have her brought in tomorrow, Prof. She's fresh enough."

"Do you mean she's new?" Mary Jess asked.

"No. No. Not that." Once more the wheezing, the really whistling, laugh sounded. "Fresh means she's had a baby."

"Oh." Her sober eyes studied the case. "Fresh like Mamma?"

May's head bent of itself. Into the silence came Benton's raw voice. "That's enough of questions."

From under her upper lids May could see that the child's eyes still asked for an answer.

Mr. Ross puffed deep on his cigar and blew rings of smoke and stuck the cigar in the center of one. Mary Jess wasn't diverted.

"I should have said it's a calf." There might have been a glint in the glance Mr. Ross shied at her. "This one, why, he eats grass." He deposited Mary Jess, got up and put on his derby. "Tomorrow, then, Prof."

Mrs. Ross hesitated at the door. "I want to take you to the ranch as soon as you're settled," she said to May. Her voice seemed to carry the lonely murmur of wind. "And, if it's all right, I'll come to see you when I'm in town?"

"Of course. Please do. Any time."

A small smile contracted the wrinkles. Then Mrs. Ross started to turn, thought better of it and bent to say into Mary Jess's ear, "Your mother is beautiful."

They were hardly out of hearing before Mary Jess said, "Father, she told me Mamma was beautiful."

"Of course she is. Didn't you know that?"

Mary Jess retreated a step and pressed the back of her head into May's apron. The act seemed almost defensive and somehow altogether pitiful. "She's Mamma."

❧

Well, it was done, or some part of it. The washing. The hanging on the line. The putting away of possessions. The cleaning of lamp chimneys. The filling of lamps. The care and nursing of Tommie, who looked frail and slept maybe too much. The sweeping and dusting. The visit, made hasty, of the next-door neighbor, who spoke friendliness in wretched English and asked if Mary Jess couldn't come play with her girl. The firing and shaking down of the range. The cleaning up of it. The making of a sketchy meal in between times. The disposition of Benton's purchases, including those evil necessities, bed vessels.

Benton, for what he called homecoming, had splurged on a round steak, which she'd have to beat tender with the edge of a plate, having no hammer. And he'd bought potatoes, a small one of which she had used to stopper the stopperless kerosene can, and canned tomatoes and dried peaches and dried apples and dried apricots and dried limas and Sunday-breakfast salt mackerel and dill pickles, a nickel's worth. Other things, too, all expensive, such as canned tomatoes for fifteen cents or two for a quarter. Did Arfive never savor a muskmelon?

When Benton tried to help around the house — which wasn't often and shouldn't be — he was funny. He couldn't even fry an egg right or a strip of bacon, always using too much heat and ending up with "Confound it!" But he was good about dumping the slops and bringing in coal and wood, though he sometimes forgot.

There was still supper to get, an ample one, for Benton ate well, and a myriad of things to do, now and later, if she set herself to them; but first she would freshen up — that word again, now to be smiled at — and change her housedress. Benton had gone to see a man he called Mr. McLaine.

She felt draggy but would not complain. It was better for everybody if she wore a bright face. And she would be sprightlier soon. It was the first few weeks, held secret for some reason, maybe uncertainty, maybe first and sole ownership, that troubled a mother-to-be.

Tonight, with all the things done that time and strength would allow, there would be bed, and there would be Benton.

All right. Right, no more and no less. Right, and often expected, and right. In her head, as many a time before, ran the
words: *Doubt truth to be a liar; But never doubt I love.* That
much she remembered from *Hamlet*. That much was cher-
ished and true.

She was about to put on her dress when she heard Benton
come in. She hoped he had borrowed a book. He was lost
without something to read. But his footfalls led to the
kitchen and then out the rear door, and she knew he'd remembered about slops and fuel.

He had these chores done when she came out of the bedroom with a smile she had put on for him. He looked her over
and said, "Well!" and smiled, too; and a knock came at the
front door. He added, "Oh, no."

A man and a woman stood on the porch just outside. In a
big voice the man sang out, "Brother Collingsworth, welcome!
I am your pastor, John Wesley Harrison, and here is my wife."

Benton shook hands, nodding. "Please come in."

"And here's your better half." Though May hadn't offered
her hand, he extended his. His grip seemed to want to seal a
compact in righteousness.

In soft tones Mrs. Harrison said, "We're so happy you've
come to Arfive." She was, May thought with a touch of guilt, a
preacher's wife all right — small, somewhat dumpy, faint-
spoken because it was her man, not herself, who had heard the
call and uttered the Word.

"A great boon to us, your coming," Mr. Harrison said in
that big voice, a voice that seemed bigger because it mis-
matched his size. She thrust from her head the memory of a
little man who had been one of Indiana's champion hog
callers.

"We don't have to stand," May said. "Come in and be
seated."

But it was a little time before she could get them to enter

the parlor, for Mr. Harrison had put his arm across Benton's shoulders and was saying, "It's no accident that you are a Methodist. It's an answer to prayer." He patted Benton's back. Inside his clothes, May knew, Benton was flinching. He disliked effusiveness and hated familiarity.

When they were seated, Mr. Harrison went on in his pulpit tones, "We are a little church, naturally." His gesture wasn't quite deprecatory. "A little church, but we have put our hand to the plow."

He had an earnest face, she decided, earnest and innocent and artlessly lined, as if all the furies had left him in untouched dedication.

"Not so small," Mrs. Harrison dared interject. "Ten families, at least."

"And more to be saved. Brother Collingsworth, have you noticed the names of our townspeople?"

Benton answered, "Only a few."

"Well, I can tell you. They're solid American names. Hardly a Roman in the lot. And not a black man in a hundred miles." He paused as if to let the information sink in. "Nevertheless, we are a wicked town. Saloons and — other places. So many souls to be rescued!"

"And bodies, too, I presume." Benton's inflection was as dry as his words. On Mr. Harrison's face showed a brief astonishment.

Already, May suspected, they were on the border of disagreement. Ahead of hell's-fire evangelism and its questionable yield of straggling and individual souls brought to Jesus, Benton put an earthly and virtuous society.

"Yes. Of course." Apparently Mr. Harrison had resolved his bewilderment. "One and the same in a way, since the body is the temple of the soul. Brother Collingsworth," he proceeded, that point having been settled, "you have no idea how refreshing it is to find education joining hands with religion. Too often, it seems to me, our institutions of learning foster doubt if not downright unbelief. I pray for them."

Benton answered, "Heaven help them!"

"Right, and God bless you. Heaven help them. I say to the educated doubters, 'Read the Bible. It has the answers.'"

She watched Benton and kept silent.

Mr. Harrison got to his feet. Mrs. Harrison came up as if pulled by a string. Her voice seemed like the demure anticipation of his. "We really must be going."

May asked — Tommie was crying — "So soon?"

Again Mr. Harrison put his hand on Benton's shoulder. "You will be a tower in the church, Brother Collingsworth." Benton neither shook nor nodded his head. He just drew away from the patting hand. "A tower. And of course we will see you at services Sunday."

"'. . . for Sunday is the fit completion of an ill-spent week, and not the fresh and brave beginning of a new one . . .'"

"What did you say?"

"I didn't. Thoreau did."

"Thoreau? I don't believe I know him."

"He died in 1862."

"Oh, a writer, I suppose. Frankly, between the Bible and religious periodicals I find little time for reading."

Benton almost smiled. "He was a lover of nature."

"Good. Fine." Mr. Harrison spoke with the assurance of regained footing. "But it's hardly the same as loving our Lord, is it?"

They left then, after polite good-byes, and Benton closed the door and turned. His face wore a look she knew from before.

"Encore," he said through a tight mouth. "Jesus rides again on an ass's back."

4

THE ROYAL COACHMAN, Collingsworth decided, worked best, at least for this time and this water, though the half dozen other flies he had tried lured trout almost as well. Not trout but Trouts, with thanks to Izaak Walton. No thanks, though, for calling fly-casting dibbling or for classifying lures under such names as gnats and cow dungs.

A fish struck at his fluttering Coachman, and he snapped back too soon and felt in his fist the message of failure. He cast again.

Sometime, somewhere, someone, some poet, had given later and lovely names to the temptations offered to Trouts. The Royal Coachman, the Ginger Quill, the King and the Queen of Waters, the Parmachene Belle and the Grizzly King. A little thing called the Professor caught fish, too, but its name lacked enchantment. It belonged in the company of gnats.

Now he had a fish, firmly hooked, and he brought it to shore and got it in hand and put his rod aside and felt for his pocket-knife. He slipped the small blade through the trout's gills and, pressing up, cut its backbone. Stopped suffering. Stopped drowning in air.

He had caught enough, a nice mess, a dozen, not big but beautiful. He dumped them onto the bank from the piece of gunny sack he used for a creel. They slithered lubricously against one another and found resting places in the grass and looked at him from their pupiled sides. Silver and soft rust and pupils — their great gift before the last gift to frying pan, platter and appetite. He gutted them carefully.

Once he had them back in the bag, he washed and dried his knife and hands and sat back. It was the shank of the afternoon, the feeding time, and other fish were dimpling the water, which here was quiet, backed up by a beaver dam. A fish hog probably could land a hundred or more.

Milk and honey, he thought, and Moses dead too soon for enjoyment. In less than a half mile, whipping, until just now, only the holes, the bright, blue holes of the Breast, he'd caught supper. The Breast was better than Walton's Dove — but try, if you could, to convince the compleat angler of that.

In a brief time, in the few precious weeks before the beginning of school, he had learned a good deal about fishing for trout. And how much better it was than flinging out set lines or stringing trot lines or, for that matter, still fishing with a prayerful eye on the bobber! And how much cleaner! No messing with worms or minnows or craw tails. Just the aseptic, artificial fly. Here, while admiring the language, he inclined to leave Mr. Walton: "But if you be nice to foul your fingers, which good anglers seldom are . . ."

A V'd riffle troubled the water, its dark point moving with purpose; and now he could see the legs working and the flat tail idle in tow. A beaver, his first one, unmistakable. He breathed softly, not moving until the pistol spank of the tail startled him. Left to see was only a wash in the pond, a riffled memory of what might have been. The trout started rising again, and the out-of-sight fledgling magpies that had been trying their voices resumed their practice.

He saw himself in another time, looking for beaver sign and setting his traps and in his hunt giving names to strange streams and finding passes that later generations would travel. But for beaver he might not be here himself. He saluted the dying riffle, glad that one of his creditors lived.

If that former time was good, this time was good enough, this time and this place. That poor, often-right, sometimes-eloquent New Englander, Thoreau, whose aim was a life with wide margins and whose feet, left to themselves, always pointed him west but didn't carry him far. Here were his margins. Here was his west.

Collingsworth twisted his head around and gazed beyond the open bank that he sat on, not to make sure but to see again. There was the purple wall of the Rockies, spired in the yonder of yonders, distant but as close as one's yearnings. And there, hard against vicissitudes, stood Elephant Ear Butte like proof of forever. To the east, beyond the grown screen of the pond, the Breast Valley lay gentle. Beyond the mere saying, a man could fall in love with a country.

He almost had it. It was there almost for the reaching — no, for absorption — the ultimate why of the world, the answer, the revelation. Wait. And wait uplifted, this close to knowing. Wait and look on valley and pond and peak and feel the touch of the sun.

In other years and other places farther from disclosure he had sat with Charlie, neither of them speaking, and felt the breath of intimation while his bobber rode the water.

Charlie's slow words weren't said to break the spell. "Nice, huh, Bent? Nice."

"Nice."

Charlie, older brother, Big Bear to everyone, first in fun and first in fights and fierce in name of family. Charlie, the immortal, who had gone to fight the Spanish and been shot down by syphilis and never took to sea.

"Nice, huh, Bent?"

"Nice."

He was too young to know, his parents had seemed to think. Just don't talk about it and don't speak of Charlie's illness to outsiders even if they ask about it. Just say he's getting well. But even now his mind could see the evil chancre Charlie showed him when no others were about. And he could see the later rash and Charlie's eyes sunk deep, and he could hear the voice, once bold and cheerful, saying:

"Take a lesson from me, Bent. See how I'm paying for my fun. Bent, little brother, keep your tallywhacker in your pants."

Every day the village doctor came, an old befuddled man who mostly shook his head and lacked faith in his own prescriptions.

It wasn't syphilis that killed Charlie, though: chronic malaria won the race — which may have made his passing more respectable. Still, reason might argue that the wages of sin should be levied by a related collector.

Why, Collingsworth wondered now, should his mind have swung from high to low. Heaven knew that in his growing up he had dwelt enough on chancres and rashes and shameful disease. He had been terrified by the thought of them but, don't forget, disciplined, too. Weigh fear against discipline and count discipline a net gain.

Charlie, made whole, sat with him on the bank again under the soft, close Indiana sky. God was good, and this time was nice; and from the rear came a voice.

"What you doing, Prof? Just chewing your cud?"

Jay Ross sat a saddle horse, a fly rod in one hand. He wore a stained, open vest. Fishhooks without feathers stuck from the band of his battered hat.

"Hello, Jay. Guess so. Chewing so hard I didn't even hear you ride up."

"How they biting?"

"I never saw the like."

"Good. You're afoot, of course."

"What else? And why not? It's hardly more than a stroll back to town."

"Sure," Ross said, and for an instant was silent, his mind on some matter. "Being so close to my ranch house, you could have dropped in."

"Sorry, Jay. I cut in south of your house, not wanting to bother you."

" 'S 'all right. But I got hired hands to do the work."

Ross thrust a thumb and finger in his vest pocket and brought out a piece of bait and hooked it in place.

Collingsworth asked, "What are you using?"

"Grasshopper heads. They're hunky-dory."

"Why just the heads?"

Now a smile split Ross's squat face. "You, an educated man, asking me that, Prof! What does a grasshopper do? He hops, don't he? Gets out of your pocket and away from your fingers often as not. Ever see a head hop?"

Still smiling, Ross kicked his horse into the water. When it was knee deep he started casting. The baited hook landed gently, with no slap of line, and almost at once a fish took it. He brought it in and up and disengaged it and dropped it in a sack looped over the saddle horn, where it flapped as a killed trout did not.

Collingsworth picked up his catch. "Good luck, Jay. High time I was starting for home."

"So long," Ross answered while he hooked on a fresh grasshopper head. "Remember to drop by whenever you can, you and the family. Oh, hell, I forgot. Just tell me when, and I'll drive a rig in. Any time." He added as if here were a thing beyond comprehension, "The wife, she gets lonesome."

Walking away, Collingsworth thought he knew why. Ross spent too much time in town, often at cards, it was said. For company Mrs. Ross had the two daughters, who would be in and out, here and gone and self-concerned in the manner of youth. She had them and the wind, loneliness and the wind, as she had told May.

But there was something pathetic about Ross, about this assured, bold-eyed man who seemed not to understand. Call him a vulgarian, if you wished, but an honest vulgarian unconscious of his insensitivity. In his repeated invitations to drop by the house, to come out for dinner, there could be a sort of appeal. There could be a wish for undefined help. Whatever he was, number him as a friend. And be glad.

He pushed through a thicket and saw the town lying mellow in the long light of late afternoon, and it occurred to him that, without his willing so, his spirit had lifted again. Ross was wrong: heads hopped. Gone were Charlie and his illness and the old fears he'd lived with. At his side was a pretty catch, and the sun warmed his back, and the deep sky was glory. A man could fall in love with a country. One had.

He was amused to find himself singing, not loud:

> The shades of night were falling fast,
> Yip — i — dee,
> Yip — i — da,
> As through an Alpine village passed,
> Yip — i — dee — i — da —

To the valley about him, to the mountains behind, to the sky above, he yelled, "Excelsior."

He strode through the thigh-high redtop in the bottom, through the thigh-high timothy growing wild and quickened his pace toward home. May would be there.

5

It was a good day, not hot, not cold, just comfortable, Mort Ewing reflected as he climbed into his buckboard and sat down and idled a minute. The country could stand a rain — hell, Montana always could — but there was moisture enough for the time, barring a dry wind from the southwest. Though the ridges had turned summer tan, the mown fields had greened up.

The two hands he'd kept on after haying was over sat in the sun on a bench outside the bunkhouse, digesting the noon meal and smoking away the few minutes of leisure left. A hen announced she had laid an egg. Of all creatures he knew, it was only a fool chicken that sang of a drop.

Before he clucked to the team, he spoke again to Dunc Mc-Donald. "Positive you jotted down everything?"

McDonald grinned and took his hand from a corral pole to reach for his sack of tobacco. "Positive, boss. You sure you got the list?"

Ewing felt in his vest pocket. "Right there."

"Don't forget the thread for the missus. Last time she blamed me."

"If that's all you ever get blamed for —"

Turning, McDonald said, "Ought to get the last of the stacks fenced today."

A good foreman, a good man with a good wife who knew how to fix grub. Lucky to have them. Lucky to own a better-than-fair ranch, two solid houses, one occupied by McDonald, and a bunkhouse and whatever was necessary, all kept up and tidy. Ewing spoke to the horses.

"What you want with a gravel bar?" old-timers had asked when he filed on the home place. "You're sure hell for rocks," they had said when he added to it. They hadn't imagined, perhaps because of the cost, that the Titty could or would be drawn on to water it; and they hadn't known and he couldn't be sure that gravel bar plus irrigation added up to wild hay. Everybody knew now.

The horses trotted along, used to the road through the one or two trips to town every week. Off to the sides cows turned their slow looks on him, and spring calves suckled or followed suit, the R5 prints of the branding iron still showing bold on their young hides.

An old codger with plenty of money, he thought; and he would stock up at Merc Marsh's store and have a drink or two and maybe play poker at the Arfive House and maybe — just maybe — naw, not Eva Fox. A man's mind ought to grow old along with his body, for Christ sake. What's more, he ought not to embarrass the school or the Collingsworths, though he guessed Eva could keep up with Prof in talk about books. She had taught in a couple of camps to the south of here until the good people had found she had too hot a crotch for the class-room. So she'd gone to paid whoring, likely without shame or apology, and in time set up a house in Arfive, where the need was great in spite of some willow-smoked squaws. So what of it? It was to be expected. It was inevitable, the more so in a place where the tally of men against women ran maybe two to one. You might say it was necessary. It was better than the rape of your fillies, good people, better even than the rape of an Indian girl that the law didn't torment or hang you for, Indians being Indians.

There came to mind a time long ago when he had been riding with some young, randy harum-scarums who knew the customs; and they had flushed a lone Indian girl from a choke-cherry patch, and all but him had charged after her, the followers shouting to the lead rider.

Their old, their young cries sounded again. "Catch her! Catch her, Jake, before she sands!"

Watching, he saw the girl run, saw her, before Jake ran her down, snatch up a handful of soil, hoist her skirt and jam the dirt into herself.

Dismounted, Jake slapped the girl to the ground and got back on his horse, but before they rode on he asked as if nobody in his senses could answer, "What do they want to do that for? Goddam!"

They went away grumbling but agreed on one point: as a book might put it, sex and sand were not compatible.

Better, he reflected now, to have Eva Fox and her house — which was a long way from claiming that everything at Arfive was jim-dandy or ever would be, new high school or not or whatever. According to possibilities a man could stand up for improvement and sit down for reform.

He pulled to the hitch rack at the side of the Arfive Mercantile, tied the team and went in. The place was a clutter of canned goods and dry goods and work clothes and pitchforks and assorted containers, and it smelled, not unpleasantly, of coal oil and cured fish and candy and leather and of a wheel of cheese freshly cut into.

Merc Marsh came up and gave him the time of day. He was a small man, and prudent, who wore black sleeve protectors at work and an eyeshade with a band that hugged an always sharp pencil. He hadn't really wanted to be on the school board, maybe fearing that matters might come up detrimental to business.

"Here's a list of things," Ewing said. "The rig's out at the side. Reckon one of your boys will load up the plunder?"

"Of course. Of course, Mort."

Marsh took the list and stood fiddling with it as if he had more than the order in mind.

Ewing asked, "Some notion in your noodle, Merc?"

"Nothing important." Marsh gave one little shake of his head. "Brother Collingsworth seems to be making out."

"Brother Collingsworth?"

"That's what the preacher calls him. Seems he's going to teach the Bible class and sing in the choir. According to the reverend, I mean."

"So? I didn't look for him to sing 'Sweet Adeline' at the Family Liquor Store."

"No. Sure not. But what old Mr. McLaine said in the first place kind of bothers me. You know, about change and the town choosing up sides."

"Shoulder your blunderbuss, Merc! Tomorrow comes gunplay." Ewing paused. "Hell!"

Marsh said, "All the same, I don't like change."

"It comes slow, like gray hair and rheumatics and the coolin' off of your breeches."

Marsh wasn't amused. "I just hope our Prof isn't too forward."

"Nor backward, neither." Ewing let himself smile. "No plus or minus, eh, Merc? Just a plain cipher."

"Just a good teacher."

"He'll be that, I bet, and maybe more. Anyhow, I got to foot it. Don't forget the order."

As Ewing started away, Marsh's voice halted him. "Nicolas Brudd's in town."

"Up goes the price of whiskey, by glass or by jug. Is that it?"

Marsh shook his head. "Just renewing acquaintance with customers and also asking around, wanting to get up a game."

Ewing walked away, saying over his shoulder, "Pretty rich for a piker."

It was, too, he thought as he made for the Arfive House. Nicolas Brudd, bigwig from Great Falls, wholesaler with almost a corner on what whiskey came to Arfive, sharp poker player whose constant and fifth ace was his bankroll. In no-limit and even table-stakes games his big bets stayed not-so-fat players. All in the game, boys.

Brudd was alone at the bar, talking to Fatty Adlam, when Ewing entered. Once inside, Ewing paused.

"Come in," Adlam said. "I might start a saloon."

"Waitin' on my eyes, you keep it so dark."

Waiting, he put Brudd together — chicken-hawk nose over gray line of mustache, head bald as a china knob under that hat, indoor and grubworm complexion, sagged shoulders, rich belly, rich watch chain, rich boots. It slid through his mind, not for the first time, that here was something unpleasant to think of the touch of, like that of an oyster against the bare skin.

"Buy you a drink," Brudd announced. He held out his hand as Ewing approached. They shook.

"Thanks. Just a beer, Fatty."

"I been telling Adlam a little about how to run a saloon," Brudd said. His tone and manner seemed only part joshing. Adlam drew a beer.

"Place suits me," Ewing answered. "Best stopover in camp."

Adlam had time to say, "Thanks, Mort."

"None so good it can't be better." Brudd kept his voice on the edge of agreeable. "Look here," he went on. "I'll tell you.

A good saloon man, he promotes business. Let a slow crowd come in, and he sets out a round on the house. Same thing if later the party seems likely to tail off. He lets the roof leak again."

"What difference to you, Brudd?" Ewing asked. "Here's how." He lifted his beer. "You sell to all three saloons. You got the whole town sewed up."

Brudd replied, "How," and drank.

Adlam put his hands on the bar. They were small, neat hands, like the starved tips of his heavy forearms. "I do not choose to run my business your way," he said to Brudd. "I will not push for profits if it means getting customers drunk. Drunks are bad medicine regardless of money."

"Christ help the kindhearted."

"But seeing it's you two," Adlam continued, "have a drink on the house."

He served them and stood silent. He must be too fat for comfort, Ewing reflected, yet he moved with light ease, and his hands had light grace. And what was strange to such poundage was dignity.

"Do business your way then, Fatty." Under the chicken-hawk nose a smile spread the thin line of mustache. "I was just trying to help." Brudd straightened and faced the door. "Any live ones around?"

"Jay Ross was in earlier. Said sometime today he'd hook up with Judge Secrest."

"You for a quiet game, Ewing?"

Ewing shook his head. "Thanks."

Brudd walked toward the door. "I'll see what I can round up."

After he had gone, Adlam asked, "How would you grade him?"

"Same as you. Not might-and-main dangerous. Likes money, no matter how got."

"Likes it enough, was it there, to tank up the town, mammas and babies included."

"Why, sure."

Adlam sighed, leaving himself looking shrunken by more than the breath. "It makes a man wonder — a man in my spot."

"It makes a man wonder."

After another sigh Adlam asked, "Crib?" and at Ewing's nod reached to the back bar for the cards and the cribbage board.

They played half a dozen games, chicken-feed games, and then Ewing called quits. He had time for an afternoon bite at Soo Son's before dusting off to the ranch.

Walking to the restaurant, he guessed he should have called on the Collingsworths. Now the hour was too late, and, besides, he didn't reckon Brother Collingsworth would appreciate him showing up with beer on his breath.

There were just two other customers at the Chink's, drummers by the looks of them. Ewing took a stool and returned Soo Son's smile. "Pie and coffee," he said.

"Apple?"

"No question, Soo Son. That's all you got."

"Not light," Soo Son answered, and reached to the board behind him. He held out an envelope and with the other hand gestured toward the curtain hung between light and darkness. "To you, soon you come, she say."

"Pie and coffee, Soo Son."

On the envelope, written in a sure hand, appeared:

Mr. Morton Ewing
Kindness of Soo Son

Inside were just a line and the name he knew would be there.

Please, Mort, see me.
Eva

6

If a man wanted to talk to Eva Fox privately, he went up the side steps and knocked at an unlighted door. Beyond the door was a small sitting room into which Eva retreated to rest or to read or to enter in her journals the number of tricks turned by the girls or to talk business unconnected with bed.

Ewing mounted the steps, just as well satisfied that the darkness pretty well hid him. Not so long ago, he thought, he wouldn't have cared. He didn't give too much of a damn now, just enough of a damn not to want to walk open. Mark it down funny.

He knocked twice without answer and then tried the knob. The door swung to his push.

The lighted room was just as remembered. There were a desk and a chair and an easy chair and a sofa and a bookcase crammed full. A couple of pictures decorated the walls. She had always been a great one for drawings of castles. It was a foolishment to imagine she dreamed herself into one of them, palace mistress of a bevy of whores. The floor had a carpet on it and a bearskin with raised head and glass eyes and ivory teeth opened wide for a bite, the gift maybe of some former admirer, himself maybe gone, along with hide, eyes and teeth.

Eva must have got wind of him, for on a low table sat a bottle of whiskey, two glasses and a pitcher of water. On it, too, rested a small, engraved cowbell which, he knew from before, came from France. He poured a drink and sat down.

It was early yet, too early for much in the way of high jinks. The voices and laughter that sounded from beyond an interior door were subdued, and the piano was silent. He guessed there were a couple of young fellows in there, feeling their oats but shy about sowing them. A few drinks, and they'd be loud and lusty. Trust the girls to oblige with the booze.

The old saying was that a man had it made if he treated the nice girls like whores and the whores like nice girls. Like other wisdom, it wasn't so wise. Like honor thy father and mother, no matter how mean.

He picked up the bell. It rang to his one shake, rang not loud but pure and reaching and fetchful as a man might expect of the Gabriel horn. Almost before it quit singing, Eva came in.

"It's good of you to call, Mort," she said, offering her hand. "Sit down. Sit down. Of all the men in Arfive you're the only one who uncovers and gets up when a lady approaches."

"Not quite," he said, and settled back in his chair. "The new schoolteacher would."

For a second the words seemed to stop her, seemed to put in her eyes more than the mere comment called for, but all she said was, "Oh." She rounded the desk and took her businesswoman's chair and looked at him.

Both time and her trade had been kind to her. Always a sizable woman, she weighed only a pound or three more than he first remembered, and her face was still cleanly defined and had none of the puffiness that so often seemed to afflict the profession. Even in repose it was lively, and her brown eyes, even level-aimed, eloquent. Another woman would have worn frilly clothes. She wore a black outfit high in the collar and relieved it with just one white breastpin. No necklace, no bracelets, no rings. A man never close to her might have thought her unwomanish.

She said, "Sweeten your drink, Mort, and pour me one, please."

"Two fingers and two fingers of water."

"Good memory."

After he had fixed the drinks and sat down, she said, "You've come a long way in life, Mort." As if to prick him, she added, "Even the town's named after your brand."

"Aw, stop it. You know the town was named before ever I bought that old brand. But did you call me here just to puff me up? No."

She put her elbows on the desk and rested her chin in her hands, taking time for her answer. "Did I ever ask you a favor, Mort?"

"I'm obliged to you, if that's what you mean."

"It isn't." Again she appeared to hunt words. "What good is your money to you?"

"To spend. To be comfortable on. To see to my old age and bury me proper. Now what in hell's the idea?"

"You never married and so gave a poor girl a home."

He had to smile. To irritate her, he asked, "You want to get married?"

"Jesus Christ, no!" If she got worked up enough, her language would jump clean over the fence.

"Then who's the lucky lady?"

"You never got on a ripsnorting spree and threw your money around."

"Not lately. Should I?"

"And never sat in a game that lost you even your saddle."

He rose to pour two more drinks, knowing Eva wouldn't come to her point until she got good and ready. No good to prompt her. No good to push. Be patient. Let her come to the end and be done. He skirted around the ivory teeth of the

57

bear and the glaring glass eyes, saying, "That's an ugly bitch of a thing."

Eva might not have heard him. She just nodded in thanks as he set her glass down.

He moved back to his chair. "Next chapter."

There was a little silence. "Mort, how long have you lived in this country?"

It was an idle question, and he answered her idly. "All my life. Born in Kentucky, baptized in Oklahoma, consecrated in Texas, sanctified in Montana. What else?"

"You got here early," she said, as if she had not heard him. "You were smarter than most men and still are. Better educated, though you stick to your old cowpuncher lingo. And more industrious than most. You arrived at the right time, and you saw farther and did more."

"That's handsome, Eva. Dock off a few words and chisel the rest on a rock."

She leaned forward. "And you hogged the water!"

"Hogged nothing! There's a law that reads first in time first in right."

"And you had the first and biggest of the big ditches, and you hogged the water."

"Do I have to explain what you already know? I took what I needed, sure, and maybe a little to boot. But the court's acted. The river's adjudicated. My rights to my water stood and stand up." He paused, wondering at the drift of all she had said. "What's the idea, Eva? You tell me I never got married, never got stumble drunk, never pissed off my roll at a card table. Guilty on all counts, your honor. That adds up to a water hog, does it? What I did was build up my own place. My men are well paid, my word is good, and no one can say that ever I crooked him. I've never been sued, much less damned by the law."

Her voice was softer than her leveled gaze. "There's a law against fraud, I believe."

"Why, sure thing."

The fingers of one hand played on her desk, going one two three four five, one two three four five. "That's how you got most of your land, by fraud. No-good cowpunchers filed for you in their names, ranch hands, drunks, even businessmen, people who hadn't the get-up or means or desire for homesteads and ranches and were glad to transfer their titles to you in return for the dollar an acre you paid them."

It had been hard to hold in and allow her to finish. When she had, he said, "Good God Almighty, woman, that was the way of it everywhere. That's the way of it still, what with the free range going or gone. How else put together a ranch? My titles are good. Fraud, my ass!"

"You might read your land laws."

"You might tend to your whorehouse?"

Of a sudden she laughed. Hers was a big woman's laugh, a sort of timed chuckle like the sound of a flushed prairie chicken. He felt the fizz leaving him, but before it was gone he said, "That loop you're swinging won't fetch many favors."

She answered, "I hope so," and counted her fingers some more. "Mort, you're a good man. I guess you're the best man I ever met. But when have you looked at yourself?"

"This morning, shaving. Can't say I fell in love."

"You didn't see a lucky man and a shrewd one, with land in his name and beef on the hoof and money enough? You didn't see any self-satisfaction?"

"Just the same old map."

She put her hands together and looked at them and sighed and said, "Maybe I've gone about this all wrong. Maybe I shouldn't have lit into you. I wanted you to see yourself. I wanted you to feel thankful — and guilty to boot."

"Thankful to who?"

Her hands came apart in an open gesture. "How do I know? To this country, to good breaks, to your pa and ma having a lay and accidentally teaming up on a mind that you didn't build. Someone deserves something because you got so much."

"Good Christ," he answered, partly faking outrage, "you talk like a Socialist. I'd have you remember, ma'am, I'm straight Republican."

"Straight Ewing."

"Or you talk like something out of a book. One of Bret Harte's fool stories, maybe. The big-hearted outcast. Eva, the role doesn't suit you."

"Don't you think it might, for once?" A shadow fell on her face. "Don't you think it might, for once, for both of us?"

"Eva, if you're hard up, if one of your girls has a bad dose —"

She waved that talk aside. "I may be hard up but I take care of my girls."

"All right. What is it?"

"I know you're an honest and just man, Mort, but how long has it been since you went out of your way to do a kind and generous thing?"

"The Good Samaritan don't tally his charities."

"There are reasons I can't do it myself — money, reputation, influence."

"Remember to prod me when you get to your point." He came to his feet and mixed drinks for them both. Back in his chair he said, "Lot of dusty words on the trail to the railhead."

"It's a girl," she announced then.

"One of yours?"

"No, but she's in the house."

"Well, tits on a snake."

"Uh-huh. True all the same."

She sipped slowly on her drink as if lining her thoughts out, point, swing and drag. While he waited for her to go on, he rolled and lighted a cigarette.

"She's all alone, Mort, with never a soul on her side unless you count me. A stranded, lost orphan of fifteen or sixteen. A kid without kin. Goddam, but it makes me mad."

She was so sore put that he had to leave off his fluff talk. "Go ahead, Eva. I'm riding along."

"Her father was one of those itinerant editors, the kind with a shirttail of type and a headful of classical references — just enough stuff to put out a newspaper in camp after camp. Always it was go bust and go on."

"To puff up a new Eden until he ran out of apples. Sure. Booze hounds, mostly."

Her head nodded agreement. "He died of the snakes four months ago. That was at Single Tree up close to the border."

"Good place to die. With the gold petered out, the camp's on its last legs. I s'pose the girl had a mother?"

"She doesn't remember her. I imagine the mother flew the coop once she was rid of her egg."

"So the girl's here?"

Eva took a deep breath and then, as if one weren't enough, took another. "Whatever her old man was or did, he taught her to read. He gave her a real liking for learning and books. Mort, she's smart. She's read everything I have in the house. Maybe it wasn't smart for her to come here, but she had a reason."

"Which was?"

"Not yet. Not the why of it yet."

"All right."

"So the old man died, and there she was with maybe two

bits to her name, a frazzle of clothes, one pair of beat-up shoes and a couple of hairpins. That was her inventory, or just about. What equipment he had went for debts. She took work as a hired girl."

He said, "Sensible."

"You think so, do you?" The blood was rising in her face. "Her boss was some goddam widower with a ranch a day's ride from nowhere. That son of a bitch raped her, and she just a young girl and unknowing. He raped her not once but again and again."

"Seems like she could have run away."

"She did. He caught her. Why are men such bastards, Mort? Such dirty bastards?"

It dodged in his head that, but for men, she wouldn't be a prosperous madam, but he thought of the Indian girl and the sand and said, "Peckers."

"A young hired hand found her crying and guessed at the reason and sneaked her back to Single Tree, riding double on his horse."

"He wasn't such a bastard. Must have cost him his job."

She waved the interruption aside. "From there she begged wagon and buggy rides when she could and walked when she couldn't and so showed up here."

"What for — to ask a dumb question?"

"Up at Single Tree she had heard of my house." Eva's mouth came down at one corner. From the side of it she said, "Her drunken newspaper daddy was against sin." After a pause she added, "But that's what she came here for, in a way."

Ewing got up and stretched and walked around the bear-skin rug, wishing he could hush Eva and get back to the ranch. After he had reseated himself, just tentatively, he said, "Sin's what she'll get then. Case dismissed."

She clapped the desk with the palm of her hand and

brought her head toward him like a bird dog on a point. "No. No. She doesn't belong here."

"Plenty of jobs for hired girls."

"For her! Again! Good God, Mort, she's just a child. She's got a fixed notion about hired-girl jobs from that nightmare position she had. She'd rather whore, if she could, than be raped. Then she'd have some say in the matter."

"But she can't?"

Eva sighed, and it was as if some of the strength left her. "I could stand another drink."

After he had served them she went on, not looking at him but at the top of the desk where words and the records of deeds might have been. "I let her try twice, Mort, and both times she came crying later to me, and the customers complained and demanded other girls free. She couldn't cut the mustard, that's all."

"Not one swath, huh?"

"I guess not. Anyhow, who wants a scared and weepy lay?"

"Except the gentleman rancher out of Single Tree."

Her face tightened and came up to meet his as if he might be the gentleman himself. "He ought to be cut! He spoiled her. He gave her a fix against the most natural thing in the world, a forever fix." Her eyes fell to the desk again, and she went on as if talking to herself. "The poor thing will never be any good, Mort, not just no good for a house but no good for one man, no good for womanhood. It happens often, oftener than you'll ever know. Frigidity, I mean. Why I don't know, except in her case I do. It's sad."

Here she was, he could almost think, the enemy of wives and sweethearts, operator of a house of ill fame, pussy peddler, corrupter of men, and here she was bleeding for all the cold, somehow-castrated women who hated her because she supplied what they wouldn't or couldn't and anyhow didn't — the most natural thing in the world. Go a step farther, and a man might understand her interest in the girl, who had nothing to offer a man whereas Eva and her crew owned a galore. Guilt through possession, maybe. Pity through guilt. A sort of Socialism except the property couldn't be divided.

What he said was, "But her coming here? That doesn't figure."

"Oh, yes. She told herself she could do it. She vowed she would. She swore she must."

"The trail's petered out. Why?"

Eva cleared her throat harshly, as if to allow no dispute of what was to follow. "For an education."

Any man would have to laugh, no matter Eva's glare. "I be good goddammed," he said, "if she didn't come to the right place!"

"Morton Ewing," she answered — and her tone now might have meant pity for ignorance — "I've told you her background. She was going to save every penny."

Before he could answer, she stood up and announced, "It's time you met her."

For the first time since the start of the talk he took notice that the noise sounding through from the parlor had increased. Someone was playing a rinky-dink tune on the piano, and deep and shrill voices rose in words and laughter, and over all came a rowdy bass that he recognized. "No fools, no fun, folks. Here's to stud duty."

He turned to Eva, who stood at the side door. "Him?"

She nodded. "Sarge Kraker. Compliments of the house."

"Cheating jackass."

She said, "The law," as if the two words were explanation enough, and before closing the door after herself added, "I have never let her appear in the parlor."

A quick one wouldn't hurt him, he reckoned, but it wouldn't do him any particular good. The hell with it. And the hell with Sheriff Harry Howie, that weak-gutted Republican who had named Kraker his deputy. Matter of simple appreciation, boys. Matter of recognition. Thanks for votes, of which Kraker had delivered considerable. The damn Krakers of the world always had toadies, always had half-fearful, follow-the-leader bums whose votes were as good as any, if you please, fellow Americans. So compliments of the house. Free booze and bed with your badge. One of these days Sheriff Howie could expect another talking to.

A quick one wouldn't hurt after all, being as he was about to be introduced to what was a virgin by rights. Here's how, being as Eva would suck him into some deal if he didn't blow back.

A damsel in distress, huh? A candidate, maybe, for the pages of Sir Walter Scott? More likely, almost surely, a draggle-tailed, bleating ewe lamb from the hospital band. Why wait, having heard enough? Why wait when he ought to be on the way to the ranch?

He was standing by the table when Eva herded the ewe lamb in. The lamb wore a simple blouse and skirt. When she turned to Eva, as if for direction or assurance, he saw she wore her hair in two braids, brought together in back and tied with a ribbon. Leave it to Eva to outfit her for a part.

Regardless, she was a small girl with the fresh, the pitiful curves of first womanhood; and she looked at him out of wide, blue, fearful eyes set wide beneath a height of brow. In the silence that Eva let go on while he sized the girl up, he marked the short upper lip, the rather wide mouth, the cheeks planing down clean to the smooth round of chin. But the face didn't smile. It seemed beyond smiling. It flicked across his mind how they catalogued Thoroughbred foals in Kentucky: by sire, out of dam, by dam's sire. She was by Illusion, out of Spring Day, by — by Disenchantment.

Eva said, "Juliet, I want you to meet Mr. Mort Ewing. Mort, this is Juliet Justice."

He answered, "Howdy, miss," thinking that only a down-at-heels editor with Shakespeare and Old Crow in his head could have named her.

The girl made the beginning of a curtsy. "How do you do, Mr. Ewing?" She spoke in the lingering tones of childhood.

"Mr. Ewing is one of our foremost citizens," Eva told the girl. If there was a touch of mockery in the words, there was none in voice or manner. "He used to visit us rather often. Now it's a special occasion." She paused. "Julie, I'm afraid you haven't met many good men. Mr. Ewing is a gentleman."

The girl's face changed. There came on it the look of haunt and yet of submission. Her young voice got out, "If you want, Miss Eva —" Then, unaccountably, the blue eyes brightened.

It took Ewing an instant to see it was tears that gave them a shine. It took him another to catch on. His voice came back to him loud. "Good Lord, child, no! Eva, for God sake!"

"Nothing like that, Julie." Eva spoke softly. "Not again ever. I just wanted you to meet a friend you can count on."

A slick surround, Ewing thought, one he should have resented. Some kind of commitment, some sort of obligation he signed by silence while he looked at the girl. Damn Eva's heart!

Eva went on, "You may go back to your room now. Side stairs and back."

"I know," the girl said, and turned to Ewing. "Good night, Mr. Ewing." Unexpectedly she offered her hand. It was a small, firm hand, and for a second it fitted in his with a seeming trust that made him feel untrustworthy. Call it the devil's tickle that he would play for even one flash with the thought of erasing that abused innocence.

After the girl had gone, Eva said, "Well?"

"Well yourself."

"Sit down. Don't you like her?"

"I don't grade that fast."

"Then take my word." She had put herself back in her chair, and now she put both elbows on the desk and rested her chin in her two fists. That position meant business. "You don't know it yet, Mort, but you're going to let her have a try at school. You're going to put up the money."

"So now I know," he said, and had to laugh. "Eva, you're back to yourself. Except in books, it didn't go with the breed, that wholehearted act. But big-hearted at my expense? Yep."

"You can afford it."

"If I want to. Don't know as I do. By God, Eva, you salted the mine, putting her up in pigtails and little-girl gear."

The girl's face showed behind the words, the girl's just-bloomed and violated body. There was her bloodline, not by Disenchantment but by Violation.

"I dressed her right — and you can afford it."

"I'm not tight-ass, it don't matter what you've said. You know so. But crucified Jesus!"

She had begun by roasting him, thinking that way to make sure he was tender. She had basted him with some compliments, too. Then she'd gentled the girl into the kettle. Some mulligan!

She asked, "You doubt my judgment?"

"Sure. Go to school? Go to school where? Couldn't be here."

"Has to be," she answered through a mouth tightened by the fists on her chin. "Where else is a friend?"

"She stays at a whorehouse and goes to high school! Eva, you're loco."

So she was. Loco and, to boot, out of character. By rights she was a hard-headed woman with an eye for a dollar. Let a girl cheat on her, and out she went. Let one get too old and too worn or too bottle-fed, and she had to go, with a tear, maybe, and just a little something by way of good-bye. Let a seller, any kind, hike up his prices, and he sure God learned better. A keen businesswoman, that's what she was.

"Not that loco," she said, and let the rest wait.

A good businesswoman somehow gone soft, no matter if she did want him to put up the money. The ruler of the roost pulled from her perch, pulled by a sorry-faced child who had been forced to yield what the house sold. Right there might be an answer — the child. Supposing in Eva was an old wish for motherhood, say now for someone to mother. A mule, always barren by some act of God, always was trying to take charge of a colt. And a hot crotch cooling off with the years maybe could nurse regrets at the lack of results.

Now her hands came from her chin. They were small hands, not overused, expressive as the wave of a wing. "Will you listen and not interrupt?"

"What have I been doing? Crying an auction?"

"No one knows Julie, no one to speak of."

He had to put in, "Except you and me and your girls and the two sports she couldn't sport with."

"Will you hush? My girls never blab. They wouldn't want to and wouldn't dare to. The two sports were strangers, greenhorns bound over to Oregon. Here, come and gone." One hand made its one wave. "Once she's out of the house, I won't know Julie, not to anyone's knowledge."

He couldn't quite believe what he said, but some doubt made him say it. "You just plain want to get rid of her."

"Have it your own goddam way! Sure. She's no use to me."

"Cool off, Eva."

She leaned back and folded her hands on the desk, and her face went from angry to grave. "Of course, Mort. It was normal and maybe part right, being I'm who I am. But about Julie, no one will know."

"It's a cinch to get out."

"The two men are gone. The girls won't tell, and I won't tell, and you won't tell. She won't even know you're paying the freight."

"Who will, to her thinking?"

"Fatty Adlam. I've talked to Bertha."

"Bertha?"

"Mrs. Adlam. In secret. By night. In public we're strangers."

He said, "I'm a son of a bitch."

"Make it double if you ever tell. Not here, but once I knew her as one of the girls. There's a fine woman, Mort, with a reliable husband and a nice child. Get that fool look off your face! Cross off the good wives who used to be whores and cross off the good get that they got, and in the west it's a long haul between stage stops. You know it damn well."

Part of it was true, but only a part. In her count Eva scanted the fillies who'd come west to take jobs teaching school and wound up as wives. She scanted the remembered sweethearts that men had sent for or returned east to get once they had stake enough.

In the silence between them the noise in the parlor beat at the door — the shrieks, the whoops, the pound of piano.

"That free-pasture jackass brays loudest," he said.

Eva didn't answer. She might still be thinking about once-whore wives and their proper manners and prime pups and the hauls between stage stops.

He said for lack of something better, "I thought it was whiskey settled the west."

"Will you please swallow your head? Fatty and Bertha will take Julie in. She'll help around the house. Not enough, though, with school and her studies. The price is twenty dollars a month, out of which the Adlams, who can use it, will get a little something and Julie will get bed, board, books and duds. There you are, Mort Ewing."

"There I'm not. There's school and how she gets in. You think Prof will take into high school someone never finished the grades? You think he won't have to poke in her past?"

"That's where you come in. You recommend her, telling the teacher about her life with her pa but docking off rape and the rest. You can fill in with some story about the time since he died. Long as you back her, the teacher won't poke."

"And she'll come out at the head of her class, huh?"

"She's smart. She'll pass examinations, if any. Have your professor test her and see. After all, you're on the school board."

"Not to sneak a poor whore into high school. And I wasn't elected to fuddle the teacher."

"He doesn't need to know. He'll never know."

"It will come out." He got up and poured her a drink and said, "Take this and come to your senses.

"Look, Eva," he went on as he sat down again. "Total it up. We don't know that the girl has learning enough to enter high school. All right. All right. Maybe she has. I bid a pass there. Second, her past will catch up with her, sure as scours follow spring grass. Next, Collingsworth is not a man to play foxy with."

"I never knew you to be afraid of a man."

"Aw, bullshit. I respect him. I'm leaning to like him, him and his family."

"It couldn't be the money you're thinking of?"

He had to grin. "Fair is fair. I fed you a cactus, and you feed me one back. Only yours hasn't got any stickers on it. No, it's not the money. It's just I be damned if I take it on me to risk the new school and schoolmaster. They would both be deader than General Custer's command if the girl was found out."

"You're concerned just with yourself."

"Wrong. Happens I am thinking bigger than me. Collingsworth would have to be told. I don't have to guess at his answer."

Both her hands waved out now, indicating, maybe, defeat. "I should have known. In some ways you're such a moral bastard."

"Jesus don't think so."

"All right, Mort." The words came out on a sigh. "Will you talk to the professor then, plain as you care to? Damn it, will you try?"

"Nope," he said, and got up. "Nope. Thanks for the drinks."

She came from behind the desk and stood close to him, though not as if hoping to soften him by the offer of her soft self. Perhaps she knew that old trick wouldn't work, not now, not here, not even with the help of come-on perfume.

Close as she was, somehow he didn't feel close to her but at a far remove from the flesh he had known. It was almost as if he never had bedded her and stood cut off from what he had done. Between them only the knowledge remained, and what the hell did it come to? Old days, old ways; and a man almost could smile at the eagerness of men and women, some women, to get their mucous membranes together.

As he took a step around toward the door, she put a hand on his vest. "Please, Mort." Then, "Socialist, it's what you owe."

"Owe, hell!" he said, and took hold of the door knob. "Keep up the good work, Eva."

He clattered down the stairs, not caring whether the noise could be heard above the noises of the goddam whorehouse. He walked the darkened street to his team. The horses had been too long without water. Merc Marsh ought to have a goddam water trough next to the hitch rail. As it was, he'd have to angle off a couple of hundred yards to the goddam creek.

Not until he was lined out on the road home did he take

note of the moon riding quarter high in the eastern sky. Once he had thought of the moon as being wild and free and hopeful as a full pocket of gold. Once. Out of Illusion.

He hoped Marsh had remembered to include the thread in his order.

7

AFTER THE SERVICES Collingsworth took Mary Jess by the hand, shook hands with the preacher and started home, feeling an unwelcome dissatisfaction with fundamentalist doctrine — which was all one could expect from John Wesley Harrison and the Methodist Episcopal Church. He was, he knew, closer to Unitarianism than any other faith, but even there he had reservations. The idea, refusing to recognize the evil that flourished or lurked all about! Calling it an absence of good!

Mary Jess, skipping along at his side, said, "In Sunday school we sang 'Jesus Loves Me.'"

"That's good. That's just fine."

How many times had he been through it in country church houses in Indiana, in open-air and tent revivals? How many times had he listened to preachers who used as their sole items of trade the fear of punishment and the hope of reward? None ever spoke of goodness for goodness' sake. How many prayers had he heard, uttered in the close ear of God? How many hymns? How many responsive readings? For today's readings the Reverend Mr. Harrison had gone, not strangely, to the first chapter of John. The words sounded again in his head, rolled out by the minister, murmured by the members.

In the beginning was the Word, and the Word was with God, and the Word was God.

The same was in the beginning with God.

All things were made by him; and without him was not any thing made that hath been made.

A wind from the southwest had sprung up, a dry wind that carried grit with it, and twigs and weeds gone to seed. Mary Jess turned away from it and walked backward and asked, "Will Mr. Ross be waiting for us, Father?"

"I think so, sweetheart."

"I wish Mother could have gone to church with us."

"She will when Tommie gets older."

So she would, but she hadn't missed inspiration today. Mr. Harrison believed in the Bible. He believed its every word. It would have stunned him, no doubt, to learn that the King James Version was hardly contemporaneous with Jesus. He believed in a burning hell and a beatific heaven. He had fear of God's wrath and faith in God's mercy. He cried out for sinners, praying they would repent, not so much for the improvement of earth as the assurance of eventual bliss. And, Collingsworth suspected, he counted on God to fill his mouth when he took the pulpit without preparation. Well, at least God had filled it with evangelical resonance.

As he turned the corner just west of the church, he saw the Ross buggy and team tied up at his side fence, the tails of the horses waved by the wind.

"Mr. Ross doesn't go to church ever, does he, Father?" Mary Jess asked. The wind was worrying her braids. She knuckled an eye that some speck had blown into.

"I imagine, sometimes. Remember that he lives out in the country."

The reply seemed to satisfy her. He knew, though, that Jay never did. Oh, maybe for funerals and an occasional wedding.

74

Probably, in Memphis, Missouri, he had grown up as untrained as a bramble.

It was Jay's loss, Collingsworth reflected. Preachers might be stupid, doctrine myopic and Methodist hymns flushed with militancy, but one reared in primitive ritual found in it something not only familiar but dear. Take "There Is Power in the Blood," which the choir had rehearsed at Mr. Harrison's suggestion and sung today, aided, or rather, disconcerted, by a few uncertain voices in the congregation. The words and music stayed with him, stayed in the idle and echoing part of the brain so often dissociated from thought. "There is pow'r" — and then, with the high note held, the deeper-voiced reassertion, "There is pow'r." And, farther along, "In the blood" — and again the affirmation, "In the blood."

"The wind holds my breath, Father."

"Put your hand to your face, Mary Jess. It's not far now."

The church house itself wasn't bad, rustic in appearance, mostly shingled on the outside, but not bad. The inside was ample, for the perhaps fifteen to twenty adults and their broods who seemed to constitute the usual congregation. The dais provided room for the pulpit, an eight-member choir — though only four singers so far had volunteered — and a pump organ which Miss Eleanor Nagle, wispy as she was, played with great enthusiasm when the time was four-four. Back of the pews were two Sunday-school rooms which a rolling door closed off when need be.

The choir was less than good, he thought as he turned his face from the wind. Worse than that: fierce. Old Mrs. Weaver, if ever she could sing, now sang in a quaver. Bill Robinson, a clerk for Merc Marsh, liked to show off his wail of a tenor, which was often off key. It was good, then, to think of Miss Margaret Carson, whose voice was true and, in view of her size, surprisingly strong. He had been lucky to get, out of

Ohio, an assistant schoolteacher like her, lucky to find a religious and seemingly resolute girl who could sing but, more than that, knew her language and history.

At the preacher's request he had stood again but reluctantly at the door to meet the worshipers as they came in. Already he had some acquaintance with nearly all of them. Yet nothing would do but that Mr. Harrison introduce him as if he were some prize exhibit, by miracle just come to Arfive. "God bless you, sister. Bless you, brother," he kept saying. "Have you met Brother Collingsworth? Yes. Yes. All of us are, indeed, glad to meet him."

It had butted into his mind, as he looked down from his place in the choir, that churchgoers too often reflected failure outside of the faith. It was as if God would make up for their shortcomings on earth once they passed into the Kingdom of Heaven. Here were old Mr. White, who did nothing, and his wife, who washed clothes and in repose shook a little as if her hands still labored the board. Here were Wilbur Webster, sometime bookkeeper, and Albert Garner, who could affix a notary's seal. The hefty man was Gene Trescott, handyman. He appeared — that lurking and idle part of the brain always kept coming up with the inappropriate — uncomfortably flatulent. By contrast, almost sole contrast, there was old Mr. McLaine, who sat thoughtful, apparently reconciled to himself, his beard like a bit of summer cloud. That evidence to the contrary, successes had no need of salvation.

But they did. If not of salvation then of grace. Fundamentalist or not, this church, this one church in town, was an influence for good. Men needed faith, not just in their selfish selves but in the capability of the human being to reject evil and embrace good and create the society that Jesus spoke for. Whether they came to that faith through dogma or thought mattered little. How many had ever suffered through an overexposure to doctrine? Doctrine, though later to be examined, still gave right directions.

Mary Jess stopped and lifted her face. One eye was crying from the speck the wind had blown in. He got out his handkerchief and pulled down her lower lid, found the speck and dipped it away. The hair under his hand, the whole shape of the skull, testified to things beyond knowledge, beyond feeling and thanks.

After she had thanked him, she asked, "Will it blow all the way to Mr. Ross's house?"

The sun focused on him from its mirror of sky, but gray wind clouds hung behind and over the Rockies, and a veil of mist was sweeping the face of Elephant Ear Butte.

"I'm afraid so," he answered.

"I wish Jesus would stop it."

"In time, dear. In time."

"I mean now. He could, couldn't he, Father?"

"Oh, pshaw. You can stand a little wind. Let's not ask tiny favors from God."

But there you had it, he thought. There was the contrast between fact and faith in a personal god. There was the chasm between broad belief and narrow, between the embrace of the universe and the catch-hold of — all right — superstition. And there, his hearers taken into account, was the reason the Bible class had been indifferent to the words spoken today. The members wanted the clean choice of bliss or brimstone. Answers they wanted, absolute answers to the unanswerable, for God was close and jealous, the god of Mr. Harrison.

He had chosen Philippians for today's lesson, not because the book was short or altogether because he hadn't had time to organize a course, but because there were lines in it that spoke to him and for him. Reading them, he had to steady his voice.

> Finally, brethren, whatsoever things are true, whatsoever things are honest, whatsoever things are just, whatsoever things are pure, whatsoever things are lovely, whatsoever things are of good report; if there be any virtue, and if there be any praise, think on these things.

The Lord knew he had thought on these things, had thought on them and lodged them in him, mind and heart; and in the preparation of his lesson it had seemed to him not inappropriate, though not biblical, to quote enforcements recent by comparison.

After reciting the passage from Scripture and commenting on it, he feared feebly now, he had said to the class, "Both inside and outside the Bible, unto even our own day, we find declarations in parallel to what you've just heard. Mr. Emerson said —"

The reference left everyone blank except for Mr. McLaine, who nodded his head and stroked his cloud of a beard.

"Mr. Ralph Waldo Emerson, the great exponent of good, the great philosopher, spoke to us not much more than half a century ago, saying:

" 'As when the summer comes from the south, the snowbanks melt and the face of the earth becomes green before it, so shall the advancing spirit create its ornaments along its path, and carry with it the beauty it visits and the song which enchants it; it shall draw beautiful faces, warm hearts, wise discourse, and heroic acts, around its way, until evil is no more seen.' "

At the path's turning Mary Jess slipped her hand from his and ran for the front door, calling back, "Hurry up, Father. Get out of the wind."

❦

Jay Ross drove a spirited buggy team of matched bays, which kept fighting the snug hold he kept on them. The perhaps not oversnug hold, May Collingsworth thought as surrey and team spanked through the town, drawing glances from here and there of what might be admiration or envy.

Seated in back, with Mary Jess on one side of her and Tommie in a blanketed laundry basket on the other, she clasped both the rim of the basket and Mary Jess's hand. It did not add to her ease when Jay turned his head around and, smiling while he held to his hat, said over Benton's shoulder, "How's your copperosity suggastuatin'?" He was always putting that question to Mary Jess.

May said, "Sweetheart, don't look at me. You know what Mr. Ross means. How are you?"

"Just fine, Mr. Ross, but I wish the wind would quit blowing."

Jay glanced ahead and turned back. "Lots of ways to look at it, Mary Jess. Don't see any mosquitoes around, or horseflies, do you?"

"The wind blew them away?"

The words themselves, spoken in a child's frail voice, might have been blown away, might now be whispers echoed afar.

"Sure thing." Mr. Ross — Jay, he wanted to be called — had heard after all. "Blew them away or chased them to cover, one or the other."

"I wish I was a fly then."

Jay laughed his hoarse, wheezing laugh. Looking at his squat, big-mouthed face, May thought his would be the prize voice in a pond. But the notion, if not quite uncalled for, still was unfair, and she put it out of her mind.

Benton tugged his hat snug and let his hand fall and, too late, grabbed for the brim again. The hat had sprung from his head and was flying off to the side. With an effort Jay pulled the team to a stop. He was grinning. Benton said, "Confound it!" As if haste were unfitting, he stepped to the ground.

He was, May knew, vexed with himself — which meant he was vexed with everything and everybody. The hat had lodged against a bush, invitingly. He marched to it, as if it were the offender, but, just as he thrust his hand out, the wind tore the hat free and tumbled it on. And on. There was nothing else for it then. Benton ran.

When he returned, breathless, he had the hat jammed so far down on his head it would be a wonder if it ever fit properly again. A new hat, too. Five dollars. He got back in his seat without speaking.

"I've lost mine a hundred times, I bet," Jay said in easing tones. It wasn't the first time he had surprised her. He put the horses to a trot.

Benton answered, "So," not as a question.

"Just one of the little prices we pay, Prof."

"So?"

"Wasn't for the wind, what would livestock do? Go hungry, maybe starve, or have to be kept close and fed all the time." Jay was speaking to all of them now. "Come winter, the wind clears most of the snow from the ranges. Lets stock get to the grass."

"I see, Jay," Benton answered. The edge seemed off his irritation.

"That's why this eastern slope is so good, because it's windy. It's a chinook blowing now, warm from down the mountains. Later on you'll welcome it."

The ill wind that blew somebody good. But not now. Not her. Even hatpins, a veil and, last of all, a tied-over scarf were hardly enough a secure her own hat. The wind dusted her white gloves, which were a sight already. It parched and wrinkled the skin, which she could feel drawing tight. It whipped grit in the mouth and grit in the eyes and kept flapping back the blanket meant to cover Tommie. Even the horses, manes and tails whipping like tattered pennants, stepped along with heads aslant.

Indiana winds mostly murmured. They breathed mostly soft, through remembered oak and maple and sycamore and the great tulip tree that flowered in the back yard. They idled along, playful with leaf and with blade. So might this wind, once it had screamed over the miles and found what it looked for.

This country was too big for the heart, too vast to contain, too wild for love, too empty for home. Where was the end of it? What was the end? The nausea she had thought over with made her swallow.

Tommie began to fret. He was a little thing and frail for his age, little and frail for time and place, too; but in a God forsaken land what did God care?

Feeling disloyal, she pushed back her depression. Here was Benton, and Benton rejoiced in his love for the country, forgiving — little thoughts helped — the snatch of his hat. If Montana suited him, so would it her. What he loved she would learn to love, too. Where he was, there she would be. World everlasting.

Jay pulled up in front of his house and cramped a wheel for their exit. From somewhere a dog came barking a welcome, its tail wagging, its hair patterned like blown grass. "Be right along," Jay said after they had dismounted. He drove toward the barn.

Mrs. Ross came to the door and, having opened it, shrank back. "Quick!" she said. "Such weather!" Once the weather was closed out, she welcomed them.

"I can put Tommie down anywhere," Benton said. He was carrying the baby, basket and all. Tommie had quit crying. It was as if all he had wanted was haven.

Mrs. Ross extended her hands for the basket. "Please," she

said with what seemed more than manners in attitude and tone. "Let me put him down."

As she returned from the bedroom, Jay ushered in Mr. Mc-Laine and Miss Carson. They had traveled together, it became evident, in Mr. McLaine's buggy. Both looked blown, even Miss Carson, whom one would almost have thought inviolable. The Ross girls, Jane and Beth, came downstairs then in a flutter of Sunday dress and greeted the company nicely.

With Mary Jess on her lap, May glanced from face to face while pleasantries were exchanged in the parlor. Mr. McLaine she knew for a gentle and educated man, the only man in town with intellectual kinship to Benton. The Ross girls, both pretty, were to young to assess except to note that Jane was reserved and Beth bouncy. Miss Carson, unruffled and starched, might be superior to the world's foibles. Loud though he was, or perhaps because he was, Jay seemed misplaced in this, his own home. It was as if, by talk and gesture, he would make room for himself in a circle he knew closed to him. Or that he defied the strange boundaries. He was a lusty heathen who had blundered into a meeting of the Ladies' Industrial and sought to make the best of the circumstances. May thought him a little pathetic. She must remember to describe her impressions to Benton.

But it was Mrs. Ross who drew first attention — the sad but eloquent eyes, the appearance of beleaguered gentility, the suggestion of fret almost despaired of. And the face with its fine network of wrinkles. It occurred to May that each harsh breath of air might have left its little etching on her skin. To her, she supposed, Mrs. Ross always would be the woman of the wind.

Mrs. Ross excused herself and went through the dining room to the kitchen, presently to come back and announce, "Dinner is ready." She looked a little flushed from her chores in the kitchen, though, as May knew, she had a hired girl to help her, no doubt a raw one.

The table was set right. Against the fresh linen gleamed silverware properly placed. For a centerpiece someone had picked wildflowers — goldenrod and daisies and unknown fall blooms. At the head of the table were roast chicken and dressing and side dishes, each with its fresh-polished serving utensil.

When they were seated, Jay said, "Well, folks —" but halted at his wife's frown. "Oh, sure. What I mean is, will you please ask the blessing, Prof?"

Benton made it simple, as always, asking that God bless the food to their use and them to His service. Mr. McLaine and Miss Carson echoed amen.

Before starting serving, Jay unfolded his napkin and industriously polished his silverware, this time not catching Mrs. Ross's expression. It was habit, May knew. She saw him in untidy restaurants and beside the greasy cook wagons she'd heard of. Were bread on the table instead of hot rolls, he'd probably butter a whole slice at one time.

With the plates served and the side dishes passing, Jay asked, "What's a feed minus the oysters? Ham without eggs."

"I told you none were available." There was a touch perhaps of asperity in Mrs. Ross's reply.

"It's September," Jay said. "R in it."

It was Mr. McLaine who broke whatever tension there was. "Interesting thing. In Montana and, I suppose, in neighboring interior states people crave seafood. We may find sometime that it provides an element missing in our diet. But, Mrs. Ross, surely no one can complain at this fare."

No one could.

May had cut up the portion of chicken for Mary Jess and served her small helpings from the bowls that were passed. Now, as they ate and paused to make conversation, the spoken words drifted around her, hardly heard. She ought to pay more attention, ought to participate. But let the men talk. Benton and Mr. McLaine were playing around with the question of whether things not sensed in fact existed. To both of them the idea seemed interesting but empty. Did a mountain come into existence only when seen? Aw! Jay had no time for such speculation, counting it a crazy waste. He said, "Tell me the soil and the climate, and I can say 'grass' with my eyes closed, my nose plugged and me in a barrel."

Across the years she heard the repeated advice of old Professor Elrod of Earlham College. "Never think small!" He was a slight, gray man with a big head, a sort of Quaker evangelist, though Quakers didn't go for evangelism. "Don't think small!" She had been guilty, or almost, in her unspoken picking at Jay. So what if he polished his silverware and called a feast a feed and would have buttered a whole slice of bread? Did those things count in the last summing up? He knew not what he did.

Not that she herself would diminish or forsake the amenities. On going out, she would wear dress gloves always and, heaven knew, a hat, and not just for church. She would lay the table as it should be laid, even for the family alone. It would be nice, for company, to have sterling instead of common plate. For Benton's and the children's sakes as well as her own, she would watch her grammar, which needed small watching, and forego slang if only because it smacked of vulgarity. But the proprieties could be carried to the point of absurdity. For instance, this matter of engraved calling cards, which after formal afternoon visits the departing ladies left on little silver trays provided for them. The practice suggested that the lady of the house had no memory for names but surely could read and recall. It made insistence on some other conventions seem a bit silly — to one who had no engraved cards.

Jay asked, "Now just what are you grinning about, Mrs. Collingsworth?"

"Oh, oh, nothing," she said. He kept his bold eyes on her. "Excuse me. For a minute I was far away." Feeling somewhat mischievous, she added, "A thought was calling on me."

"Hmm. Nice visit, seems like." Jay dismissed the subject with that.

When all had eaten to surfeit, Jay pushed his chair back. "I guess the ladies will excuse us," he said.

In the parlor Collingsworth took the cigar that Jay offered, thinking something could be said for a luxury he couldn't afford. Mr. McLaine took one, too, and the three of them lighted up and settled back, hearing the comforting sounds that women made in tidying up after a meal. A back door opened and closed, probably after someone on the way to the privy. Despite all niceties the natural functions had a way of announcing themselves. It must have been embarrassing, for women especially, on the Oregon Trail without even an outhouse in hundreds of miles.

As if just to make conversation Jay said from the comfort of his leather-lined chair, " 'Bout time for school, Prof."

"Tuesday morning. There'll be a class of eighteen or so, maybe half from the country."

Mr. McLaine tipped a little ash from his cigar. "You have had time to form some perhaps lasting impressions, about Montana, I mean?"

"It is hardly what I expected."

Jay asked, "No?"

"It is better than that. Written accounts had led me to believe men in town would be wearing guns, whereas they're not. There are Indians, of course, but no painted braves as often reported."

"Sorry lot," Jay put in.

"But from what I've seen I'd say the magazines and newspapers back east were wrong — anyhow exaggerated — in other directions."

"What?"

"For instance, about the copper wars. About William A. Clark and Marcus Daly and Heinze and all the rest. About vote buying and bribery and general moral delinquency."

"Aw, that's Butte's business and Helena's. Hardly touched us. Never has."

Mr. McLaine leaned forward and gestured mildly with his cigar. "Not all the truth, Jay. Editors and newspapers were bought this side of the mountains, not to mention our honorable lawmakers. And it nauseates me to think how the copper trust brought the state to its knees, forcing the governor to call a special session of the legislature and the session to enact the special legislation the trust demanded. What a disgrace!"

"I'm not about to puke," Jay answered. "Sure, to get them to do business again, to put a lot of hungry men back on the payroll, we gave the trust what it wanted. But what went before the trust, before Daly and Heinze and Clark sold out, why, that was just one big poker game. Bet, call and bluff. The best bluffer won, or the high hand."

"Or the most money. The most money generally wins, Jay." To Collingsworth Mr. McLaine's measured words seemed to have a hidden significance. "The big bankroll has a way of adding to itself."

"Losers weepers," Jay answered. Whatever point Mr. McLaine had tried to make had failed of its purpose. Softly he added, "Winners keepers."

It could have been by common consent that they changed the subject.

After a while, after the cigars had been smoked down to stubs, the women came in with Mary Jess tagging along; and presently Collingsworth suggested it was time to start home. "I have to milk that good cow," he said to Jay, "then go to evening services."

May came immediately to her feet and, after good-byes and

thanks, Jay rolled them toward town. The wind had blown itself out, had hurried on from nowhere to nowhere. The leaves on the clumps of willows they passed were as still as paintings, and a lone cottonwood stood as if it had never known fury. Here, now, as happened so often when the sun notched itself in the mountains, was the hour of no wind. Some words of Saint John, written far back in his memory, came to mind. "The wind bloweth where it listeth, and thou hearest the sound thereof, but canst not tell whence it cometh, and whither it goeth . . ." Had John never known the quiet time, when earth and air were at peace, and the creatures thereof?

After a long silence Jay said, "That looks like Mort Ewing's saddle horse in front of your place. Yep. There's Ewing himself on the yon side."

8

COLLINGSWORTH HAD LISTENED with due patience to Mort Ewing's story, though he had known for some time what the answer must be. It was difficult, however, to pay whole attention to a matter already settled; and, as Ewing tried to tie up whatever loose ends he'd left, he kept finding a part of his own mind wandering off.

He had to call this his office, this mere corner of Woodmen's Hall closed off from the rest by movable screens. Unseen beyond it were ranged student desks, which for Saturday-night dances would be moved to the sides to provide room for cavorters and seats for occasional sitters, wallflowers and drunks. But now, on this last day before school, the hall was empty and met well enough Ewing's insistence on privacy.

Ewing, he reflected as Ewing's useless words continued and stopped and continued against his own silence, must have regarded this arranged interview as an occasion, one so special as to call for a complete suit and tie, though his cowpuncher boots were out of keeping. Even his talk was dressed up, free of range-country habit, conformity or pretension. More important, though he had started his story on the flat, as if to lay the whole case bare and leave it to cold judgment, his voice as he proceeded had gained warmth and strength. It was the conviction, Collingsworth thought, of a man who had convinced himself, not by the facts but by his own recital.

"That's the whole of it, and that's the truth of it. I am willing to swear by that," Ewing said. His eyes were questioning.

"On what authority?"

"My own eyes and ears."

"And you can swear that you saw and heard all of it?"

Ewing shifted in his chair and brought a hand out, one finger pointing for emphasis. "Prof, you can have your own ideas of Eva Fox, and I won't argue too much. But whatever Eva is, she's not a liar. And remember, I saw the girl."

"She now stays at the home of a saloonkeeper."

"She is staying at the home of Mr. and Mrs. Adlam, where she helps with the housework, for pay enough to see her through school."

"Mort, there's just one answer. You surely realized it before you began."

"I know your answer now. I knew it before, if I read your face right."

"You read it right."

Ewing sighed and sank back. "Not that I want to, but what would you think of taking the case before the whole board?"

"No! Confound it, no! This is an administrative matter, not one of policy. If the board voted unanimously to let the girl in, I'd say no if it cost me my job."

Ewing said, "Good man," and no more.

"If I admitted this, this girl — what's her name, Juliet Justice? — and her past became common knowledge, the school would be dead."

"Hurt, maybe. But it isn't the school that's the first thing worming around in your head, Prof. And, I give you credit, it isn't your future here."

"What is it, then?"

"It's your feeling for what's proper. It's your sense of morality."

"Tell me, what's wrong with that?"

"No use my saying, but it can eat a man up."

Out of respect for Ewing, Collingsworth considered the words, though in application to him they seemed idle. Simple decency didn't eat any man up: it kept him whole. By being whole, by acting whole, he helped repair his community. He set standards. Still? For an unwelcome instant, for no relevant reason, there came to his mind's eye one John Wesley Harrison, a whole man and a fool. He said, "Has it occurred to you, Mort, that the girl might revert to her old ways?" The words were no sooner out than he wished he could swallow them.

Ewing shuddered his chair back and got up. Of a sudden he seemed out of place in his suit, too big for the shoulders, too untamed for a tie, too natural a man for a townsman's disguise. He said, "Good crucified Jesus!" and stood there towering.

For the first time it occurred to Collingsworth, without fazing him, that Ewing could be dangerous. He had never feared any man. But from Ewing came a special and inner force that battered him, as some of his statements had battered him earlier. It was the emanation of a man who was a man, whole or not, and it was unwelcome.

Ewing was going on. "Old ways, for God sake! Haven't you listened? To your notion have I been lying? Whoring isn't her old way. Not new either. What she's trying to do is get back to herself."

Collingsworth held up his hand, but Ewing ignored it. "You think you're going to have a bunch of goddam, simon-pure virgins in your school? You going to protect them all from the evil call of the flesh, them that ain't heard it already? Crucified Jesus!"

Collingsworth stood up. "I've heard enough. What seems right to me, that will I do."

"All right. Then will you see the girl? Will you test her for what she's learnt?"

"No."

Ewing swung about and pushed a screen aside, pausing just long enough to fling out, "A religion that don't have room for redemption or some such is a closed-in shit house."

Of a sudden, hearing his boots march him down the hall toward the entryway, Collingsworth found the answer. He had been a fool not to see it before. He hurried past the opened screen and called, "Mort," and saw Ewing turn at the door. "On second thought I'll see the girl. I'll test her for entrance."

Ewing gave an abrupt nod and disappeared.

One Juliet Justice would be given her test all right, all right.

After he had eased himself, May Collingsworth knew, Benton would tell of his troubles. It was often if not always this way, the physical urgency in him demanding discharge before he could be the kind and thoughtful and confiding partner that was the true man. She disliked to think of the days ahead when, for the sake of her unborn, she would have to refuse him.

He had come home straight-mouthed and short-spoken this afternoon and at supper had distressed Mary Jess by saying in his hard voice, "Can't you watch what you're doing!" when she had spilled her milk. It was a time, then, for silence. No use to ask him what was the matter. It had to lie in him like indigestion.

Now, with the act of love done, he would talk. But sometimes it seemed not so much the act of love as a fierce drive for relief that allowed no time for approaches, for the preliminaries she would have welcomed. No matter. He was Benton and, the deed done, the need met, would open his heart. She brought a hand up and soothed his brow and said, "Benton."

He told her then, gently, about Mort Ewing and his plea for a girl who had been abused and later retreated, or sought to retreat, to a fancy house with the aim of making money for school — all this, mind you, according to Mort, who might not know the full facts himself. No doubt he didn't. It exceeded the imagination to believe that here was the whole and true story. Prostitution for education indeed!

"But, Maysie," he went on, "even supposing there's nothing hidden from Mort and nothing from me by Mort, what then? Let the report be true, let the girl be all she's made out to be, I can't gamble the good name of the school. Under the best of circumstances she's got to be a casualty."

"The poor thing," May said. "I can sympathize. I can understand."

He chuckled and felt for her hand. "You can understand, huh? Not much, I'll warrant. How can you understand, you, the innocent?"

"No woman is innocent, Benton. Women are born not innocent, most of them anyway. We know but keep still." She could almost hear him fumbling the words in his mind and had to smile to herself. "You tend to think, Benton, that we have no understanding beyond our experience. No imagination, no sympathy outside personal occurrences."

"I didn't say that, sweetheart."

"But it's true. Limitations don't ensure innocence in women, you innocent yourself." She gave him a small nudge. "Men just like to think they do." Here was an interesting line of thought, not altogether new but never before expressed, but it was off the subject, and she decided not to pursue it save for a conclusion she thought afterward was rather smug. "So men make the rules harsh: women make them tolerable."

"So," Benton said. She knew he was amused. "Is class dismissed?"

"Except that I sympathize with that girl. I understand."

"Forget it, Maysie. I haven't told you, but there's a sure way out."

"Yes?"

"I'm going to see the girl. I'm going to give her a test, you bet, a test that even a college graduate would fail. Then, phhft!"

The words brought her up in bed. "Benton Collingsworth, you'll do no such thing! You mustn't. You can't. I refuse to believe it's in you to do so. You'd be false to her and false to Mort and false to yourself." She added as an incidental, "I just hope you and Mort can patch things up."

All he answered was, "I'll see."

First day of school over, students gone home or wherever. The opening had gone well enough, Collingsworth thought. Young people always were fidgety when faced with indoor discipline after outdoor anarchy. Not that some of the ranch boys, several of whom were domiciled in town with family friends, hadn't worked, during calving and lambing and haying and such, but even they stood in need of severity if they were to learn. He had given an object lesson to all by ejecting one unruly lout pending the time he could mind his manners. Respect for authority came first, then, it was to be hoped, admiration. Thank the Lord, that small Miss Carson commanded attention. A well-known and frequent fault of women teachers was that they couldn't enforce discipline. Miss Carson was a notable exception. He was beginning to think of her as a little Napoleon.

He sat waiting. One of the screens of his office was half-folded to allow entrance. He snapped his pocket watch open. It was time, or almost, she arrived. Best not have it appear, though, that she alone kept him after hours. He shuffled the students' personal-history cards on his desk and gave them idle attention. It was then that a timid knock sounded on the screen's upright. He looked up and asked, "Yes?"

The girl seemed to shrink from his gaze. "I — I am Juliet Justice."

"Come in and be seated." He had thought not to get up but did so. Habit, he told himself. "I was informed you would be coming."

However misguided in other directions, Mort Ewing was right in his surface impressions. The girl was dressed properly in a blue blouse and pleated skirt, obviously freshly ironed. She wore no rouge, though he had wondered if she might not. Her hair was parted in the middle and drawn back severely, by braids, he supposed. He couldn't see from in front.

For an instant, after she had seated herself with what a man would have to call prim grace, he continued to appraise her. Her forehead was high. It held room for brains. He wondered if she had a back to her skull. Phrenology was buncombe, but he always had had some doubts about the intellectual capacities of people whose heads in the rear were flat with the spine. Surprisingly, her face with its blue eyes and lean planes was delicate. It would have softened the judgment of many a man.

"You want to go to school?" he said to the waiting eyes.

She answered, "I'm going to, somewhere."

It was a declaration, a statement of purpose, a vow muted but taken.

"That's to be seen," he said. "There has to be preparation for high school."

She didn't reply. She just sat, her young face waiting. It was, he saw now, the face of fear, the pleading and piteous face of a fear perhaps stamped there, as Ewing had said, by the outrages of men. Men were damned brutes, or could be. Even now another man might be thinking of the budded breasts, of the sleek treasure of thighs, of the young mouth crying while the young body yielded. The devil with such! Hell, if it burned anywhere, had special fires waiting.

He said, "How old are you?"

"Sixteen next month."

"And where have you gone to school, to grade school, that is?"

"Here and there, sir, and never for very long. My daddy was my real teacher." She paused and added with a gravity that outlawed ridicule if not doubt, "Please, sir, he was a learned man."

"Yes, of course." At this point it was all right to sound dry.

Before he found more words, the girl said, "The bottle got him. I tried my best, sir, but booze killed my daddy. It was a bad thing."

"It always is," he answered, feeling weakened by her candor, by her young fellowship in the recognition of evil. He would have to admit her, for a trial anyhow. That decision had been forced on him, maybe by Ewing's words, maybe by May's. May seldom disagreed with him but had an annoying habit of being right when she did. Infernally right. Still — confound it! — a weak sympathy was a poor assessor of merit, else idiots would inhabit the classroom. More than that, this girl must not think that a pretty face and a fearful mien alone got her in.

"All right," he said. "Nothing so far necessarily rules you out. Now, then, you have permanent quarters?"

"Yes, sir. With Mr. and Mrs. Adlam. I help Mrs. Adlam, and I like it there."

"Whereas, if I understand rightly, you didn't like it before?" Even as he spoke, he knew the inquiry, though more or less veiled, had the whiff of prurience in it. But the question was asked and had to lie there.

The girl's eyes looked naked into his, and a mist came over them, and a spasm twisted the delicate face. And it seemed to him that hers might be the face of Mary Jess later if the fates had their frolic with her; and lines of remembered verse posted themselves in his head, lines about another prostitute, dead:

> Take her up tenderly,
> Lift her with care;
> Fashioned so slenderly,
> Young, and so fair!

"Forget it!" his voice came to his ears in a bark. "Forget it!"

The mist had grown into unheeded tears. The broken mouth said, "Daddy said, no matter what —"

"I know. An education. Now I said forget it."

She took a handkerchief from her sleeve and wiped her face, and he waited for her composure, wanting crazily to reach over and take her hand. She rose and took a step away, her expression too tight and too old for her years. "All right, sir. Good-bye."

"Wait! I didn't mean that. You are admitted." The words had come out in an unthinking gush.

Her face changed slowly. "Am I? Oh, am I?" If Mr. John Wesley Harrison thought the saved sinner wore the look of seen splendor, he should see this girl.

"Report in the morning."

She moved one pace toward him, as if to shake his hand, then turned and made off, her head lifted to unveiled Olympus.

So much for that. So much, now, for that. He should have posed a few simple questions, at least, to test her knowledge of grammar, arithmetic, history, as he had planned. Instead, he had let the flush of unworthiness dictate his decision. It wasn't the Lord who worked in mysterious ways: it was the devil. Still, it occurred to him as he got up to leave, he felt strangely good.

9

Saturdays were good days, and today would have been a good day in any case. Mid-September had been squally, and between wind squalls six inches of wet snow had fallen, leading a man to wonder why the equinox, that temporal settlement between night and day, should bring unsettled weather. Then, like an apology for breach of truce, had come the chinook, warm as a sighing breath, and water had run in the paths that did for sidewalks and over the planks at the intersections; and who, wanting to hurrah, cared much about mud? Housewives. One indulgent housewife smiling while she plied broom or mop.

Now, in early October, the paths were dry, the sky smiling, and Collingsworth, walking to the drugstore and post office, went along slowly. Why rush when the air was tonic and fallen leaves whispered under his feet? There was green in the cottonwoods yet, along with new-come gold, and now and then, at no urging of breeze, a leaf fluttered down, somehow both melancholy and gay in its good-bye to season. The high lifts of the mountains to westward wore a mantle of snow above the stone blue of their bases. On the slopes of the benches to eastward grass had cured on the stem. It was the color of a mountain-lion pelt he had seen at Merc Marsh's store.

More than anything else, though, it was the size of this world, the generosity of it, that won a man over, that made him want no other. Depth of sky, reach of miles, elbow room for mind and muscle. Here was a country to live in. All right. Be sensuous: it was a land a man wanted to wake up with.

Wanting that much, he wanted to know more about it. What was loved had its warm antecedents, warmer here, if imperfectly sensed because history whispered to ears that were open. It spoke in a couple of arrowheads he had found while out hunting. It murmured in the just-dead brain of an empty buffalo skull he had kicked up in a wallow used not so long ago. Only two lifetimes took a man back to Lewis and Clark, who had looked on this land and, despite all, had found it teeming and fair. Almost just yesterday the fur hunters had roamed it, setting foot, free and ecstatic, where no white man before them had set theirs. Then had come the buffalo hunters and wolfers, some of whom still lived, and then in due course the cowpunchers whose hi-yis, even now, were joining the reverberations of history.

He wasn't sure how much this train of thought had been directed by the sight of old Charlie Blackman, who was shuffling around in front of his shack. The shack was part tin and part scrap wood, and around it were angled or strewn other pieces of board and other rustings of tin that might come in handy someday, together with used remnants of leather and rope, a sagging grindstone and beaver and muskrat traps partly repaired, for when Charlie was not making do by swamping saloons he earned a few nickels by trapping. St. Louis, he had said, was still the best market for furs.

Collingsworth called out, "How are you, Charlie?"

Charlie came forward. He was whiskered and dirty. His gums worked on a chew of tobacco. If he spit oftener, which was often enough, maybe he wouldn't be drooling. Despite his age he could, when he wanted to, move with sure purpose, Collingsworth had observed. For the most part, however, he shuffled. Indifferent to the man, indifferent to the past of which they were beneficiaries, alive only to his age and outworn occupation, people were inclined to smile when his name was mentioned.

"Har you?" the old man said. "Dogged if you don't always sing out hello."

"Fine." Collingsworth gestured toward the traps. "Going out for beaver."

"Or muskrat or mink. Whatever fur comes to the bait. Won't be much. Not anymore."

"Not like old times, I suppose."

Charlie spit and looked into distance, and the shimmer of remembrance shown in his eyes. "I can call to mind," he said, and let his subject trail off.

"Yes?"

"Course, I wasn't around when doin's was real high, not for beaver. But buffalo, man alive, and wolfin' along with it. I seen anyhow a thousand head centered here where we're standin' and wolves taggin' the cripples. Man alive."

Charlie dug his chew out with a forefinger, studied it and, apparently deciding it was dead as old times, dropped it at his feet. "In them days," he went on, "the Injuns was smart, the women leastwise. Ain't anything like it used to be."

"I suppose not, but cheer up, Charlie. This is still a young land."

Charlie's remembering eyes came to focus in what might have been pity. "Young? To you, I'm thinkin'. Whatever is old to the young? Tell me that. Nothin', that's what, except old men like yours truly."

A young country grown old through aging vision, Collingsworth reflected as he walked on. The eye of the beholder. But not entirely. Things had changed since Charlie's youth and would change still more, not the mountains, not the sky, but the earth and the habits of men. People would come seeking homesites. The straggling forerunners, indeed, were already coming, bringing plows and grains and garden stuff and hope and the seed of their loins. When there were enough of them, what would be left? What of the old times of uncluttered acres, of hope that no homesteader could hope for, of blithe and unstudied assurance? Would the likes of Jay Ross and Mort Ewing disappear, their deeds unknown, their voices unheard, their philosophies outgrown and uncomprehended by a new manner of men? What of the free-and-easy attitudes for which, for all their flagrancies, something could be said?

Here, as schoolteacher and even as churchman, he felt a touch of discomfort, for he was part as well as agent of change. To his inner ear came the words of old Mr. Mc-Laine, said after dinner one night — words emptied of pomposity by reason of person and content.

"Change is the order of nature," he had said. His beard swung to the shake of his head. "It is in our nature somehow to resist while forwarding it. What comes comes, to our dismay or delight or more likely both, and both diminished."

So be it. Change. Push, man. Sing hello and sigh goodbye.

As he approached the Adlams' white frame house, he caught a glimpse of Juliet Justice in the back yard. She was raking leaves. There was grace about her, a fluid economy of movement that would have caught any eye. Far more important, there was discipline. Here was a task to do, there in school a lesson to be learned, and there the tease of an idea to which she rose — well, like a trout to a skittering fly. Best student of all, he was about to admit. She wore a red scarf and didn't look up from her raking. It would be questionable for him to call out a greeting.

But there was one change to rejoice in. Whatever his doubts had been, however insufficient and tainted his test of her, she was a prize — so far. The gem of purest ray serene had to wait further assay.

Sauntering on through the rustling leaves, he wished all the students were as eager, as perceptive, as Juliet. Only three, maybe four, were close, including, thank heavens, Jay Ross's girl Jane. Still, he had no complaint. By George, the school was doing well. For the most part these cow-country boys and girls were receptive. By cuffing one, he had cowed the three young ruffians who had thought to play hob with system. He would cuff the others if need be. He had order in his school, and respect for authority and even a liking of regimen and perhaps even a distant liking of him. The students might like Miss Carson as much or more. Certainly those youngsters who wanted to learn must. One thing for sure, they all respected her.

Once he turned to the boardwalk of the main street, Collingsworth quickened his pace. Always he felt not timid but ill at ease, like a man in the dock, when, in passing, he sensed the boozy inquiry of the Family Liquor Store and the Arfive saloon. A piece of foolishness, of course. A dodge away from conviction and manhood. He slowed back to his saunter. The mail might not even have arrived yet. The stage was uncertain since Mort Ewing had disposed of his contract.

Ewing didn't call around at the house anymore. At the last school-board meeting he had been pleasant enough but aloof. It was as if their one quarrel had put a lasting distance between them. Yet Juliet was in school, wasn't she? She was recognized as a superior student. Here together were concession and apology, if unspoken, and neither nor both dented Mort Ewing's shell. Yet he must have known of the high reports the girl won. He would have heard of them from the Adlams, who surely knew. Or from the girl herself. Twice, with his own eyes, he had seen the two together in outside conversation. Twice. All right, he supposed. All right, no matter the past. But confound the man!

It was when he was almost in front of the Arfive saloon that a man with a star on his chest swung out the door. Kraker. That was his name. Kraker, deputy sheriff. After him came two others, by appearances sometime cowpunchers, gone-to-seed rowdies.

Kraker said, "Afternoon, Professor."

"Good afternoon."

Kraker slanted over and blocked the way while the two men looked on. His mouth smiled, and his breath stank of drink. With what might have been mocking assurance, he moved his arms to akimbo, one hand close to the revolver he sported. "How you findin' things here?"

"First rate."

"Guessed you would." The man's left hand came out open as if in acknowledgment of things men held in common. "Who wouldn't, with all them cuties?"

"What are you saying?"

"Oh, nothin', Professor. But it sure is nice to have a filly that needs no breakin' in."

Collingsworth took one step and swung. Kraker went down. He lifted himself with an elbow. At his hip a hand fumbled. Collingsworth kicked it away. With it went the revolver. It skated off the boardwalk. Kraker was licking the blood from his mouth.

Collingsworth went on. There was the mail to get.

10

Mort Ewing was coming from the barn when Fatty Adlam drove up. Damn shame, he was thinking, to have a good saddle horse foundered and ruined forever, all because someone had neglected to close the door to the feed shed. The dog by his side wagged cheerful agreement, then ran out to bark.

The sight of Adlam in a buggy, holding in either hand the reins to a livery-barn team, submerged his annoyance. A chicken, dusting in a patch of sand and sun, cackled out of his way.

"Can't be. Not you, Fatty," he said. "Special occasion?"

Adlam drew a breath into his big belly. "Special but bad."

"How so?"

"The professor! He cleaned up on Kraker."

"And you call that bad?"

"The worthless son of a bitch. Kraker, I mean."

Ewing rested one arm on the rump of the nigh horse. "I vote aye."

"Mort, there's one thing I guess you have guessed — which is that I know. But nobody ever heard it from me." The fat face above Ewing wore the look of distress. The mouth was as apologetic as a bullet hole. "My hunch. Little Julie."

Ewing said a slow, "So," for no yet defined reason feeling the blood rise. "Spill it all."

"It happened in front of my place, but it's hearsay I go by. Kraker, tailed by a couple of no-goods, slaunched out and braced the professor. He said a word or two, and then he was on his ass. The professor booted his six-gun away."

"Any mention of the girl?"

"Not as I get it, but Kraker was hinting around at all, and I guess especially one, of the schoolgirls. Made out the professor to be a lucky stud."

"Then somebody in the know told him."

"Sure. But who I'm thinking about is the professor."

"What! Oh, I see. He ought to be decorated."

"Yes, but the way it is, Mort — and that's why I came — he's apt to wind up in court."

"For what?"

"Assault. Resisting the law. Whatever. It all could come out."

"Hank Howie, that pus-gut of a sheriff!" Ewing removed his arm from the horse and stepped back. His dog brushed against him and licked at his hand. A couple of chickens trailed by, cheered by the prospect of feed time and roost. Out of sight a hired hand was pounding, putting in shape a piece of equipment for now or next season.

"Anyone can file charges, Mort," Adlam said, not as if to defend Howie. "Then, under the law, right or wrong, the sheriff has to act."

"Thanks," Ewing answered, and smacked the dog away. "Since when does a ruckus go on to court?"

"But it was the law he whopped."

"Yeah. Bad as pissin' on Old Glory." Ewing motioned toward the kitchen door. "Light, Fatty, and tie up. Then go inside and rest yourself. There's a drink or so in the cupboard."

"What do you figure to do?"

"Stop it. Stop it before it goes any farther."

"You can, if anybody." Adlam sighed, then took a quick breath. "But see here, Mort."

"What?"

"There's a story I heard about you. You in action."

"That was away back." To dismiss Adlam's worry, Ewing smiled. "What I'll use is what they call gentle persuasion."

Lightly, as if his weight were more float than burden, Adlam got down from the buggy and tied the team to the fence. For an instant Ewing watched him on his voyage to the kitchen door, then strode to the corral and saddled the one horse inside it.

He put the horse to a steady lope, counting hill and gully as measures of progress. He could stop the sheriff if he got there in time, but damn Howie, damn Kraker, and damn the good people if ever they heard.

It was dusk when he pulled up at the sheriff's office. It was a stone building and served as jail, too, and had bars across the windows in back. He swung off the horse, threw the reins over the hitching post and went in.

Howie's eyes rose from his desk. Under his hand was some kind of paper. He had the look on his face of what passed for thought. "Have a chair," he said. "Glad to see you."

Ewing sat down.

Howie took time to light a lamp. In its yellow glow his eyes might have been oiled. He hitched in his chair and pulled at the belt that was always working down the slope of his belly. It struck Ewing that there were two kinds of fat, one unclean.

"Little action in town today," Howie said.

"So I've heard."

"I've been debating, Mort. It's a problem I got, but only one answer to it." The face asked for sympathy. "I guess you know that damn teacher of yours hung a haymaker on Kraker.

Disarmed him to boot. What maybe you don't know is that Kraker's faunchin' to swear to a charge."

"Why not let him faunch?"

"Because he's got cause. Assault and battery on an officer of the law. Mort, how you going to abide that? Where's your respect if you do? A sheriff's got his duties, you know."

"One of them is to use his head. Use it, and you won't cite Collingsworth."

A shadow, maybe of irritation, crossed Howie's face and left it bland. He picked up a gnawed piece of cigar and lit it by means of the lamp. "Sure, you got the school to consider and all, but I got the law and respect for it and a man hot to use it like it was intended." He looked to Ewing for an answer and, getting none, went on. "I haven't seen you and Collingsworth hobnobbin' much lately."

"Makes no difference."

"No? Then what's eatin' you, Mort?"

Ewing waved the question away, but it had been a good one. School was eating on him, and Collingsworth, the proper bastard, and, damn it, the girl. Three times he had talked to her, three times since school started, and each time, like the old fool that he was, he had thought of young things in spring sun.

Howie put his cigar on the edge of his desk and spit out a shred of tobacco that clung to his lip. "You being a good Republican, you got to remember that Kraker swings quite a few votes." He spread his arms out like some hill preacher bringing in the sheaves. Then one hand went to his chest, and a finger touched the star there. "Wasn't for him, I might not be wearing this. It was that close."

"Pass that for now. Just tell me what made Collingsworth mad? What did Kraker say?"

Howie's eyes slid away. "Aw, nothin' as I know of, Mort. Just some little josh of a thing."

Maybe. Probably not. But Kraker could have lied in reporting to Howie. Time would tell. Ewing leaned forward and pointed a finger. "Now about Kraker swinging votes."

"He did!"

"Uh-huh, but aren't you forgetting something?" Howie's gaze asked what. "Your name was on the ballot, put there by vote of the county convention."

It took Howie an instant or two to understand. Then he said with a throw of his open hand, "Mort, you wouldn't!"

"The next convention might. It might figure it could put on the ballot a stronger candidate for the office. How many votes could Kraker turn for you then?"

As if that one little outburst was all a good politician could allow himself, Howie shook his head in unbelief. "By God, Ewing, I thought you were my friend. You mean, come convention time, you'd fight my renomination?"

"It's a little something to think about, but we haven't come to that point."

As he finished speaking, the knob turned, the door opened, and Kraker came in. He wore a patch over the side of his mouth.

Ewing pointed to a chair. "Sit down, Kraker."

Taking his time, Kraker slouched over and sat. He had retrieved his revolver. The eyes in his long face with its jut of a chin were sullen. About him was not so much an air of defeat as defiance. Ewing guessed that at least some of his scrubby followers had deserted his line and made bold to rag him. Fallen, the mighty always were sore. Here was no Sheriff Howie, to be reminded of the facts of political life. Here was a sulky four-flusher, a man to be buffaloed as he liked to buffalo others. It would be easy enough, too easy for a man's taste.

Ewing said, "You been shooting off your face and so got it closed for you."

"Be smart-ass. I don't have to answer to you."

"I'm thinking you do or you will." Ewing kept his voice down. "Keepin' quiet won't set well."

Kraker's eyes went to Howie. "You goin' to let him bully-rag me?"

Howie answered mildly, "Best speak up, Sarge."

"Boss's orders," Kraker said then, making out that without them he would have kept still. "What the hell you want to know, Ewing?"

"What you said to Collingsworth."

"Nothin' to speak of. It was horseplay is all."

"Don't bullshit me!"

"Ask anybody."

Howie broke in. "Answer up, Sarge."

"Boss's orders again. You want the truth, that's what you'll get."

"Get to Collingsworth."

"What I did was I just kind of shied a word at him about a girl, a girl I know about, one of Eva Fox's once. And by God if she ain't in school now!"

"Where'd you hear so much?"

"Eva Fox, she fired Adelaide and —"

"Eva did?"

"She did, and damn if that wasn't dirty after Adelaide workin' her ass there for two-three years."

"Skip your opinion. Go on."

"Well, a couple of nights ago I and Adelaide had a few drinks, and she spilled it. You doubt me, I can name you this chippie. She's —"

"No goddam names!"

Howie interrupted. "All right. All right. We hear you, Mort."

"So who all have you blabbed to?" Ewing said.

"I ain't. That's who."

"How come that?"

"A smart man keeps his powder dry."

Ewing turned. "You believe him, Howie?"

"Sarge don't lie to me."

The question would have to rest there, Ewing decided. There was a chance, fat or slim, that the thought of riper occasions — say campaign time — had kept Kraker mum, some or mostly.

But something didn't jibe. "What about court, then? Likely it all would come out."

Howie cut in with, "No court. No charge. Hear that, Sarge?"

"I figured so," Kraker answered as if grudging the order. But it could be, Ewing thought, that he had figured out for himself that running to court would only cost him more rank.

"That's sensible," Howie said.

"But damn him, I'll get even!" It was hurt speaking. It was the blister, the fester, of comedown.

"No, Sarge. Easy, now," Howie replied as if understanding the blister. "Tell you what. Tell your friends it ain't the function of law to bruise up the voters. Tell 'em that's orders from me — and what could and what can you do long as you're deputy?"

Kraker thought about it.

"One thing more," Ewing said. "That's to shut up. No leaks anywhere. Not even a whisper. Not from us. Not about Collingsworth or the girl or whatever."

Kraker had spirit enough to ask, "Orders?"

"Call it advice. Not everybody knows it, but it could be spread around good and wide that with your badge you been sponging pussy and booze off Eva Fox. Lots of voters don't like spongers. Hardly anybody. So, was I you, I'd keep my trap shut."

"He will," Howie was quick to promise. "Strikes me we got a full understanding. Here's the deal — no charge against the professor, like I already told you, and no loose lip from Kraker or me. Not a word." His eyes raised in a question. "And none from you. Right?"

"Seems likely."

"That's the deal, then," Howie went on. "And I'll tell Eva Fox she don't necessarily have to let Sarge make free with her merchandise. That suit you, Mort? All hunky-dory?"

"Suits," Ewing said, and got to his feet. He had done what he could, all any man could, except that he would go see Eva Fox now. It was then that an oversight flashed in his mind. Jesus, he was fat-headed! The lamp flickered as he put his hand on the desk. "Where's that damn Adelaide?"

A glance passed between Howie and Kraker. With a thumb Howie motioned over his shoulder. "In back."

"Jailed?"

"Just sleepin' it off. We done it for her own good. Right, Sarge?"

"Sure. She was screamin' around crazy, indoors and out."

"Close to the snakes," Howie added.

Ewing said, "I'll have a look."

"No law against it," Howie answered, "but she's likely still cuckoo. Might be better to wait until Soo Son sends over some grub."

"I'll see her now."

Sighing, Howie reached over to the wall and took keys from a hook. "Bring the lamp, Sarge." He lifted himself from the chair and hitched at his belt with one hand, stepped to the back and unlocked and swung open the thick door, letting Kraker go ahead with the lamp. The door opened on an aisle, which was flanked on one side by two cells.

This much Ewing knew from before, having bailed out a

seasonal ranch hand or two. What was new was the smell of the place.

Kraker said, "Holy goddam!"

Howie was late in getting the scent. He halted and sampled it and blew out his breath and stepped ahead of the lamp, the keys swinging from his hand. He fumbled for one and turned the lock. "Bring the light." The two pushed inside before Ewing and came to a stop.

What Ewing saw first was the mussed bunk with nobody on it and the pot that stood at its foot. Then he moved to one side and could see the woman on the floor.

Howie was calling, "Adelaide. Hey, you, Adelaide!"

The woman had discarded most of her clothing, torn and discarded it in some dark frenzy, and lay almost naked on her stomach. She had fouled herself fore and hind, and her face rested in her own vomit.

"Adelaide!"

But one look was enough, one look and the smell of the place to which, it seemed to Ewing, death added its stink to indignity.

While he waited for decision to come to him, Howie began swinging the keys. They ran shadows across the floor and up the side wall.

"How long since you checked on her, Sarge?"

"Not since early this morning. Hell, I've been out."

Howie nodded. "Me, too." Then, as if there were nothing else for it, he went forward and stooped. He pulled one of the woman's arms out from her body and felt for the pulse. He took hold of her back hair and lifted the face away from its smear and half turned the head and with the thumb opened an eyelid. "Closer with that lamp, Sarge."

After his examination he stood up. "I'm afraid she's damn dead," he said, looking at Ewing. "Too bad, but nobody to blame."

"Nobody," Ewing answered, and turned and walked away from the stink.

Outside on the darkened street he was tempted to mount his horse and take off for the ranch. Enough was enough, and yet not enough. There remained Eva Fox and an accounting.

Here and there lights were on, shafting yellow into the night. A team and a saddle horse stood hitched to the rack at the side of the Arfive Mercantile; but most people were home at this hour, relaxed and ready for supper or already stuffing their mouths or digesting what had been set before them. Early for this time of year, not to be explained by the weather yet, but overhead wild geese were honking, bucking up one another for this too-soon trip through the night. And there was a good girl in school and a poor whore who had conveniently died because barkeeps were happy to sell to her and there was a pursy sheriff and a dimwitted deputy and a game and stiff-backed professor and Eva Fox and himself, the champion fixer. And shit.

Merc Marsh was locking up. He came forward as if wanting to talk, no doubt about the set-to this morning; and Ewing went by with only an "Evening, Marsh."

He didn't take the side steps to Eva's. He mounted to the front door and found no one in the parlor and made his way to Eva's office and entered it without knocking.

She looked up from her desk, smiled and asked, "Since when don't you rap, Mort?"

"Since today."

She indicated a chair. "Take the load off."

"Yes," he said. "I will."

She waited, impassive, only her eyes seeming alive in the calm of her face.

"You know about Collingsworth and Kraker this morning?"

"More or less vaguely. Your professor must be quite a man."

"You know the cause of it?"

"As much as anyone seems to know. Some slur on the professor and his girl students. No names."

"And you can sit there, calm as you please, and it was you that tied a can onto Adelaide!"

She leaned forward abruptly and began to shake a hand at him, yet her actions seemed defensive. "Of course I fired her. She was a drunk and a cheat."

"And she blabbed to Kraker. What the hell did you think?"

Eva brought her hands together. Her eyes went away from his. "I was afraid, Mort, afraid when I heard about the ruction this morning, but I swear I never thought Adelaide would tattle. Damn her soul to hell! Now you leave Kraker to me. I'll shut him up."

"No need to. But what made you think Adelaide would keep mum? Why didn't you give her some going-away money?"

Eva came forward again, and again her hand shook at him. "I tried to. I offered more than enough to take her from town. But you know what she wanted? She wanted three hundred dollars. Said she'd stay right in town and hook on her own unless I gave her that much. I got mad. Dammit, you think I can come up with three hundred dollars for every chippie that ever works here?"

"You didn't get in touch with me."

"You wouldn't have come up with it, and I wouldn't ask."

"I'd have come up with something. Acting on your own, you've put the professor and me and Juliet Justice in a spot, and I don't know for sure I can wiggle us out. I think maybe. Maybe I have. But it's a cinch you haven't kept faith. You plain let us down."

"Have it your way, and I'm sorry, sorry about Juliet and all, as sorry as I've ever been." With sudden concern, or what passed for it, she asked, "You're not giving up on her?"

"Nope. It's you that did that."

"That's not so, and you know it, and go to hell, Mort! Bad as it came out, I did what I had to, the only thing that I could. I'm not rotten rich like some I could name."

A muscle ridged itself against one point of her jaw, and it seemed to Ewing, looking at her, that what he had considered the clean lines of her face were the lines of hard cash. Who could say, considering this and that and the other? Anyhow, the time came now and then that cash put its brand on the whole herd.

Eva asked, "You wouldn't want me to take Adelaide back so as to hush her?"

"No," Ewing answered, and rose and made for the door to the outside staircase. He had his hand on the knob when she said, "Adelaide was a good girl once."

"All of them were once." Before he closed himself out, he added, "I reckon she's a good girl again. Anyhow, she's dead."

He didn't wait for her answer.

11

As soon as school let out on Monday, Collingsworth walked home, not tarrying, as he usually did, to consider papers and problems. Though nothing pointed had been said and nothing open done during the day, the atmosphere had altered. The students kept looking at him, with questions and speculations in their eyes, and between classes and at noon had gathered in twos and threes for conversations that ceased when he approached. Little Miss Carson gave no indication at all that she had heard anything. She wouldn't have, anyhow. Always she was strictly business in school. If Juliet Justice knew of the reasons for his punching Kraker, she showed no sign. It would seem that all were aware of the fact and no one aware of the cause.

Though he had felt uncomfortable, something like a bug under a microscope, it was just as well, he supposed, that the students knew what he'd done. He'd have no more problems, or fewer problems, with discipline. But a sidewalk altercation was a poor way to get it.

The sun was about to sink over the mountains, leaving as proof of its trip a great arch of cloud, honey-colored, beneath which fires burned. A beautiful sight, he thought, yet somehow ominous, as if the heavens were showing what might they could exercise.

After he had opened and closed his front door, May called from the kitchen, "Benton? Brother Harrison's waiting to see you."

He went into the sitting room and received Mr. Harrison's hearty "Good afternoon. How do things fare with you, Brother Collingsworth?" The man's grip was possessive.

Collingsworth answered that things fared all right and asked Mr. Harrison to sit down again.

Mr. Harrison laced his fingers across his stomach. The vague grooves of trouble troubled his face. "I have come for advice," he said.

"If I can give it."

"You have heard of the death, the death of that poor woman, I mean?"

"No."

"She died in jail Saturday, the result of too much strong drink. She was a wanton" — Mr. Harrison had lowered his voice — "a fallen woman."

"Yes?"

"I have been asked to conduct the funeral services and so find myself in a trying situation, one I've never before experienced in a long ministry. Not that I haven't presided at the last rites for sinners, though not of this sort — but always something hopeful, something kind, some bit of amelioration, could be said for them."

"Who asked you?"

"That adds to my difficulties. A note came from that woman called Eva Fox. Brother Collingsworth, surely she wouldn't profane the house of God with her presence?"

"I don't know, but you could hardly conduct services at her house."

"Oh, no! Goodness, no!"

"Conduct them at the graveside. Isn't that best?"

Mr. Harrison nodded, it seemed a little unwillingly. "Yes,

though I'm not sure that such was intended in the request. Besides, graveside services always strike me as bleak, as removed, so to speak, from the seat and shelter of worship."

Collingsworth kept silent, though he was tempted to say that on occasion God must journey forth from the church.

Mr. Harrison went on, "So far as I know — and I've asked around quite discreetly — there's not one single thing to be said for this lost soul. Why, not even her last name is known. What words can I speak in her favor? Where is one covering grace?"

Twice now, twice recently for no reason except some relationship of subject, lines from "The Bridge of Sighs" sang in Collingsworth's head. The poem was no more than a highly adroit exercise in sentimentality, but still the lines sang:

> Owning her weakness,
> Her evil behavior,
> And leaving, with meekness,
> Her sins to her Saviour!

Aloud he said, "Why a funeral oration, Mr. Harrison? Why must it be personal?"

"It's part of the service. It's always expected."

And usually wrong, Collingsworth thought, usually in bad taste, usually embarrassing with its charitable exaggerations of perished and personal graces, if any. "Read some prayers and something out of the Bible, like Psalms. That's my advice."

"Well," Mr. Harrison answered, counting his fingers, "I may do just that, but it's so true, isn't it, the wages of sin?"

"If death is the proof, then we're all paid in the same coin."

Mr. Harrison thought a minute. The smile that he turned on Collingsworth then had in it the pinch of reserve. "The hereafter — but you're just trying to guy me a little. I'm on to you, Brother Collingsworth."

Collingsworth answered, "I knew you would be."

The reply appeared satisfactory. "I'll surely think on your suggestions," Mr. Harrison said, but made no move to go. His mouth shaped a word but left it unuttered. At last he ventured, "You didn't linger after services Sunday."

The statement required no response, and Collingsworth made none, though he suspected what now was on Mr. Harrison's mind.

"You've had your own trouble, I know, Brother Collingsworth. I shouldn't burden you with mine."

"What did you hear?"

"It's common knowledge. That you knocked down the deputy sheriff." Mr. Harrison extended a generous hand. "I am not being inquisitive, but if it would help you to talk about it?

"I am sure you had good reason," he went on, apparently encouraged by silence, "but as it is, in the dark, so to speak, what can your friends and supporters say except that the incident was unfortunate?"

"Nothing."

"Mr. Marsh and I were discussing it."

"And both regretted it?"

"Well, you know, yes."

"Forget it. It's done. That's that."

"Don't get me wrong. I'm sure there was real provocation." Mr. Harrison's gaze came up, still hopeful of an answer.

"Good."

Slowly, as if under the weight of things unsettled, Mr. Harrison rose to his feet. "Thanks for your advice, brother."

As they went to the door, Collingsworth answered, "Any time." He said good-bye and swung the door to.

People with their certitudes! People with their pushing curiosity! Mr. Harrison, as sure of the Word as he was lost for an explanation! Certitude and curiosity, and the devil take both!

May came from the kitchen with Mary Jess trailing along. An apron circled her just-swelling front. A lock of escaped hair dangled over her forehead. She listened an instant as Tommie cried from the bedroom, the look of care deepening on her face. "I'm glad you contained yourself," she said.

"I'm glad someone is. Numskulls need kicking."

"Hush." May made a backward gesture toward Mary Jess.

"Who, Father?" Mary Jess asked. "Who do you want to kick?"

"Whom," he said.

"No one you know," May told her.

The truth shall set you free, but fibs were the ticket for children. "I didn't go for the mail," he said. May looked at him. "People and their infernal curiosity! I won't put up with it."

"What will you do, Benton? Wait till it kills all the cats?"

"All right. All right." He didn't feel like grinning.

"Then you can pick up some onions. I haven't a one for the stew."

He was at the point of asking why not, since the grocery wagon took orders and made daily deliveries, but then he took note of how worn she appeared. He told himself, not for the first time, that he ought to make a habit of being more thoughtful. "Sure, Maysie. No trouble," he said. "Anyhow, Merc Marsh will want a look at his gladiator."

Outside, dusk was coming on, delayed by the bright sea of sky in the west. Above the sea, like an inverted bank, the long honey arch rested, a shade darker now, the color of wild honey taken from bee trees in boyhood Indiana. Out of the north, the limitless north, came a breeze with tidings of winter. Soon, he supposed, men lucky enough to own buffalo overcoats would put them on, glad to be warm though weighed down. He snugged his own old cloth coat about his neck.

He could do with a new one, but, Lord, May came first and

Mary Jess and Tommie and the house and the baby a-coming. All on a schoolteacher's salary. Thank heavens, neither Maysie nor he was overfond of possessions, never having had many. Even in old things, a man could keep himself presentable by means of a whiskbroom and shoe polish so long as he remembered a tie.

Already the store was lighted, but the lamp shine that came through the windows seemed pallid and false as against the western sky's permeation. Seeking the light, men put a match to a kerosene wick.

Inside were just Bill Robinson, the choir's faithful quaver, and Merc Marsh himself. Marsh sat on a high stool before a high desk, pencil in hand, eyeshade drawn down, sleeve protectors in place. He looked up as Collingsworth entered, then returned to his work.

Approaching, Bill Robinson asked, "Yes, sir, Professor?" It appeared to Collingsworth that there was more in his eyes than the request for an order.

"A few onions. That's all tonight. A small sack."

After Robinson had complied and marked down the charge, Collingsworth stepped along the aisle, carrying his purchase. He stopped in front of the high desk and said, "Good evening, Merc."

"Good evening, Professor Collingsworth." Marsh's face wore no expression at all. It was as vacant as a blackboard, innocent of chalk, misspellings, constructions and Q.E.D.'s. Profit above position. The face of business. He did volunteer, "Nice out." Then he went back to his pencil work.

Collingsworth waited an instant, but no more was coming. He went to the door and let himself out, imagining that Marsh's gaze had been fixed on his back.

He was a little astonished, walking on to the post office, when a man he didn't know said to him, "How are you, Professor?" Apparently the man was a lounger, a roughneck possibly, but his expression was friendly and smiling, and his eyes projected no questions.

Collingsworth answered, "Fine. Thank you."

He came to a group of three men then, two of whom he knew by name only, and, as old Charlie Blackman would have said, they sang out hellos. He replied civilly, brushed by the sense of initiation into an unknown and unlikely fraternity.

Fatty Adlam stood in front of his place and stepped out as Collingsworth neared and stopped him almost at the very spot of Saturday's trouble. His expression wasn't belligerent. It was as grave as a headstone. He extended a hand that might have belonged to a lady.

"Professor Collingsworth," he said, "may I make bold to thank you?" He added, "For many things."

Quickly, then, as if not expecting or wanting acknowledgment, he turned his great hulk around and disappeared inside.

After Benton had gone, May picked up Tommie and changed his diapers and brought him to the kitchen and fed him. He could eat porridge now and mashed vegetables and bits of graham cracker that drooled from his mouth and had to be spooned from his chin and reintroduced. He had taken to a bottle readily enough, though sometimes he still nuzzled for her as if his little mind could recall better sources. She put him back in bed with a warmed bottle slanted down from a pillow.

In the dining room Mary Jess was setting the table, being exact about it as she'd been taught. Even the napkins, rolled in their rings, were put each in its proper place. Already the child could read the inscriptions. She could do more than that. Once she saw the shape of a printed word and heard the sound of it, she didn't forget.

For such a daughter, thank the heavens, and thanks for Tommie, too, and, pray God, let him grow big and strong. One thing, he ate well enough.

The stew was simmering. In addition to meat, she had put into it potatoes and rutabagas and carrots. It lacked onions, which would be supplied shortly, and okra, which no one in town seemed to have heard of. At home a stew without okra was hardly a stew.

She put a basin of sour milk in the churn and sat down and began paddling it, half aware that the paddle rose and fell to the pace of her thoughts.

Some people would have thought and some people did think Benton a difficult man, as, to be truthful, he could be. But those severe in their judgments, as her own parents were wont to be, did not know the man. Noting his aberrant moods, they went no further. They didn't know the depth of him, the rightness and virtue, the enduring commitment to family and the good life. He needed understanding, to be sure, and he needed returned love. But they were all he needed, and he had them; and his unaccountable humors melted away as a consequence. Underneath, he was a tender man and one as capable of fun and merriment as any husband known.

She could smile, as many times she had, at a remembrance now stirred somehow by the splash of the paddle. It was early in their married life, and they were abed at night, and she had asked Benton please to get up and bring a glass of water. "Why," he had answered, "get it yourself." It was then, and never after, that she had thought to leave him and go home.

What foolishness! She had been spoiled, as all girls were spoiled, by the silly customs of courtship. Maidens were to be wooed. They were to be danced attendance on. They were to be treated, not just as precious, but as helpless, fragile as a piece of heired china too fine for use. They had to learn later, as they should have been taught, to get their own water, barring disability alone.

She stopped churning when Benton came in. He laid a sack on the table. "No mail. There's your onions."

"Thank you, Benton. I'll put them right in."

"And the so-called schoolteacher, better known for his fisticuffs, now will go milk."

He went to the back entryway, shed his coat in favor of an old sweater and drew a pair of overalls over his trousers. Then he picked up the clean pail and went out.

May peeled and quartered three onions, dropped them into the stew kettle and moved the kettle to a hotter spot on the range. The fire was all right. It was Benton that wasn't.

Later she took the foaming bucket from him and strained the milk and set it aside to cool. "Supper's ready," she said.

After grace, which Benton said as if hard put to find blessings, they ate in silence. Even Mary Jess had come to respect her father's moods. The little thing beamed when he beamed and sobered when he did.

Afterward Benton went into the parlor, probably to read more of Hawthorne, whose works he was going over again; and, with the help of Mary Jess, May took the dishes out to the kitchen, dipped water from the reservoir at the end of the range, made it hotter with an addition from the teakettle and started to tidy up.

She had rinsed the last dish when she heard Benton's laugh. The why of it she couldn't imagine. What was funny in *The Scarlet Letter?* But it was as if a cloud had lifted, and she gave the dish to Mary Jess to dry and went into the parlor.

Benton was chuckling now. On his face was the twisted, slightly impish, wry-more-than-mirthful smile that incongruity often brought to it. The opened book lay face down on his lap.

"Guess what?" he asked.

"Tell me."

"Before you you see not only the preacher's doubt and the storekeeper's discard but also the ne'er-do-wells' choice and the saloon owner's friend."

"What, Benton?"

"Maysie, I've swapped constituencies."

Part Two

12

COLLINGSWORTH SAT in study hall after school was dismissed, for the moment preferring this second-floor space to his downstairs office. Motes of still-unsettled dust patterned the sunlight that streamed soft through the westward windows, but silence had come and quiescence after the coughs and questions and fidgets of students; and from here, if he went to look, the view, right or left, was better than from below. But it was good just to sit. It was good to think the time was May, the tender month, the beginning burgeoning, the last month of school.

How different from just six weeks or so past, when a spring blizzard had struck and left lambs dying and dead all over the Breast River country. Poor Jay Ross, who like many another had switched from cattle to sheep, in prosperity calling them the golden hoof. Now the frozen hoof was more like it.

The scene flowed before him. All the land a glare of snow, small-humped where it glistened over downed lambs and old ewes, and Jay, bundled and booted, his face expressionless as he and his men had pitched carcasses into hayracks pulled by teams breathing white. Free on that Saturday, he himself had taken a hand.

Pausing once after having flung a lamb in the rack, Jay

smiled a smile not of defeat. "I'll wind, Prof," he said. "Now the missus will have more ammunition."

Collingsworth looked at him and gazed around. The sky was a far frozen shield and the sun a frozen stare. When a man tried to look across the fields of snow, his eyes pinched up. Not a breeze moved. The wind was as dead as a carcass.

"It's not just the wind sets her off," Jay went on as if noting the stillness. For an instant a glint of dumb puzzlement came to his face. "I don't know, Prof, but was she a horse, I'd think about loco."

All Collingsworth could think of to say was, "She's just upset. It will pass."

"Hope so. Like hard times; they'll pass, too." His thoughts, Collingsworth guessed, had shifted to sheep and losses and bank account and to days ahead. On his face grew the look of resolution, of utter confidence. "I been in worse fixes. Something weak in a man who hollers out uncle."

It struck Collingsworth that Ross spoke for himself alone. Out of his own energies, his native wit, his inward faith, his managed luck he would master the fates. From this fierce but lovely young land he would wrest fortune. He envied Ross's animal confidence, wondering if education would have altered and weakened it. Books made a man wonder. Books made the whole man, and the whole man doubted himself. But it was difficult to think that anything ever would have changed Ross, that ever his native hue of resolution could have been sicklied over with the pale cast of thought. Himself he was born, the seed sown with conception.

Collingsworth rose from the desk and went to an east window from which he could see most of the town. Yonder was the new courthouse, made of native stone hewn from Breast Butte, and to his left the grade school that matched it. They looked a bit like buttes themselves, fashioned and turreted buttes fitting to countryside. By contrast, his high school, made of buff brick, stood boxlike and alien to its surroundings. But it could be said in its favor that it was a far cry from the old Woodmen's Hall. It sufficed and would do so long after his tenure.

Long after his tenure, though Arfive was growing. Seven years — and already it was half again as big as when he first saw it. Idly, without order, while he watched the occasional stirrings of town, he let drift through his mind the additions to be counted since that long-ago but not-so-long-ago time. A bank now and a store to compete with Merc Marsh, both run by Jews. A resident doctor. A resident dentist. A resident lawyer. A third high-school teacher. A four-page newspaper that alcohol edited and occasionally didn't. A couple of questionable land locators, for the flow of homesteaders had become somewhat more than a trickle. A commerical club, no less, of which he was a good if questioning member. A telephone system, already once improved, which not everyone could afford to subscribe to. Some of the close-in ranchers, like Mort Ewing, had connected, however, though wet weather grounded the top wires of fences used for telephone lines where fences existed. There was talk of a post office divorced from the drugstore. There was talk of electric lights and a railroad spur from Great Falls. The town should incorporate, the commercial club believed. Growth. People and more people, drawn by real or imagined opportunity in commerce and field.

Beyond the town, beyond the wintered trees of the valley, the cemetery lay on the slope that led up to the benchlands. Its headstones, catching the afternoon light, looked like the remnant rubble of a forgotten upheaval. The cemetery had grown along with the town. In its population now were the two he had had to put there — little Tommie, who had withered to death, and Charlotte, the baby, who had lived hardly long enough to be named.

To his ears came May's cry, the never-answered cry of all those bereaved. "Why did it happen to us? Why did it have to happen?"

"Bronchitis," the doctor had said.

He turned away from the window and followed the sun across the room to the west. From here he could see Cashman Coulee, denting the bench that slanted down to the valley. Part of it was shaded and part of it still bright with sun, and all of it lay secluded and private as it had since old Johnny Cashman, in years that only the oldest remembered, had tried to make a go of things there and gone off defeated, leaving the work of his hands to the work of the elements. There remained of ambition forsaken only a board or two, a stone, a shoveled hollow, as remote in time as a teepee ring and as unobtrusive.

A man hunting, feeling the whispers of old return about him, always could bag a brace or two of teal in the potholes of the coulee. Or, feeling older whispers, he could hunt for arrowheads, left or lost by untamed Indians who had driven buffalo to wreck or death down the leftward bluff and so made meat for winter. Or he could sit among the sandstone toadstools and listen to the wind that carved them.

Farther west, snow-patched and purple, the mountains cut the sky. The lonely mountains, he thought, the lonely purity of mountains, with Elephant Ear Butte standing grand like a guarantee of grace.

He had supposed the school deserted, but now he heard footsteps and voices and looked toward the door and saw Miss Carson coming in. With her was a dark, thin girl, part Indian by appearance, whom Miss Carson had to encourage to come forward.

"Excuse me, Mr. Collingsworth," Miss Carson said. "I wondered if you had a minute?"

"Of course," he answered, and motioned toward the closest row of desks. "Won't you sit down?"

"May I introduce Marie Wolf?"

He acknowledged the introduction, thinking the girl was probably French and Indian. Lame Wolf or Hiding Wolf or some such variation might be her Blackfoot name.

While they were seating themselves, it passed through his mind that he would always have time for Miss Carson. She was a faithful, no-nonsense, excellent teacher, grown better and better with years. Praise be she wasn't one of those just-graduated, fugitive misses who taught for a term and got married. Her first interests were the school, the students and church. And it was pleasant to know she was loyal.

"Marie wants to go to school here next year."

He said, "I see."

What his eyes saw was a girl with that first flush of beauty, that fugitive flush, that part-bloods so often had. It was likely she'd become a fat and unlovely squaw, but now she was trim and dear and graceful as well, if what movements she'd made were indicative. In the thin, copper face the eyes were enormous, enormous and liquid, perhaps with fright.

"Marie's been going to school at Shaw Academy," Miss Carson continued. "It was there I met her."

"Last year?"

"Yes, of course. During that inspection they asked us to make."

"You weren't impressed."

"Maybe that's why the authorities appear to have shelved my report. But I was impressed with Marie."

"Indian schools are hardly up to standard," he said. "As you reported, only two instructors and those ill-prepared, health and sanitation indifferent, church dogma put above education."

As he spoke, he was seeing the Indian encampments that, fall and spring, sprouted on the south edge of Arfive, seeing the tattered teepees, the cayuses, carts and wagons, the dirty curs, the relict bucks and squaws and progeny, all squatted at this point between school and reservation. It was a celebration, this accompaniment of pupils, and it was noxious, and it was pitiful.

"Marie is as much above the Shaw standard as our standard is above its," Miss Carson was saying. "She's much the best student of all. I've checked the record and I've talked to her, both there and here, where she looked me up. Shaw has no more for her."

"Without more proof than the records at Shaw, it appears irregular," he said, somehow not wanting to close the door on this war whoop, as superior white men called Indians.

"If I remember rightly, Mr. Collingsworth," Miss Carson said, smiling, "you ventured irregularity once before — and with no regrets."

He had to smile in return. "Your memory's in good shape. And now you want me to push my luck."

While they waited for him to go on, he looked again at the girl, who had hardly moved since sitting down. Was there, in those dark eyes, in that tan face, the appearance of intelligence? Winsome she undoubtedly was. Too winsome probably. He could imagine, looking ahead, the agitation of some white father whose son insisted on courting her. But pretty was as pretty did. Did winsomeness combine with wit? Could education overcome the teepee? Was there any back to her head?

He must admit somewhat in her favor that the Indians never had had a chance. Nor had they now, they or their hybrids. They had been proud once, maybe clean, though certainly pagan, and they had been chivvied and cheated and altogether debauched, and who cared? It was still felt if not often said anymore that death made a good Indian. To be sure, the little breeds from the south fringe of town went sometimes to grammar school — from shacks and cabins that discouraged brooms and mops. They came from families too poor for a pot. They came lousy and often enough smelling of skunk, for skunk meat was better than none. They came bewildered, out of place, minus grounding. They came and failed and disappeared, untouched or hurt by experience. Never before had one sought admission to high school.

"I was woolgathering," he said by way of apology. "Where would you stay, Marie? With your family?"

The girl gave a grave shake of her head. "It is too far. They are poor," she answered. Her voice was soft, not coarse or shrill as he had rather expected. She spread her small hands. "All of us are poor." Her tone was matter-of-fact, not resentful, though he supposed she meant to include the whole tribe.

Miss Carson said, "If you take her, I'll sponsor her. Actually, I'm tired of one room. Even before Marie looked me up, I had arranged with Mr. Leonard Wither to rent that little house of his next fall. You know the one — kitty-cornered from grade school? It's adequate for two."

"We would have to take you on trial, Marie," he said. "Your grades would be important, more so than in most instances. They'd have to be good."

What the girl was feeling, he couldn't tell. Except for the luminosity of eye, her face didn't speak. Indians, he knew, could be like that, impassive as statuary, impassive in her case as a figurine.

"I'll help her if need be," Miss Carson said.

"Yes," the girl answered him. "I know. I will."

"Then let's call it settled."

"I'm so grateful, Mr. Collingsworth." Miss Carson got up. "Marie?"

The girl rose then. "Thank you many times."

"Your thanks go to Miss Carson," he said. "She's responsible."

The two started for the door. Then the girl paused and turned and said, "I'll do good. I promise."

Her grammar, Collingsworth thought as they disappeared, could stand some help, but for that matter what student's couldn't? Except for one, and she was gone. Except for one he'd admitted with doubt as he had admitted this little Marie.

Though the memories of satisfaction held constant, the years fused and mixed. It was difficult to believe that four school terms had passed since Juliet Justice had made her address and that fall had gone on to the University of Montana at Missoula where, this very next month, she'd receive her degree. Three years in high school, only three years, and those remembered as image rather than time, and then graduation as valedictorian.

To think of her was to see her. To see her was to canvass the adjectives. Neat there in the front row. Prompt. Cooperative. Gracious. Alert. Even radiant. But adjectives were empty. In the field of C minds, she was the sport, the A-plus; and there was the teacher's reward.

Sin, he thought, wasn't always the winner. If her past claimed any due, it was negative and reverse. It was her seeming indifference to boys. Save for public functions, which she attended with other girls and sometimes Mort Ewing, her excursions from the Adlam household had been pretty well limited to weekend and vacation visits to the R5, proper and rightful visits, no matter how gossip might have it, to the home of her known benefactor. If also, in the absence of kin, she had come to look on Ewing somewhat as a father, fine. There was no doubt about it, Ewing had found a daughter, found her and paid for her education and been proud. He had let it be known that he would go to Missoula for her graduation.

Maybe, just maybe, this little Marie, this shy offal-eater from the reservation, would turn out well, too.

Collingsworth took the watch from his vest and flicked the lid open and saw it was time to go home. The soft, lengthening days had a way of confusing a man. First, though, he must arrange a table and chairs for the confounded school-board meeting tonight.

�

It appeared to Collingsworth that Jay Ross never ran out of cigars — his vest pockets bulged with them — nor was he ever reluctant to pass them. As he was about to finger some out, he asked, "Sure the smoke doesn't mortify you, Miss Stonehouse?"

"Not at all. I enjoy it." Miss Stonehouse was the newly elected county superintendent of schools and as such sat in on board meetings, not altogether to the delight of the men members. Having taught first grade for a couple of years, she was abundantly qualified for her position. Besides, she had had no opposition.

The room would have to be aired out later, Collingsworth reflected. He had to admit he liked tobacco himself, but it would not be fitting that young people enter a room heavy with dead smoke.

"Full tally tonight," Mort Ewing said needlessly as he looked around the table at which they all sat. It had been plain from the first that he didn't much like to preside.

Not in seven years had the board changed — which testified to public satisfaction or apathy. There was the new county superintendent, of course, and there was Bill Robinson, Merc Marsh's man, now acting as paid clerk, but here were Ewing and Ross and Merc Marsh and old Mr. McLaine whose hand, raising a match, had a tremor at odds with his mind.

Ewing rustled the few papers in front of him. "Y'all have a

copy of what Prof figures we'll need, come another school year. I reckon you've read 'em." He had a habit of relapsing into southernisms when presiding, as if formality goaded him. "Total count, near as he can calculate, comes nigh onto two thousand dollars. Biggest single item is to outfit two classrooms we've left bare until needed. Time's come, he says, or next fall will catch us. There's coal to buy, too, and supplies and whatnot. But you know all that a'ready."

"I believe," Merc Marsh said, his smile maybe asking forgiveness, "that procedure requires we approve the minutes of the last meeting first."

"You're a great one for order, Merc."

Mr. McLaine leaned forward and shakily tipped the ash off his cigar. "I move the reading of the minutes of the last meeting be dispensed with." No one voted nay. "Now," Mr. McLaine said, "we all know that the school needs these things since Mr. Collingsworth says it does. Surely there's no disagreement. And so I move to approve —"

"Just a minute," Marsh broke in. "I may be a little ahead of myself, but still it's a thing we have to discuss. No disagreement about the items, I'll grant. But about the cost?"

"Of course it's an estimate," Collingsworth said, "but an estimate based on the comparative prices in a good many catalogues. Possibly we can purchase for less."

Marsh spoke to the rest of them. "The professor's not a businessman and not supposed to be. I'll guarantee that figure can be cut, just how much I don't know. What I mean is that I'll undertake to get it for less. Naturally my store has connections."

Ewing said, "So? Just leave it to you, huh?"

"That way we'll not only save money but keep it at home. You'll admit that's desirable?"

"Yep." A little smile played on Ewing's face. "All the desk carpenters we got around here and the coal miners and them as whittle chalk and mold inkwells — they got to come first."

Collingsworth saw the blood starting up Marsh's face. Except for Ewing and Mr. McLaine, he couldn't be sure the others saw the real issue in the proposal, though Ross could be expected to back him. Miss Stonehouse, sitting prim, appeared to be thinking. Robinson had his pen poised over his tablet, no doubt hoping to record that his boss had been granted the contract.

"It would be against my advice," he said then.

Marsh asked, "Why?"

"Because you're a member of the board."

"It's known as a conflict of interest." With his snowy beard Mr. McLaine was remindful of a picture of Moses. "You would have opposing concerns, your own and the school's."

"Even if I could save the school money?"

Ross moved in his chair. His cigar had dropped ash on his vest. "Sure, Marsh. Can't you see? No matter what, it would look bad for us. A put-up job, people would say."

"And you got a boy about ready for high school," Ewing added. "Thinks high of you, I bet." He said no more, choosing, Collingsworth supposed, to let this aside move into the current of thought. He fashioned a cigarette with the skill of long practice.

"I give up," Marsh said, summoning his storekeeper's manner. After all, here were customers. "Sure has its twists and turns, this being a board member."

"I move we approve the list and ask for bids, if it appears to Mr. Collingsworth that's the best way," Mr. McLaine said. "He knows the school-supply houses."

Ross seconded the motion. It passed without dissent.

"All right," Ewing said, picking up a page of paper. "Under new business here's another thing. It's a letter from Mr. Nicolas Brudd. All hands know who he is, I reckon?" His eyes questioned the others. "Miss Stonehouse, he sure must be a name to you. Big liquor distributor out of Great Falls, not to mention other interests. Got a wad that would plug a culvert. I'll pass this letter around, but what he offers to do is to give a twenty-five-dollar prize for the top student in each class every year."

He gave the letter to Ross, who read it and handed it on. For a moment, after it had been returned to him, he sat silent, apparently waiting for comment.

At last Miss Stonehouse ventured, "It would be an encouragement, a boost, if I may say so, for greater application to studies."

She was an addlepate he'd probably have to set right, Collingsworth reflected. With an effort he kept silent, reminding himself, before he forgot, that he was the instrument of the board's decisions. Legally it was for the board to set policy and for him to carry it out — which made him a eunuch if he obliged.

"Sure thing," Marsh said. "Brudd can spare it, the kids can use it. Open and shut, I would say."

"Anyone else?" Ewing asked. "No? Prof, what's your notion?"

Collingsworth pushed back his chair and got to his feet. "My notion is no," he said, letting his voice be as harsh as it wished. "Respectability for that man! Even the odor of it! No! He wants to buy it, not having any. He wants good will for ill deeds. Call it vanity in him. Imagine it to be restitution. Say it's business promotion, as in large part it must be. No matter. It's bad."

Ross said, "Whoa, Prof. It's still money."

"Tainted money. That man has done more to corrupt this whole section than any other man you can name."

Ross would support him, Collingsworth knew, but from loyalty more than conviction. Even obvious moral considerations like this one were likely to be unclear in his mind.

"It's for us to decide," Marsh said, not looking at Collingsworth. "What does it matter, the source of the money? Good kids would get a reward."

"Not while I'm principal."

Now Marsh looked his way. "Professor, that sounds mighty close to a threat."

"Make it a fact."

Smiling, Ewing raised his hand, palm out. "Easy, Prof."

For a moment more Collingsworth remained on his feet, then sat down slowly.

"I move," Mr. McLaine said, his beard moving to the involuntary shake of his face, "that the board decline this kind offer."

Put to a vote, the motion passed, only Merc Marsh dissenting.

A quotation ran through Collingsworth's head. "So are the ways of every one that is greedy of gain —"

"That's all," Ewing said. "Anyone want to adjourn?"

❧

Outside the school building Ewing exchanged leave-takings and started up the boardwalk with Jay Ross. "Save walkin'," he said to make conversation, "if we'd drove our rigs here, 'stead of tyin' up at McCabe's."

"Yep." Jay was wearing that damn derby hat. Wanted to be a nabob, maybe, or to josh them as thought they were. The moonlight played on the hat.

They walked on in silence until Ewing said, "It's hell to be right."

"Anyhow, all the time," Ross answered. "If anybody is."

Somehow Ross's remark put the mind to working. Collingsworth had been right all right, yet dedication was one of those jim-dandy words that, if practiced, a man shied away from. It was too sure. It didn't allow for any maggot in virtue, not even so much as its opposite owned up to its maggots. But a man had to go along with Collingsworth. No maggots there.

What he said was, "It's not only hell but damn lonely."

"I don't know. Teaching. Church work. Tuba in the Silver Cornet Band. And his wife leading those teetotal biddies. What do you call it? The Women's Christian Temperance Union."

"Anyhow, we're lucky he stays on — iron face and iron voice and all, when he gets r'iled."

"Sure," Ross said, and after a while added, "Nick Brudd's in town. He won't like it much."

"You scare me."

"I bet I do." They had reached Adlam's saloon. "Come in and have a drink."

A half-dozen men were in the place. Brudd stood at the bar, talking to Adlam. He turned his head at the sound of their entrance. "Live ones," he said. "Fatty, bring drinks to the gentlemen." He moved to the back, rested a hand on the table and waited. Arrived there, Ross shook his round, derbied head.

Ewing said, "We been savin' your hard-earned money, Nick."

Brudd narrowed his eyes. Ewing thought he saw a gleam in them. "First turndown but who cares? There's other schools eager. Unanimous, was it?"

"Nope," Ewing answered. "Merc Marsh was all for it, him being so sensible."

"But you two?"

"Was in the majority," Ewing answered.

Brudd made a show of shaking his head, as if in dumb wonder, but the eyes at the sides of his hawk's beak of a nose gave the lie to his act. "A man would almost think that preacher-principal had something on you."

Before Ewing could speak, Ross said, "He has. What he has on us is that he's maybe got the best school in the state. If we don't always see eye to eye with him, like I don't, we figure likely it's because we're cock-eyed, and so we string along. You better believe it."

It was a long speech for Ross and warm-spoken, too, and Brudd answered, "Aw, pull up, Jay. Nothing meant." He pushed his hat back on his bald head and so put his face out of true. His brow was too high for a bird's. "It's just, well, a good-intended man gets a kick in the ass. You know how that is. But that hand's been played, and it wasn't much stakes in the first place. Speaking of that, how about a friendly game? Judge Secrest said he'd come along by and by."

"Not tonight," Ewing answered. Friendly game, Brudd had said. Like always, but now maybe more so, he meant cut-throat. Ewing turned and walked out, giving Adlam a wave of good-bye on the way.

There were four of them at the table — Nick Brudd, Jay Ross, Judge Secrest and a visiting wool-and-stock buyer named Tevis, whom Adlam hadn't known before. They disdained chips — each had brought his stake with him — and they had agreed to play no-limit straight stud and to discard the joker, though in cow-country games it was usually played as a match for an ace and a wild card in both straights and flushes.

A sure-enough gamblers' game, Adlam thought as he re-turned to the bar after serving them and began dousing glasses. Big stakes and let losers cry. A kind of worrisome thing if you had a friend in the play. But let the chips — the bills — fall. He hadn't promoted the game, except to sell two decks of cards and provide a table and chairs. He took no cut and never had, wanting the layout to be a convenience for cus-tomers who liked modest play. What little profit he made, aside from whatever good will totaled up, he made from the sale of drinks and decks.

"Yes, sir, my friend," he said to a customer who looked like a drummer. He poured a shot and drew a small glass of beer for a chaser.

"Private affair?" the man asked, looking back toward the players.

"Unless you're loaded."

The man shook his head, drank shot and chaser and went out.

The two other customers at the bar, Adlam knew from before, would spend an hour in occasional conversation over one beer apiece. His attention went back to the gamblers. He couldn't see the actual play.

He drew on his knowledge. Ross was a bold player, a frequent bluffer who, like many a one, hated the thought of being bluffed himself. Secrest had been a judge all right, by appointment, and still practiced law here and there while drawing a salary from the federal government for some vague services in connection with the public domain. He played a close, lawyer's game and would take care of himself. Combine bankroll, bumptiousness and craft, and you had Brudd. Tevis was new to Arfive.

"Bring us a round, Fatty," Brudd called.

At the table, after he had set out the drinks, Adlam lingered long enough to see that Brudd was bulling the game. Raise and stiff raise and raise again. High and mighty poker — but there was no rule against wielding your roll. Bar luck, it was bad poker, though. Bar a sweet run of cards.

While Adlam watched, Brudd fifth-carded Ross, drawing an ace to his hole card to top Ross's kings. The pot was better than sizable. "Shit will do for brains if you're lucky," Brudd said, adding the pot to a pile that had grown.

Three customers came in, and Adlam returned to the bar.

One of them, after a pull at his beer and a glance toward the rear, said, "We was hopin' to work up a game, but not tonight, huh?"

"If you'd staked out the table earlier — ?"

"Sure, Fatty. Forget it. How does it go?"

"How would I know without horning in? Seesaw, I s'pose."

"Yeah. Hell and gone both ways, too high and low for the likes of us. Fill 'em up again, will you?"

It wasn't being too bad a night, Adlam reflected after the three had gone and still other drinkers dropped in. Nothing big, like Christmas Eve and the Fourth of July, but big enough to keep a barkeep fairly busy. He wished he could find a good, steady man to fill in so that he and his wife could go to Missoula to see Julie graduate. The trouble with fill-ins was they drank up the inventory and, stewed, kept serving drinks on the house.

A lull came now, and it was time the house bought for the poker players. They had paid for five rounds in four hours or so. He arrived at the table during a hush. His "The roof leaked" didn't break it. He placed the glasses, saying no more, and stood back.

Every man had stayed, and every man was paired in sight. Ross had tens to a jack, Tevis kings to an eight, Secrest nines to an ace and Brudd only treys to a deuce.

"Pot right?" Secrest said, holding the deck. The pot was a ragged clutter of bills. "Here comes the bad news, gentlemen." With a judicial air he began calling the turns. "A jack to a jack and two pairs in sight. A four to the kings and no visible help. A trey to the treys and three of a kind. The dealer draws a deuce." He glanced at the hands. "Your bet, Mr. Brudd."

Brudd fingered the bills at his side. "Three lousy treys don't like to buck pairs in sight. Won't risk more than fifty." He fluttered a bill into the pot.

Secrest said, "Dealer folds," and pitched in his hand.

Ross chewed on his cigar, his face showing nothing. Finally he said, "Call and raise it two hundred."

His bet revealed to Adlam what his face didn't. He would have been a fool to try to ride his two pairs over Brudd's three of a kind. He had a full house, either jacks and tens or tens and jacks.

Tevis turned over his cards and threw them in.

"Well. Well." Brudd had a habit of smiling, his mouth did, when he played poker. He looked at his treys and then gazed around. "The beauty of the game is you never know. You never know until showdown. Is Jay thinking he can run a wagon over yours truly? Hmm. Could be. I've known him to bluff. Shall I call? Shall I raise?"

Ross said, "Take your time." The others were silent.

"Well, then, I will see you, Mr. Ross, and bump fifteen hundred."

In what must have been his courtroom voice, Secrest said, "Fifteen hundred!"

Brudd looked innocent, if he could. "I understood this was a no-limit game." He fluttered out the call and the raise.

The raise was too ungodly steep, even for this game. It suggested a bluff. It suggested a cinch. A man from the bar, Bob Franklin, came from it and stood in the archway, looking on. Likely he had heard Secrest's voice.

Adlam's thoughts pushed at Ross: Careful, Jay, careful: could be a bluff, but remember the fourth trey hasn't shown. But Jay knew that much and wouldn't pay heed, even if the warning could have been spoken. He brought a steady match to the stub of his cigar.

"I figure the pot's worth the gamble," Brudd said, his eyes going from one to the other as if all must agree.

"I'll see you." Ross took from his mouth what was left of his cigar, examined it and dropped it in a spittoon. "Have to draw shy." He put in the pot what he had and drew to the side of it what he hadn't.

Brudd turned his hole card. It was the fourth trey.

As if nickels were stakes, Ross said, "Beats a full house." He showed his hand, jacks and tens, and took a checkbook from his hip pocket and with a stub pencil made out what he owed. "Not my night," he told everyone, pushing his chair back. "So long until next time."

"Winner'll buy a drink."

"At the bar for me," Ross answered, and got up. "This sitting has put a crimp in my tail."

Adlam followed him and poured him a shot, letting the others wait. Ross took it as always, not gulping but taking three measured swallows. "See you," he said as he finished it.

Adlam followed him to the door, bid him good-bye and stood breathing fresh air. A crimp in the tail wasn't all that Ross had. Lamb loss, poker loss, crimps in his bank account sure as taxes and hell.

Ross hadn't turned up the street toward the livery stable. He had turned down it. Well, if it was that and she suited him, that gladsome wife of a here-and-gone husband? If she cushioned his loss? Anyhow, though Ross was cagey, might as well try to advise him about pussy as poker. The hard-headed, the horny, the kind of pitiful son of a bitch. Goddam it, Jay!

Inside, Brudd was calling for service. Out loud Adlam didn't say: Piss on you, Eagle Beak! He went to pour drinks.

13

A MAN COULD SAY Missoula was a lost-and-gone town for a plainsman to get to, Ewing reflected as he sat in the smoker of the Western Express. No matter how figured, the trip took the better part of two days if a pilgrim wanted to arrive in time for a shindig set for 2:30 P.M.

Team, Great Northern and now the Northern Pacific's Express — that was the order, along with a choice of long waits in Helena. It was just as well he had fixed on the longer one so's to arrive in Missoula at night. This way had left Julie's afternoon open for last-minute stuff. She hadn't been obliged, as she sure would have felt, to show him around. Tomorrow and commencement were time enough.

There were quite a few men in the smoker, most of them landseekers, he reckoned, some of them in rough clothes and lace boots and some out of stores or offices back east. With their hands they kept shading the windows as if, looking out in the late dusk, they might see dollars growing out of the ground.

The man at his side took his hand down. He wore a red mustache and bib overalls and smoked a pipe that would have gagged a gut wagon. "Goot country, dey say."

"You hear it, all right."

"Minnesota, I bane. Nort' Dakota. Vind, it blow seed hell and gone. Cold, too."

"Worse than Norway?"

"Norvay all right, you bet," the man answered as if a trifle offended. "But, you know, little and too many dere, and vere is land to settle? Four small vones, I have, and my vife, and ve look for better."

The poor bastard, Ewing thought. All the poor bastards looking for Eden, looking beyond Norway, beyond Europe, beyond desk and counter, beyond east and midwest to full bellies and barns and glutted root cellars. And the only crop they could count on was kids. "Sure, I know," he said. "You'll make out all right."

"You bet. Goot country here." The poor, hopeful bastard got up. "Excuse. Now I go see how family make out." He walked down the aisle and went through the door.

Tobacco smoke dimmed the dim lights of the coach, which smelled of pipes and cheap cigars and the remnants of home-readied lunches and of the sandwiches and candies the train butcher had sold.

Ewing slid over to the seat the Norwegian had vacated and, shielding the lamp glare from the glass, peered through the window. The train, he supposed, now was rolling down the valley of the Clark's Fork of the Columbia. The stream shimmered and rippled in the late light, its meanders ruled by the shouldering mountains. A man of the plains felt a sort of doom in this pinched wrinkle of rock — or would but for what lay ahead. He couldn't see far enough, to the upcoming or downgoing of sun or the touch of sky against the lip of the earth. Closed in, he was, like a prisoner, his eye balked and his feet stopped by walls.

Ewing reached for papers and tobacco, rolled a cigarette, struck a match and waited for the sulfur to burn out of it before lighting up. The smoke he puffed would add to the total just about as much as one drop would add to a bucket of water.

One foot was a little stiff. He straightened his leg and moved the toes in his boot. Too much strolling around Helena while he had waited, though he had sat down for a beer or two and joined three old codgers in a few games of solo.

Helena wasn't such a grand town, even with the capitol building it boasted about. All gold camps tended to peter out sooner or later and mostly sooner. Bannock, Virginia City, Confederate Gulch, Gold Butte — what were they now? Gold didn't breed like cattle or sheep and couldn't be seeded like oats. Wash it out, dig it out, make a splurge and be off, leaving the worked gravel and holes in the ground to show what wasn't there anymore and never would be again.

Copper was different, though taking any part out meant the less there was left and, in the long run, none left at all. But the city of Butte had a whole mountain of it, a hill reckoned everlasting or at least thereabouts. Dig it, boys.

He dropped his dead cigarette on the floor. It seemed a long time ago he had come to Montana. He was old for a fact, as proved by thoughts that wandered to ghost towns and gutted gulches and what was being called conservation and to copper wars and to Helena and how it came to be capital. A big fight, that, between Anaconda and Helena, and millions spent by the opposing high cockalorums of copper, and men bought and sold — and for what? So one town or the other could have a State House and play host to legislative windjammers who ended up doing what copper demanded, its voice being single since the high cockalorums had sold out to the trust, to the Anaconda Copper Mining Company.

Ewing consulted his watch. Barring delay, it was time the

train got there. From the window the late twilight looked smoky, as if from the output of what would be lumber plants. He saw lights. The train slackened speed, its wheels clicking the slow and slower beat of arrival. From the end of the coach the conductor called, "Missoula, Missoula. This way."

He rose and stretched and took hold of his war bag — a valise, Prof Collingsworth would have called it — and edged into line.

The air outside was different but hardly better than that inside. It carried a definite whiff of stink, a mixed odor that suggested chickens and pigs and — not so bad — horses. Side-by-side planks led to the station, put there, he supposed, against the chances of wet weather and mud. Walking, he heard the groan of a pig changing bedtime position. For an instant the sound took him back to Kentucky.

He jostled through the station and opened the door, and the shouts of hotel hackmen beset his ears. "Hotel Shapard." "Right here for the Missoula Hotel." "Savoy Hotel. All modern conveniences." Their turnouts stood ranked along the sides of the station.

Then, frail but clear above them, came a voice he wouldn't forget. "Mr. Ewing! Mort! Mort!"

With a swirl of skirts she came rushing to him. "Oh, Mort," she said, and kissed him, her hands tight on his arms. She looked in his face, her eyes wide and glad under a flat, funny straw hat he would have called a boater; and he remembered that once he had thought Disenchantment a sire in her pedigree. "I'm so happy you came."

"Course I came, Julie, but I telegraphed you not to meet me."

"I can't read."

A man had come up, a youngster with a foolish cap that decorated the back of his head like the crest of a woodpecker.

He stood quietly by, and then Julie, slow to see him, dropped her hands and turned and said, "Mort, this is my friend Rex Emmett. Mr. Ewing, Rex."

The young fellow plucked off his crest and shook hands. "I've heard a great deal about you, Mr. Ewing."

"Pleased to meet you."

Julie said, "Rex was good enough to come with me."

"Good. Fine." He hesitated just for a breath. "Now the next thing for me to do is hole up. Looks like a hotel over yonder." He picked up his war bag.

"No," Julie said. "Not over there. I've spoken for a room for you at the Florence House. That's where you're to stay."

"All right, Lieutenant, even if you don't get your commission until tomorrow."

"We have a carriage," the woodpecker said. "Here, sir, let me have your valise."

Ewing thought of protesting. Christ, did he look so old he couldn't tote a poke? He let the young fellow take it.

The carriage was a two-horse, closed-in rig with a driver's seat perched outside at the front. Its sidelights outlined the dismounted driver, who took Ewing's bag and turned to stow it away.

"Rex," Julie asked, "would you mind sitting up with the driver?"

Before Ewing could say he would sit there himself, Rex answered, "Of course not. I was going to."

As the cab started to roll, Julie moved closer and whispered, "He's a good boy, Mort."

"Seems like."

"He's graduating, too."

Ewing waited for what was to come. Waiting, he reminded himself that long expectation went mute at reunion. Always there was too much to say, too much remembered, too much in changes in person and upshot, and so nothing was said.

At last he asked, "Yes, Julie?"

She was a moment in answering. "The Adlams sent me a purse, a lovely one, and such a good letter." Her voice sounded far away. "And Eva mailed me a bracelet. How is she, Mort?"

"As to that," he said, "I don't know. Been a long, long time. Downhill, they say."

She said in his ear, "A long, long time," and there was a catch in her voice, and her hand came to his, her confiding hand, and he held it while he thought of the time she was thinking of, too. Who said Disenchantment was not of her blood? He put her hand aside.

"Sun's up for you, Julie, so buck up. What's a degree for? The desponds?"

Now she could laugh a trembling laugh. "You're a dear, Mort. You always were. I wonder how ever I ever can pay you?"

"You have, so don't try."

The rig pulled up in front of the hotel. "I have to get back," Julie said. "Rex will see me home. Now you have it straight, Mort? Main Hall at two-thirty o'clock. I'll see you right afterward." She pecked him good-bye.

"Sure. Sure." He stepped down to the street. "Night, Julie."

Rex had taken his bag and was striding ahead. At the desk in the lobby two people ahead of them were about to sign in. The boy put down the bag. "It won't be a minute, sir," he said.

So this, Ewing thought, looking, was the new way to dress up. Turn up your pants at least half a handspan so's to harvest a good crop of hayseeds. Wear peg-top trousers, which weren't pegs but flares and made a man look like a squaw spread by many a birthing. Have wide lapels, low cut in order to be able to jump through the collar if a rope got under your tail.

The boy said with that pitiful, that right, earnestness as they moved toward the desk, "She's a wonderful girl, Mr. Ewing, if you'll allow me to say so." He had a good face and a body that looked to be strong, no matter the way he decked it out.

"Top cut," Ewing answered.

They shook hands good-bye, and Ewing put his name on the register.

"A nice room on the second floor," the clerk said. "In a minute there'll be a bellboy to help you."

"Never mind," Ewing answered. "I'll make it myself." His bag wasn't so goddam heavy.

14

HE WAKENED EARLY and stretched and looked at the ceiling from which an electric lamp hung. Lighted, it would look like a hairpin burning in a bottle, as some graphophone joker — yeah, Uncle Josh — had cracked wise.

A rancher, a busted-down trail hand, always got the wide eye at sunup or earlier, while men who decorated their vests with gold chains and their heads with hard hats slept their paper-work sleep. One of the hands at the ranch would be milking already, and Mrs. McDonald likely feeding the chickens or readying flannel cakes for the men's breakfast. Nice day for it, it seemed, if ever there was a nice day for milking. When canned milk had come out, some cowpuncher galoot had written in praise of it:

> No tits to pull.
> No hay to pitch.
> Just punch a hole
> In the son of a bitch.

He yawned, wishing he could catch a wink or two more, and rolled up in bed and reached for tobacco and papers. The room, with the first sun beaming in, seemed almighty hot. That was the way of town — the sick heat — and a man who knew weather first-hand felt a fever. Better a hot wind and a scorcher of sun than this walled-in and dead insolation.

The cigarette tasted like mold. He went to the bathroom and flushed it away. No doubt here was an improvement, the patent toilet, but it took something away from the pleasure of a man's morning chore. No buzzing of bees. No visits of curious chipmunks. No rustle of breeze. No idle fingering through last year's Sears Roebuck catalogue, if it lasted that long.

He was out of date all right. Mr. Darwin's evolution was bringing out a fartless new breed, and the hell with the old save maybe a few, preserved to show what ancestors looked like. An old dear, he was. Julie had said so.

But his ass to these dismals. When a man thought low, he was low sure enough. When he got to looking back, dreading the downhill, the goddam grave sneaked up on him. Safe in the arms of Jesus.

He bathed and shaved. In the mirror he had to grin at himself, inside and out. The weather had put seams in his face, and he had put a few in on his own and didn't regret the occasions. As the years added up, a man didn't feel bad so much about what he'd done as about what he'd missed. Now, before long, those squinched eyes of his that had seen many a thing would see Julie graduate. Who said there was nothing new under the sun?

He should have hung his clothes up last night. They showed some wrinkles as he took them out of the bag. But the suit was a new one and, to boot, no Monkey Ward bargain. If the pants didn't turn up at the ends as if the tailor had forgotten to dock them a handspan, if the coat collar was snug enough to keep him from jumping clean through it if anyone goosed him, if the britches didn't flare so's to make him six ax handles across, then that was that. His hat, a low-crowned Stetson, would do. What tormented him was a tie.

At last, good enough. Now out on the town. He could hear it coming to life.

At a counter he ordered coffee, sausages and a short stack. The hot cakes were heavier than Mrs. McDonald's.

He paid up and moseyed onto the street. First thing a man did in strange settings was to see just how he was set. From this side of the main road it looked like the settlement was sunk in a bowl. He crossed over so as to see what the buildings in back of him hid. Here was a bowl all right, open only to birds. Reaching for distance, the eye bumped up against mountains. Not that he had anything against mountains, just so they didn't crowd in on him.

The town wouldn't let the stranger forget where he was, he thought while he idled along, careless of where his feet took him. Every sign, every firm name, had "Missoula" in it and once in a while "Garden City." And there were plenty of outfits — saloons called wine houses, restaurants, drugstores, general mercantiles, abstract offices, sheet-metal jobbers, Chinese laundries, stationery and wallpaper firms, hotels and more than enough real-estate joints. Professions like banking and law didn't lack nomination.

He paused in front of one of the real-estate offices. The door was open, and a man at a desk was gesturing at another as if offering all the best of Montana. From somewhere inside a third man came out and said, "Howdy, friend. Won't you come in?"

"I'm just lookin' around."

"You're interested in land, perhaps?" The man was half-bald and had the look in his eye of an indoor fisherman.

"I am."

"Then let me tell you. You should dismiss the mistaken idea of taking up a vast tract of land, if that's in your mind.

People out here are making a comfortable living and saving some money on a five-acre tract, raising fruit and chickens. Ten acres will insure a handsome income."

"Sure enough?"

"Sure enough. Now I have any number of places for sale, priced from two-fifty to five dollars an acre. They are all excellent buys, but I would recommend the latter."

"Fruits and berries, huh?"

"Just name it and grow it."

"And chickens?"

"A profitable enterprise. An easy one. And here's another thing, friend. Hard work is for young men. Not that you're not in the prime of life, as you plainly are, but all of us as we get older like to let up a bit."

"I was thinkin' on that. Berries have to be picked — don't they? — which means stoopin', and tree fruits grow high, which means stretchin'. You got a place where a man can just set and grow rich without lookin' for eggs?"

The man's expression turned queer. "You said you were interested in land."

"Yep. I own a ranch."

The man turned and marched back in the office.

A little crowd had gathered up the street. Ewing lagged to it. What had centered them there was a contraption that any team of his would have run ass-over-teakettle away from, a contraption sometimes called in sneer or praise a horseless carriage. It looked bulgy and awkward, as the one or two he had seen always did. It was a poor-built box with a tarp for a top.

Apparently the salesman, standing alongside, had thrown out his bait and was waiting for bites. Now he turned to Ewing and made a fresh cast. "Look it over, mister. Look it over good. Best autobuggy in the whole of the land. A Winton, by jingo, that's that she is, a full six-cylinder Winton.

Takes you there and brings you back. Would you believe I came all the way from Hamilton this A.M. and never a hitch?"

"So?"

"A good fifty miles and roads not the best, by jingo. How long by horse, saddle or harness, I ask you? How long? By the looks of you, you know horses. Mister, aren't you tired of saddling up and hooking up and watching grass grow up under hoof? Aren't you tired of old Dobbin?"

"Not dead tired yet."

The salesman addressed all of his audience. "Get in, two, three, four of you, and we'll make a sashay. That's right. Make yourselves comfortable."

When three men were seated, the salesman went to crank up. He gave the engine a couple of quarter-turn jerks and then bent to his work and spun it around. But the best auto-buggy in the whole of the land wouldn't poop.

Walking away, Ewing saw generations of men, lopsided from wrestling cranks. All old Dobbin needed was, "Giddap!"

He had a drink — two might smell on his breath — and took his time over a midday meal at a place called Ye Olde Inn, which tried to look new. Lazing around afterward, he halted in front of a posy house and thought about buying Julie some flowers. In former days, in cow towns large enough for theaters, he might have sent a big bouquet on stage for some actress he happened to admire; but that caper didn't seem the ticket now. He could see himself seated in brainy, solemn company, holding the cut flowers, carnations sprouting from his bellybutton, until the last amen.

The main street was coming to be busy. Along it, together and at intervals, rolled-top buggies, surreys, buckboards, bicycles, hacks and even a work wagon, all bound south. On the sidewalks groups and couples and now and then a single marched, trigged out in Sunday best.

A lone cab was pulled up in front of the Florence, its driver dismounted and watchful for customers. He had a mustache like a boot brush.

"Graduation?" Ewing asked.

"Sure thing. Climb in."

By and by the rig rolled across the bridge over Clark's Fork, the river which he had heard miscalled the Missoula. That was the way of things, Captains Lewis and Clark. Explore a whole world of wilderness, and in a hundred years maybe your names could be found in the graveyard.

They turned to the left from the main road, and the smell of flowers, likely lilacs, drifted into the cab. Looking out, Ewing saw showy houses, some made of brick, and yards tidied and planted, and early summer in bloom. The season, he reckoned, was maybe a month ahead of Arfive, where the leaves of willows and cottonwoods still were young green.

The driver whoaed up and got down and opened the door. "Here you are," he said.

Ewing stepped out. "Can you wait till it's over?"

"No, sir. Not here. Not on the oval."

Ewing gazed around. The road made a loop, touching close to three buildings, and nowhere along it was there a hitch rack. "Hell of a note," he said. "A little horse manure never hurt anybody."

The driver smiled under the brush of his lip. "You're right, old-timer. But it's bullshit they pitch around here."

Ewing handed over two dollars.

"Well, thanks and thanks again," the driver said. "Tell you what. S'pose I show up in an hour, anyhow in plenty of time?"

"Good. Be in front of Woman's Hall, will you? And, say, how about a bigger buggy? There'll be some plunder."

The driver answered, "No trouble," and climbed to his seat and wheeled off.

At the top of what he took to be the main hall was a cupola with a clock in it. The clock said 2:17. Too early to enter.

He moved around idly, taking things in. Yonder, with the side and front porches, probably was Woman's Hall, where Julie stayed, having said nix to the little hen's clubs called sororities. They cost money, she had written, though never had he played pinchpenny.

He stepped off the sidewalk to let people pass. The grounds were well kept and maybe new-manicured for the occasion. The mowed grass led along to young and shaped shade trees, to a whole scattered batch of them, where young folks could have lolled in the night. But this ordered management of blade and leaf and shrub and walkway wasn't for him. Kept grounds were men's doing, as little and artificial as dollhouses. Give him a reach of raw land. Give him a tumbleweed.

The passers-by had thinned down almost to nothing. The tower clock said he was three minutes late. He walked up the hall steps, removed his hat, entered the auditorium, took a program from an usher and chose a back seat from which he could see.

Some opening music, mournful enough for a funeral, was fading out, and the seniors in caps and gowns were taking chairs on the stage. Julie was in the front row. After the music ended, a preacher got up and came to the front of the platform and took God's own time in making sure God would guide the feet of those about to be turned loose in the world.

A woman sang a song then, giving both lungs to it; and Ewing, half listening, ran his gaze over the graduates. The boy, Rex What's-His-Name, sat stiff at one end of the back row. Maybe the academic sky-piece was an improvement over his peckerwood cap. From what he could see of them, the girls wore full, pleated dark dresses that reached to their shoes and ruffled white blouses high in the neck. Except for Julie, they wore pins at their throats. She wore a little, more-fetching, black bow. His eyes kept going that way but slid off enough to count twenty or more on the stage. The program divided them into four groups. Julie was Literary.

The president stalked to the stand and ruffled his papers. After hemming and hawing a little, he lined himself out. His subject, the program said, was "Twentieth-Century Education." By virtue of learning, he assured all, these young people would make a better stab at things than people before had. They had the education and the youth and the will. Improvement was sure. The future shone.

While the president kept circling the same track, Julie listened, or seemed to do so. Her expression was grave but alive. Her small hands lay clasped in her lap. Attentive or not, she surely did shine. Better she didn't know his cowpuncher and common assessments of show. Better he shone for her.

After the headman had dried up, another woman sang another song; and then, one by one, the graduates filed by and received their degrees along with his handshakes. Maybe Julie had spotted him in the back row. Anyhow, unlike the others, she turned and for a little instant held up the paper. For the wind-up a third woman had to sing and the preacher to chew again on God's ear.

Julie came pushing through the crowd. She hugged him. "Why did you sit so far back?"

"No seats outside."

"Oh, Mort, at last!"

"Why, sure, girl."

She leaned closer and whispered, "I know it was dull as dirt for you — but, Mort, not for me."

"I savvy. A new world." As they moved out, he told her, "I've got a turnout waiting."

"My things are all packed and ready downstairs."

A voice called, "Julie! Julie!" and Rex hurried to her. "Your cap and gown. I'll take care of them. Pardon me and good afternoon, Mr. Ewing." He took Julie's gear and loped off.

"You must meet the preceptress," Julie said as they went on.

"Come again."

"How's proctor then?"

"Closer to the reservation."

Before they reached Woman's Hall, in front of which various carriages waited, including the bigger one he had asked for, Rex came trotting back. "I'll see that you're loaded."

Girls swirled at the entrance to the dormitory, meeting and coming and going and telling parents and well-wishers to wait just a minute. All of them seemed to know Julie. They said congratulations and hello and good-bye in the tender, overblown, blossomy way of young females. It was as if, just petaled out, they had tears about winter already.

Julie led him and Rex into a parlor, cluttered with the plunder of everyone's going. He didn't get the name of the preceptress, if that's what she was. She looked old and staid and indulgent and, while Julie listened, said to him, "Your girl's been a jewel, just a jewel, all along. I hate to see Julie go." Her eyes went wet.

"There's my luggage, Rex," Julie said, pointing. "I'll go to my room for a last look around."

"Where is your cab, Mr. Ewing?" the young fellow asked.

"No. No. Don't you trouble yourself with the loading. It will take me only a jiffy."

Empty-handed, Ewing went to the doorway and indicated his carriage and stepped back inside and waited for Julie.

She returned and hugged the old woman, and for a moment both of them cried. Then, holding his arm, she took him out.

Rex stood with the driver. "Good-bye, Mr. Ewing," he said first, extending his hand. "A great pleasure to meet you. And good-bye, Julie. Good-bye. I hope to see you this summer."

"Yes. Yes," Julie answered, and gave him a kiss that left him looking uncomfortable in front of company.

"Hop in," the driver said, combing his mustache at sight of Julie. "Hop in, you and the little miss."

Ewing saw Julie up and climbed in himself. As the rig rolled, she took his hand and looked in his eyes, and a little quirk, maybe sad, came on her face.

"Home, old-timer," she said.

15

"Mother," Mary Jess said, "some of the girls are going to meet at Smith's Ice Cream Parlor. Is it all right if I go?"

May Collingsworth looked up from her ironing. "Why, I think so. Just you girls, is it?" She smiled into the fair and innocent, the dutiful, face. "You'll need a nickel or two."

She found her purse on the sewing machine and took a dime from it, leaving five cents — for seed if ever it sprouted.

Mary Jess went out happily, not letting the door slam, and May followed her and opened it and watched her trip up the street. Let her never be hurt, she asked. Let her never be hurt more than she has been. Tommie's death and the baby's were hurt enough.

The child was so lovely, so lovely and vulnerable, so young to have deaths ever cloud the calm trust of her eyes. So young at eleven to bow to God's mercy. So young, though the virgin breasts were swelling her middy blouse, to have learned anything about the nature of boys.

It had been two weeks ago or about, and at dusk Mary Jess had run into the house frightened and crying and buried her face against May and finally between sobs — and almost as if the shame were her own — had told her and Benton that Wallace Marsh had proposed she lift her skirt and open her union suit.

Benton heard her out without comment or question and then walked to the rack and put on his hat, his face like a casting.

May ran to him. She caught hold of his arm. "No, Benton! No! Think first."

"The whelp!" He tried to shake off her hand.

"What good would it do? Whatever good?"

"I'll teach him."

"And have it known? Have it known everywhere? Embarrass Mary Jess?"

Mary Jess cried from the parlor, "Please, Father."

Benton hesitated. "I'll see his father then. I'll talk to Merc Marsh."

"Maybe, Benton. Maybe sometime. But what can you expect from him? He might try to turn it against you, against us. Don't you see? And no harm's been done. No real harm."

Finally she had managed to calm him, though her logic had been weak, it seemed to her now. What really had scared her, what had made her protest, was what Benton might do.

May closed the door and stood thinking, letting the ironing wait. To a young girl what could be said about sex except that she close her mind to it and wait the right and sanctified time? What could a mother say? Not the truth surely, lest it inflame the beginning desire and hasten experiment. Love couldn't be taught. It had to be experienced and repeated under proper circumstances with the right man. It was unfortunate, it was less than right, it was a tarnish of eventual truth to apply the word "nasty" to all acts of young curiosity. But where was a better, more discouraging word?

She went back to the ironing board. Lately, she thought, her chores took a ridiculous toll of her strength. More and more she had been scanting the dusting and sweeping, the immediate tasks seemed so many and heavy. She couldn't plead pregnancy, either, not since last summer's miscarriage. Four pregnancies, three children born live, one of them living. Now barrenness? It couldn't and shouldn't be.

Just as she finished doing up one of Benton's white shirts, there came a knock at the door.

Mrs. Ross stood outside and came in at May's invitation, stepping with a too-old precision. As always, she was carefully dressed. It was, May thought, as if some compulsion kept her immaculate, as if all of her, saving her face, had to be shielded and herself confirmed by outward appearance, like a priest in his vestments. Even now she wore a heavy veil.

"I'm so glad you came," May said, aware without embarrassment of her own worn and untidy dress. "Please, let me take your things, and you go in and have a chair."

With a sort of slow purpose Mrs. Ross removed her gloves, then her hat and veil, and handed them over along with her purse.

From the clothes closet May called into the parlor, "Excuse me just a minute. I'll put some coffee on." Mrs. Ross was seated when she returned. She took the old rocker nearby. "It's so nice to have company. So nice it's you."

"Thank you," Mrs. Ross said. "I always think of your house as a house of peace."

The fretwork of weather on the sad face had deepened and extended with years; but now, May saw for the first time, little twitches disturbed it, small, nervous eddies like the touches of wind on water. Her eyes looked unfocused and empty of thought.

"I needed someone to talk to," May said. "Benton's gone, you know."

"Oh, I thought he was helping out at the county treasurer's office." Mrs. Ross spoke as if Benton's whereabouts touched her hardly at all.

"He was, but school will start soon, so he hitched up the horse and went to the mountains to fish for a day or so. Sometimes he likes to be alone. I can't say that I do."

Still in a faraway voice, in a voice, May thought, as frail as a breath, Mrs. Ross said, "Forlorn. Ever since the girls left for college, the ranch is forlorn. But I've said that before. I've said almost everything before. They keep coming back, what I've said."

May waited. Mrs. Ross's gaze wasn't on her. It wasn't on anything to be seen. "Everyone's that way, I guess." She tried to speak lightly. "It doesn't matter. Today's such a nice day."

"I suppose so."

"And you're looking quite well, Mrs. Ross."

"Oh, yes. Ask Jay. Finer than frog hair, he would tell you."

"How is he?"

"I don't inquire." Into the eyes had come the look of haunt, of joys or nightmares remembered, the look more than ever of severance from here and now.

May excused herself and poured coffee, spilling some, and brought it and napkins in on a tray. "I remembered you took it black. I find coffee just the thing when I'm at low ebb."

Mrs. Ross didn't answer. The thin hand that held the cup trembled a little. On the back of it veins ran a pale tracery. Abruptly she said, stronger voiced, "I'm all right, Mrs. Collingsworth, righter than I've been in a long time, so don't fret yourself. Things aren't going to bother me anymore, not the sky and not even the wind."

May could think of no better reply than, "One does get used to it."

"Or away from it, my dear. I could never get used to the sky here. It is bottomless and without end in any direction, and I feel so — so flung out, I guess you could say, so bare and so scattered. It's like a jail without walls but with peepholes in it, or one giant peephole." The voice had gone weak again at the end. It was remindful of a sigh over forgotten regrets.

"Are you sure you're all right, Mrs. Ross?"

Mrs. Ross might not have heard. "I will put the wind away from my ears," she went on. "It marches, you know, always marches or charges. You can hear it before it arrives. It gathers strength on the far butte from the ranch house and then howls along like an invader, like a troop of them."

"It's good you've decided to pay no attention. More coffee?"

"If it isn't men marching, it's horses charging. They're all of them stallions."

It seemed to May, hearing and watching this thin, troubled woman, this woman too soon grown old, that the wind had dried up all her juices, leaving a dead reed of a body, a papery voice and an erratic mind. "Stallions?" she said without purpose.

"Always stallions. Jay likes to watch them, you know, when —" She didn't finish, having come as close to the fact as any lady should come.

It occurred to May of a sudden that perhaps it wasn't altogether the wind and perhaps not at all. Juices never there could scarcely be dried. And men didn't invade or stallions charge unless fear or distaste populated the winds. Poor woman, she thought, and, yes, even poor Jay, who by her guess — and by whispered report — had more than enough appetite. Poor both of them.

"We had a name in upper New York," Mrs. Ross was saying. "We still have. My family."

"Why, you have a name here!"

Mrs. Ross was a long time in answering. "Yes," she said finally. "Yes — Jay has." She got up with her frail, dry dignity. "I must go now. Thank you for the coffee."

Carefully she put on the hat and veil May brought her, carefully her gloves. At the door she said, "Good-bye, Mrs. Collingsworth. God bless you. Good-bye. I'm leaving tomorrow."

"Leaving! For good!"

Mrs. Ross turned away as if not wanting to face her. "Yes. For New York. For home. The girls will join me."

"I'm so sorry. Oh, Mrs. Ross, I'll miss you. Good-bye."

With nice, old precision, without looking back, Mrs. Ross went down the walk.

16

HERE AT THE MOUTH of the canyon the Breast River washed gravel already shining. It ran from bend to bend and at the bends tarried, green-blue and inviting in the late-afternoon light. Its surface caught the colors of sunset.

Collingsworth hitched the home-fashioned creel on his shoulder and walked on toward a turn, casting his artificial lure idly in the shallows where no trout were likely to lie. One more hole, he thought, and he would have plenty of fish, not alone for himself but for old Charlie Blackman and his companion.

He had met Charlie upstream on the shore, standing gawky as a blue heron. He held an open-topped, five-gallon kerosene can with a haywire handle. "How, Perfessor?" he had said, grinning.

"Hello, Charlie. What happens with you?"

"Me and my pardner is gophering up there on the ridge." He thumbed back toward the place with his free hand. "Might get jackass lucky. Gold's where you find it, ain't that the sayin'?"

"Gold, for heaven's sake!"

"Yep, but it's dry work. For wettin' our whistles we got to come to the crick. How's fishin', Perfessor?"

"Good, so far. I'll bring you a mess if you want it."

Blackman pushed his can in the creek, filled it and lifted it with an ease surprising in so old a man. "Any day but Friday, which today ain't." Blackman grinned again, showing some teeth. "I got scruples against fish on Friday."

Collingsworth had said good-bye and walked on. When he looked back, he saw Blackman lugging the full can up the hill.

There was no hurry. He sat down on a dead log and watched the stream flowing, saw the gravel underneath and over it the shapes and colors of sundown, plain then distorted by the fancies of water. Like men, water had to go somewhere, yet the stream would remain, new water introducing itself to old rocks, old driftwood, old twists and turns and quarreling and chuckling to itself at discovery. Old discoveries couldn't be reported upstream.

He saw the old horse again, stirred to the thought of it, he realized, by one of those frail and distracting connections that too often made thinking random. It had trotted out, sway-backed and big-headed, from the shade of old Sorenson's deserted homesteader shack as he was about to pass in his buggy. The shack was of tarpaper, now mostly blown off. Its two windows were blank, glass and frames taken by someone with use for them. Whatever there had been in the way of a barn had been torn down for firewood or planking. The old horse remained.

Collingsworth imagined he knew what had happened. The Sorensons had packed up and moved off, bag and baggage, in their dismal good-bye taking the few animals still of use or of value. But there was Old Buck or Old Blue or Old Bess, too old for service, too dear for death. And so they had left it. The horse had followed along for a mile, its heavy feet lifting slower and slower, and then had stopped and turned back and plodded home.

From somewhere now crows were yelling against the turn of the day, a nutcracker scratched the air and, close at hand, a water ouzel, fresh as creation, tried current and stone and seemed pleased with both as well as itself. Out of water, from fish to bird.

Elephant Ear Butte was shaded save at its very top, where the sun said good-bye to it or promised return. It stood lonely and eternal, itself a promise of constancy, sunrise or not, storm, time and tide or not. A man felt drawn to it, felt embraced by a flowing foreverness, felt mortal and reassured. Dying, he would know the butte rose there.

He got up and started down toward the hole, thrashing through a thicket of willows that caught at his line and rod. From the ground came the smell of mashed leaves, the nostril-pinch of bruised peppermint. Careful lest he muddy the water or be glimpsed by the fish, he approached the hole and whipped out his fly and guided it, fluttering, to a blue eddy. The fly was a new one to him, a Silver Doctor, by name a fitting companion to the Grizzly King, the King and Queen of Waters, the Royal Coachman. It answered, silver and live, to the light rein of the rod.

But, strangely, here was no strike, not even the quick glimmer of a trout tempted but wary, and he let the current carry the lure around a shouldering bank and so out of sight. It was when he was reeling in that the fish struck.

He set the hook, and the rod arched and quivered, and the line ran through his fingers to the shrill of the reel. He lurched across the stream. Here he could see and work his tackle in quieter waters and presently bring the fish to the shallows. It lay quiet there, its gills laboring. He lowered the rod to the slant of the line and, running back, yanked it ashore.

Now there, he thought, for an instant watching its spasms,

was a fish. There was a cutthroat such as seldom was seen. Three pounds at least, maybe four. No wonder no other strikes. Big fish devoured or chased away smaller ones.

He got out his knife and caught the trout by its gills. It ceased flapping the minute the blade cut through its backbone. He held it up after he had removed the Silver Doctor. Red streaked its jaws, and red washed its lower sides, and from its back and upper sides the pupiled speckles stared out. It was too big to lie whole in a frypan.

He gutted all his catch and made for camp. Camp was a tarpaulin slanted down from a rope and shone white in the gathering dusk. It was a tarp and some cook stones and a pot and a pan and some small provisions tied in a sack that he had drawn part way up on a limb against the possibility of packrats and porcupines and just possibly bears. Off just a piece was his buggy.

His horse whinnied from the patch of grass in which he had staked it. He went to it, saying, "Whoa, old boy. Whoa, Fox." The horse always disliked the smell of fish or of game, and now, snorting, kicked at him. But his luck had been too good for bad temper. He quieted it and led it to water and found fresh grass for a picket ground.

He changed into dry clothes and afterward fried out some bacon, put half a dozen fish in the grease and set coffee to boil. Bacon and fish and May's special bread. Not fancy fare but fit for a king. With coffee he permitted himself a pipe of tobacco. It tasted better, perhaps, because he shouldn't be smoking it, not on his salary of one hundred and seventy-five dollars a month, not with so many family needs, not after the illnesses and deaths that had visited them.

He supposed he ought to be earning more. There were other professions and places. But he had tried reading law and found it so dull that when he came to the study of torts he had pitched the book to one side, never to crack it again.

Other places? He had had offers, two of them, and had rejected both. The second one was the better — much better in promise and pay than ever could be hoped for from Arfive. When he had announced his decision, May had looked up from her sewing. There might have been accusation in her eyes.

"You don't agree," he said.

"I know your capabilities, Benton. Do you?"

"I know I don't want to go to a city. I don't want to have to contend with a lot of young foreign hoodlums."

"Yes," she said quietly. The one word seemed to hold both agreement and contradiction.

"It's not that I'm afraid, confound it! Don't ever think that!"

May had looked back down on her sewing.

Dark was drawing on, and the first stars appearing. He knocked out his pipe and brought himself up and, turning, saw a glow on the ridge where Charlie Blackman was camping. He could wait till tomorrow, he thought, to deliver the fish. He could turn in if he felt like it.

He took the creel to the stream and there stripped off some willow leaves and put them inside to keep the trout fresh. Then he doused the creel and turned and set out. The darkened way was uncertain at first, but soon he discovered a winding game trail — made by what and how many animals in what long ago? — and followed it up.

"Hello, the fire," he shouted when he was close enough, recalling that at night in southern Indiana a visitor helloed a rural house lest he meet with suspicion.

"Hello, your own self," Blackman yelled back. "Sing out the countersign."

"Heap fish."

"Leave the fish come ahead."

Blackman sat like a stick, like an assembly of sticks, at the side of his little fire. Near him, propped by an elbow, lounged a stranger to Collingsworth.

"Perfessor, here's my sidekick, name of Smoky Moreau. Smoky, shake hands with what I would call a goddam good man if he wasn't around." As if in an aside to his sidekick he added, "The perfessor ain't stuck on cussin'."

The man had risen to shake hands. He was younger than Charlie by perhaps fifteen years, and his face in the firelight showed swarthy. It seemed so open and guileless as to affirm the myth of the noble native.

As they shook, Moreau said, "*Comment portez-vous?*"

"He means how be ye," Blackman explained. "He can speak the lingo pret' near as good as any barroom buster, but high-toned company edges his nerves."

"Fine, thanks," Collingsworth answered.

He put down the creel and sat on the ground, watching Blackman nose sticks deeper into the fire. Farther on was a sheep wagon with a torn canvas cover and, beyond it, a knoll with the mouth of a hole in it and scattered boulders alongside. "How's the mining?" he asked.

"Leave me look at the fish." Blackman hinged up from his squat, went to the creel and dumped fish and leaves in a battered basin. One by one he lifted and examined the catch. When he came to the big trout, he said, "Now that ain't exactly a peedad. More like a wowser. Me and Smoky sure thank you."

He sat down. "We was runnin' pretty low in the feed sack. Think on it, Smoky. The perfessor, he's spelled us from sow belly and poop fruit. Course," he went on for Collingsworth's benefit, "once in a while we knock over a fool hen, but they's hard to find when you set yourself to it. That's how it is. Don't look for a thing, and it's underfoot. Look for it, and it's hell-and-gone gone. Ever notice?"

"Yes. How's the mining?"

"Now as to that, it's hard to say. We got a fair show in the first place, enough to keep our hands on the shovel. Had it assayed and all. Lately not so good."

"Kill ourselves, no," Moreau said. "Feel like work, all right. Feel not so, fine. We live."

"Likely nature's just baitin' us." Blackman shifted his old haunches. "But, long as our stake holds out, it's somep'n to do and nice place to do it. Beats hell out of the poor farm. Y'ever been there?"

"Once," Collingsworth said, remembering.

"Damn if I ever go and shuffle around with them old farts as can't open their eyes or shut off their bowels. Come winter, I'll catch a few furs and later go back to swampin' saloons. No poor farm."

"Charlie, he never runs out of talk," Moreau put in. "Most old people deef. That would scald him."

"A man gets to talkin' just because he's got nothin' to say," Blackman replied, unoffended. "And, like us, only Smoky can't read, he'll read whatever comes to his eye. And, speakin' of labels, I just learnt by heart one that come on a box that held somep'n called Force. What it was was corn or oats or wheat smashed flat as a mouse turd in a sheep wagon. Underneath the picture of a high-flyin' scarecrow was the pome.

> Vigor, vim,
> Perfect trim.
> Force makes him
> Sunny Jim.

"The horses et it, not hearty."

Moreau got out a pipe and rolled tobacco in his palm and held a twig to the fire and used it as a match. "The Indians told stories. Big stories."

"Yes?" Collingsworth asked.

"Nothing more to tell, they told stories. The Indians."

Blackman considered, then said abruptly, "Oh, sure, Smoky. I savvy. Perfessor, you're bound to have a yarn or two up your sleeve."

"Oh, no. Thanks. I haven't."

"All that readin', and no crop a'tall?"

"Children's stories. Fairy tales I tell my daughter, or used to when she was smaller. That's all. Anyhow, it's time to bed down."

"So what's wrong?" Blackman asked. Moreau's open face waited. "I listened many a time to Injun stories, some here by Smoky, and how the coyote could outslick any brute or brave, bein' able to change shapes and talk whatever tongue suited him."

"He was a smart one, that one," Moreau said like a believer.

The old horse at the deserted homestead came to mind and with it "The Bremen Town Musicians." Mary Jess had liked the story, perhaps in part because he did himself. But these grown men? "It's so childish," he said.

"So's Mr. Coyote. Speak up, Perfessor."

He started uneasily, not sure of memory, much less of audience. "A farmer once had a faithful ass —" He had apprehended a snicker here. What he got was attention. He went on, gaining confidence, gaining the voice that public appearances often subdued, encouraged by the absence of interruption or fidget. He told of the old ass and the hound and the cat and the cock and the rout of the robbers and ended with that disarming ending: "And the mouth of him who last told this story is still warm."

For a minute they were silent. Then Blackman said, "I said so, Smoky."

"Yes."

"We're a couple of old cocks but still crowing."

"Or the ass or the hound or the cat. Too old but not so."

Collingsworth got up, and, as if suddenly aware of his presence, they got up, too. "I must be going," he said.

Blackman came to him and held out his hand. "Come again, any time, fish or no fish."

"But have the warm mouth," Moreau said, taking his hand.

Away from the fire the stars fired up, and one, falling, flared its good-bye and left the congregation no poorer.

Simple stories, conceits, language, logic, history, formulas — they were all fairy tales, images and symbols, acquisitions and wisdoms that the fanciful and exploring mind had conjured and explicated. Not fairy tales, though. Wonders. Rich wonders. And hungry old men would listen.

He saw again to his horse and sat on a downed log by his dead fire. He must learn more of the stars, that final wonder of all. The Big and Little Dippers, the polestar, the Pleiades, they and a host of others were shining tonight, all on parade, at attention, close as reach and farther than thought. A night bird cried once, and a coyote sang and another joined in. Elephant Ear Butte was still there.

The night was in him, and the stars and the mountain, and a shiver, not of his making, ran over him. Afraid or unafraid, who would choose to abandon this land? Here was his homestead, his point of outlook on heaven and earth, on the world and America. And it was part of his America, part of her riches, part of her essential rightness, part of her stamina and invulnerability. Other peoples had love of their countries, none with more or as much reason as his own fellows.

He found himself saying aloud what he had memorized as his peroration to a Memorial Sunday address delivered last May.

"And thou, the spirit of my country, thou, our America, our Columbia, it is our custom to typify thee in the noblest and most beautiful form that we know. It is our pleasing fancy to think of thee as a woman. Thou art so very fair that thou dost challenge all our admiration. Thou art so virtuous that we reverence thee. Thou art so gentle that we love thee. Thou haste, moreover, the crowning grace of womanhood; thou art a mother, the mother of us all. We should all pay to thee the fullest measure of our loyalty. But, alas, thou hast those sons who are ignorant, others who are thoughtless, others still who are false, and these would do thee harm. May we who would be accounted worthier raise about thy feet a strong wall of defense as did those, our older brothers, in thy darkest hour, and, emulating them, may we see to it that thou dost retain thy place in the seats of the mighty."

He got up and sang to the listening night in a voice he never really let go in the Methodist choir:

> "Stars of the summer night,
> Far in yon azure deep . . ."

He went over and pulled his bed out from under the tarp and undressed to his underwear and lay down. As he was about to close his eyes, he thought of May and of home and the end of the stanza.

> Hide, hide your golden light.
> She sleeps, my lady sleeps.

17

THEY HAD BEEN riding horseback, up the big ditch, along the mown fields, through the grazing cattle, and on up the ridges where Ewing's horses found good feed in winter. The day was so clear that the eye ran away, ran north, south and east without end and west to the blued backbone of the Rockies. Was distance blue? Ewing asked himself. Close up, the mountains weren't. Close up, what hue was the sky?

From a height the town of Arfive came to sight. Men would be drinking there, breathing air that their crowded breath and their tobacco and bodies had fouled. Or they would be talking prices and prospects and portents of winter. Or investments and interest and what they called progress. And some would be thinking of church and school and manners, counting as an improvement in moral tone the fact that Eva Fox had closed up her whorehouse but not pausing in their satisfaction to wonder how a poor, pestered devil was to find his.

Hell, he thought while he and Julie sat quiet in their saddles and looked, sin was the invention of man. The sky didn't know it, or the beasts and birds of the field. But to man's credit were other inventions like honesty and honor and compassion and courage, and to fall short in these amounted to sin after all. Collingsworth would have said — or would he?

— that the inventions were God working through man. There was the hitch.

It struck him that here was a fine, old way to be thinking when a pretty girl, his almost daughter, sat her saddle close by him. Had she been more — yes, vivacious — maybe his mind wouldn't need to be advertised, like an animal, as lost, stolen or strayed. But she had been uncommonly silent, the sun on her face clouded by some trouble of spirit. He couldn't believe, quite, that she wasn't enjoying the outing. She loved to ride, and always she rode astride in a divided skirt, disdaining a ladylike sidesaddle. Seeing her on a horse, a rider would have said she had a good seat. Knowing her, he would have said she rode gay. Today, for a headpiece, she had chosen, of all things, a checkered and cheerful poke bonnet. Yet underneath it was thought, preoccupation or something other than cheer.

After supper with the McDonalds they sat in the beamed and fireplaced room that scarcely could be called a parlor, though Julie had given it feminine touches. It was late dusk, and he had lighted the lamps, and around them a few millers fluttered. A damn nuisance, those dusty house-loving moths.

"I wish it were brisk enough for a fire," Julie said.

"It's close enough to it with night coming on," Ewing answered. He got up and struck a match and touched off the laid fire.

When it was going well, she said, looking into it, "It's all here, Mort."

"What?"

"Nothing. Just old stuff like low lights and fire. But where's the soft music?"

"Like a graphophone racket?"

"Like 'I dreamt that I dwelt in marble halls.' "

"Who knows but you will?"

"Even there, I would think about here. I would remember

so many things, things like now, for instance, and now just swept by. Already it's a memory. That's why the now is important, because it never is."

"Whoa up, girl. It slips by you, all right. Say now and, bang, there she goes. But how come you're thinking so old? It's too early for you to count steps to the boneyard."

"It's less than a month till I leave." She was too damn young to be sad.

"Not for the boneyard!" He got up and punched at the fire. "For school and the classroom to teach, for Christ sake!"

"I still will remember."

As if he wouldn't, Ewing thought. What he answered as he turned to his chair was, "It's not good-bye. It's not forever. The place will still be here, and the fields and cattle and horses and all. They'll whet up your memories and add to the tally to boot."

She didn't speak for a minute. "Will you still be here? Will you be the same?"

"I aim to stick around as long as I can. The point is you got a whole life ahead of you. Now buck up, girl."

"That's your answer to everything, isn't it? Buck up?"

"To some things. To this thing for sure. Here you are, dreadin' what you'll enjoy. You're bound to have fun teaching school."

"I won't, Mort." Her voice was so low that he strained to hear. "I can't." She bowed her head and put her hands to her face.

"God sake, Julie. Don't get the weeps."

Her voice came out choked. "I don't want to leave."

Here was an old, old story, he supposed, one enacted and reenacted by generations of families and, for lack of a better connection, related always to the doings of birds, to the fledgling and the nest and the trying of wings. Necessity plus regret. The tearful need. Goddam it.

He found himself saying, "You don't have to go, Julie. Stay here. You earn your keep, Christ knows."

"I must make some money. I must pay you back."

"You mustn't, either."

"For my sake I must." She rose abruptly, the wet of tears on her cheeks, and sat on the floor and rested her head on his knee. His hand went to her hair.

He said, "There, now. You've braved a lot worse."

She turned her face up to his, her eyes wet and eloquent and hurtful to look at. "Mort, I want more of you. Let me share your bed. You've been so good, and I'd be happy to."

For an instant he went over her words, making sure he'd heard right. Then he thrust her head from him and arose and stepped away. "I will be damned! You've lost your head if you think to pay me back that way."

"Pay! Are you blind?"

"To what? Not to this. Think what I've done I did just so's to bed with you?"

"I'm sorry, Mort. I didn't put it right. I want to marry you."

"Me? Old enough to be your father. Old enough to paddle you, like I feel like. I can't think of one good reason you'd want to."

"Why don't you say I'm after your money?"

"Because I know better," he answered, feeling the question disarm him. "But, Julie, think on it. There's young men around, younger and likely a lot better. You can't patch up an old stag like me. The years between are too long."

"The difference doesn't keep us apart. It brings us together. It brings me to you, I know."

"Yeah. Father and daughter."

"If you were I, you'd answer bullshit."

He poked at the fire and let the alien and unlikely word

soak. Here was a Julie new to him, a Julie not just soft and sweet and filial but also resolute and blunt and desirous. He almost felt glad.

She remained on the floor, watching him. "It's either you, Mort, or nobody ever. Except for you, I don't take to men, and you know why."

"You're a poor judge of quality."

"Mort, don't you love me? Don't you ever think of me as a woman? Haven't you ever wished for me?"

Had he or hadn't he? Not openly, anyway. Not quite consciously, for what conscience he had had forbidden acknowledgment. It was the way of men, it was their rule, and it was their guilt — to wish for the shes, the lovely young shes of dream and fact and on occasion to file their allure and their temptation in the closed storage house of the mind. Fathers loved daughters not apart from their sex.

"I haven't thought about it," he answered, "but I know it's not best for you."

She put an open hand out. "Whatever you say, Mort. I'll accept it. If it's no, just forget I was ever so brazen. But please answer one way or the other. Do you love me or not?"

"Goddam it, yes."

Without seeming effort she arose and came to him. She pressed herself against him. He averted his mouth from her kiss, while feeling himself readying for what must not be.

Against his throat she said, "I know it's ridiculous, Mort, but it's too bad just the same."

"That's what I've told you."

"I mean to have at our wedding the people who've been kindest and most important to me."

"Yeah?"

"Like the Collingsworths and the Adlams and Eva Fox."

"You get crazier and crazier."

"Oh, I know we can't, but still it's too bad. And, after all, Eva shut up her house and bought out Soo Son, and lots of decent people go there to eat."

"From bed on to board and up to respectability, huh?" He had to laugh a little. "At heart and by reputation she'll always be a madam. Fancy women don't change."

Without looking at her, almost before the fool words came out, he knew he'd made a mistake. She stepped back, and the face that had been alight now looked stricken. "I see, Mort," she said. "I'm sorry I spoke. But you're wrong."

"Hold on! Crucified Jesus! I was wrong and I'm sorry."

He moved to her and took her in his arms and patted her shoulder while she cried against him. "Little Julie," he said. "Lord, Lord and my clumsy tongue. Ask me, and I'll say the man never lived good enough for you."

When she had quieted, he told her, "Now go on to your bed, Julie. Think it over. Think on it well. I'm twice your age or close to it, and a rough old customer, too. For myself I don't have to think. It's you and what's best for you I got to keep in my mind. Now be off, girl."

She left him then, saying only, "Good night."

It didn't surprise him, it was somehow in the right and due nature of things that, wakening later, he saw the gowned shape of her at his bedside. He moved over and threw back the covers.

18

IT WAS FALL, or close to it, but not too late for young things — calves and jack rabbits half-grown and on a small pond a hatch of wild mallards that could flap their wings but not fly as yet and so were called floppers. Twin antelopes born just this past spring ran away a piece, white-rumped, and turned and stood, their eyes flowing with curiosity.

And it seemed to Ewing, riding toward town, that all young things were his, his in a sense never recognized, never kindled or come to full growth till last night. He had mated with all youth and so was younger himself. Gone clean as a whistle were the incrustations of age and the habits of mind that increased the crust. He was an old fool and a young man who'd have a young wife and live young and foolish on the sap newly risen.

A man saw things different according to happenings. Which was a way of saying that the eye of the beholder didn't always behold. To get down to cases, here was the land with cloud shadows on it, here was the ripened range grass that waved to the breeze, here was the blue of sky and there the ageless blue bone of the Rockies, and the wind carried scents the nose sampled and sampled again but couldn't identify. Beauty was an empty, damn-fool word until the damn fool filled it. Until a girl filled it for him.

So he would take out the marriage license and see the sky pilot, who was young and uncertain and so better than some preachers before him, and he would try to corral the Collingsworths and the Adlams, leaving Eva Fox out of it, whether grub merchant or madam. And tomorrow he and Julie would be married with due ceremony if not in high style, for such was what Julie wished. Right now she was altering a dress that she said would suit the occasion. She would be waiting for him, and so would the not-yet-nuptial couch.

He waved to old Mr. McLaine as he passed his house. Mr. McLaine rose from his chair on the porch and signaled for a whoa. Walking down the path with his cane, he said, "I was expecting you, Mort."

"Howdy and why?"

"Looking for you, then. It seems you're always in the nick of time. Get off your horse and come in, please."

"I got things on my mind, Mr. McLaine."

"None more important than this, I'll wager. There's evil afoot."

What could be more important than marriage, Ewing asked himself? What evil could come before good? Yet he dismounted, hitched his horse to the fence and followed Mr. McLaine to the porch.

Once they were seated, Mr. McLaine asked, "Drink?"

"No thanks. I'm all business."

"I'll get right down to the subject then." Mr. McLaine raised his cane and with his closed fist worried his beard. "It's a devilish thing. The very devil of a thing."

"Now that I been introduced — ?"

"Yes. Yes. I'm coming to it. There's trouble in the school, Mort. Merc Marsh and Nick Brudd are out to get Mr. Collingsworth."

"And that makes a surprise party?"

"No, of course. But they have a weapon now." Mr. Mc-

Laine worked again at his beard. "That nice Miss Carson, Margaret Carson." Ewing waited. "Mr. Collingsworth has always championed her, you know."

"So have we. Why not?"

"It puts him in a bad position, one perhaps fatal to his post as the principal." Mr. McLaine tapped his cane on the floor. To the beat of it he said, "She is, it would appear, a deviate, a sexual deviate, a pervert, so-called."

"Her! A bitch man! A bull diker!"

"I'm not familiar with your terminology. In Old England they might have called her a faggot."

"Where's the evidence?"

"Marsh warned me," Mr. McLaine went on as if he hadn't heard the question. "He's warned Ross, too. They'll tackle you next, I suppose, he and Brudd, though —" here Mr. Mc-Laine's white eyebrows lifted and his old eyes studied Ewing "— they may be a bit timid about that."

"I doubt it."

"The two are making big medicine. For championing such a woman, Collingsworth has to go. If the board doesn't fire him, the matter will be made common knowledge, and the consequent stench will force us to act. That's the ultimatum."

"I don't aim to eat that shitty pickle."

"It's a pickle, just the same, no matter that we've renewed Collingsworth's contract."

"You haven't told me. How in hell do they know?"

"Oh, about Miss Carson. It seems Marsh's boy, Wallace, saw the two women in bed in intimate embrace."

"The breed girl?"

"Marie Wolf, I believe, is her name. I understand the boy has sworn to what he saw."

"Collingsworth know?"

"I believe not. He must be told."

"You mean I'm elected. Christ!"

"You're elected. He'll listen to you, and you can explain best."

"Just because I've been around? Even a damn rounder doesn't savvy much about such goings-on."

"But all I've learned — and it's little — I learned in the courts. And Ross is hardly the man for the job. The fact is that Collingsworth must be forewarned. Who can say that therefore he'll be forearmed? Maybe not, but in friendship and admiration, out of mere courtesy itself, we have to tell him."

Ewing sighed. "I do, you mean." He got to his feet. "All right. I'll try."

With old-fashioned civility Mr. McLaine lifted himself with the help of his cane. "Thanks, Mort."

The facts of life, Ewing thought as he rode away. The facts of sex with its twists and turns. How explain them, how make them exist in the mind of a man who probably never had had a piece in his life until he got married, who would have read about birchings and sodomy and pederasty and maybe muff-diving but in his innocence, out of his determination, might class them wth ancient history, remote from modern, sanctified sex? How much would a man like Collingsworth recognize? How much was he bound to reject? Well, anyhow, woman-to-woman love could be stomached, if not understood, whereas man-to-man love couldn't be.

He dropped off at the Collingsworth house. May Collingsworth came to the door. Somehow she put him in mind of Julie, though she looked older and tired. That lovely but uncommonly still and restrained child, Mary Jess, stood at her side. No, Mr. Collingsworth was not at home. He had gone to the school to prepare for the new term.

Collingsworth sat alone in his office, working on a graph or a chart, his necktie tucked neat in his vest. "Welcome,

Mort," he said, his face breaking into the good smile that was not so rare as some people thought. "Sit down."

Ewing took off his hat and turned the brim in his fingers. Sitting, he wondered how to proceed.

"It can't be as bad as that," Collingsworth said. "Not the winter of discontent."

"No Shakespeare, Prof. I'm not play-acting."

Collingsworth's face sobered. "Yes, Mort?"

"It's about that Miss Carson of yours."

"Mine?"

"Prof, you're in trouble."

The strong countenance darkened. "If you are suggesting —"

"No. No. Not about you and her. No."

"Go on."

Ewing had to shift in his chair, knowing that the shifting from one cheek to the other was avoidance. "It's no news to you that Merc Marsh and Nick Brudd are out for your scalp."

"No news."

"They figure to get you through Margaret Carson."

"Just how, tell me? She's the best teacher on the staff. Never a breath of scandal about her."

"There is now, Prof. It seems she ain't natural."

"What in the devil is this?"

"Mr. McLaine says sex deviate. He says pervert."

"Nonsense!"

"Women can love each other, Prof. Don't ask me why."

Collingsworth brought his fist down on the desk. His complexion never was ruddy. "I've heard enough!"

"You don't know enough. It's her and that Marie Wolf."

"Ridiculous! Two women?"

"You sure are a vegetarian."

"What do you mean by that?"

"I don't know. Innocent of the flesh, I reckon."

"I won't entertain such scurrility. It's preposterous. Two women? One of them Miss Carson? Bosh!"

"I didn't say it was so. I said it was the report. I say it can be."

"It can't."

Against some blind walls a man could use a sledgehammer to let the light through. He could tear down the corral that another man put up around himself against what he chose not to recognize. Through Ewing's mind flashed the brute, unsparing, sometimes exact expressions of the barn and barroom, though they concerned men's doings mostly. Women's hankering for women being strange, none of the terms would serve. They would only add poles to Collingsworth's corral.

Collingsworth had drawn back, his jaw tight, his whole face tight as dried rawhide.

"Prof," Ewing said, making his tone mild and reasonable, "I know it doesn't come welcome, but use your imagination. The Caesars and them are dead and damned, too, I reckon, but not what you'd call their evil and outlandish ways. We got 'em with us still."

"You're off the subject. It was women and particularly Miss Carson. And what you say can't be."

"Maybe not. Maybe she's not one of the shes that loves shes. Maybe so. Maybe she's caught in this devil's mix-up. The thing is, just as men sometimes have their quirks, so do women. It could be there's our Miss Carson."

"Who says so?"

"I forgot. Seems like there's evidence. Merc Marsh's boy, Wallace, he says he saw 'em cozying up."

"That overgrown whelp!"

Ewing got up, feeling spent and sorry somehow. "I had to tell you, Prof," he said. "Maybe you can do something. Remember, we're with you."

Now Collingsworth sighed. "Yes," he answered. "Yes."

He picked up a pencil and studied it as if to find was there a point to it.

Outside the building, Ewing decided he'd take out the marriage license first thing. Then he'd call Julie, if the barbed-wire telephone line was in order, to tell her he'd be late getting home. He ought to stay, maybe, in town for a while.

19

It was a march of only five blocks to Merc Marsh's store. Collingsworth located Marsh in his office, a cubicle which housed a roll-top desk, a neat file of papers, a couple of catalogues and two chairs. Marsh was hunched at his desk. When Collingsworth entered, he swung around, green eyeshade in place, black sleeve protectors over his forearms. He smiled.

Out of the smile came "Good morning, Professor. Have a chair, won't you? Nice day out."

He had been waiting, Collingsworth suspected, waiting with his shade and his protectors and the eyeglasses that didn't hide his eyes' satisfaction.

"I came to talk about your boy."

"Yes. Yes." The smile remained. "My son, Wallace. Ready for high school this year."

"He's no good."

The smile eased off. A man less cautious would have been outraged. "On your word, Professor? Your word!"

"Mine. Last spring he made an indecent proposal to my child. I let it pass then."

"That proves it, does it? Children shouldn't be inquisitive, and boys shouldn't be boys. Don't tell me you never were."

"Now, by report, he's telling tales about Miss Margaret Carson."

"Ah." Marsh answered as if the preliminaries were over and the right subject opened. "But not tales, Professor. The truth."

"About what could have been a mere embrace. Dirty minds are inventive. That's your Wallace."

"Call it embrace if you want to. He saw them all right, Miss Carson and that little breed, and he wouldn't lie, not to me or you, either. He saw them in bed, hide to hide, fiddling with each other, and Miss Carson had on —"

"How did he see them?"

"With his own eyes, of course. How else?"

"I asked how he saw them."

"And I answered you."

"You didn't. He saw them by peeping. You have a peeping Tom on your hands. The community has. It won't like it."

Marsh straightened. What there was in him of bluster asserted itself. "Who's going to believe you, you who's always stuck up for the Carson woman? You're out."

Collingsworth came to his feet. "How but by peeping?" he asked, and took a step forward.

"Now, now, Professor." The air went out of Marsh. "Fists aren't the answer."

Collingsworth wheeled around and marched off. He had silenced a mouth but not got at the truth.

Miss Carson wasn't in, the doe-eyed breed girl said after he had knocked at the door. She would be back in an hour or so. Would he come again? Did he want to leave word?

It was fantastic. That delicate face, slanted smooth from cheekbones to chin. Those luminous eyes. This mere child of the plains. This elf of the open.

He said, "Tell her to come to my office at once."

"Yes, sir," she answered. Was there the look of fear, of hidden guilt, in the young copper face?

He could go home. He could sit somewhere. He could visit

somebody while the clock ticked. Better a walk, though, a thinking walk, through the buckbrush and cinquefoil south of the town.

He had no more than arrived at the edge of their cover than a covey of prairie chickens flushed up, their frightened chuckles startling and foolish, told by an idiot. He watched them wing away and go down.

Sex, he thought while he meandered through the low growth. Sex, God's best and worst gift to man. Miss Carson, that excellent teacher, that good mind, that example of womanly modesty — Miss Carson a pervert! A Sappho of times outgrown and forgotten if ever true!

Yes, Mr. Marsh, he had been a boy once. He had abused himself and abused himself more with the afterguilt of the act, with the sure knowledge of penalties earned and accruing. In some cheap organ an advertisement had read: DOES YOUR URINE FLOW IN A TWISTED STREAM? There was the harbinger, the ad had implied, there the omen of dreadful developments by self incurred. But deliverance was at hand. Send twenty-five cents for the booklet. For the lack of only a quarter he had wearied on, seeing ahead the betraying pimples, then epileptic fits, imbecility and death, for these were the penalties sworn to by his parents. And his urine kept flowing twisted.

All darkness then, and all bosh, then and now. But how else discourage the secret vice? Not by taking advantage of pubescent girls. Not, as his mother would have said, by getting next to them.

Sex. It could be so right, as between him and May, so right that he recoiled from the thought of a sheath. Better the meeting of membranes, better pregnancy, than fish-skin insulation. And how could he, without embarrassment, ask for the article at the drugstore? Some things should be secret.

He came to the stagnant oxbow that the river made south of the bird cover. Suckers lay in the mud there. Watching them, he thought here he was, far off the subject. It didn't matter how urine flowed. It didn't matter how right sex could be. Sheaths didn't signify. Now he had to nose in the mud.

She was waiting for him when he arrived at his office. Trim, straight-backed, ever respectful, she arose as he entered. Always there was a stiff grace about her, a good, businesslike manner appropriate to her profession. It flitted into his mind that he had always thought of her as a neuter, as a school-teacher only.

"I came the minute I heard from you, Mr. Collingsworth," she said. "Is there something I can do?"

"Sit down, please." He went around to his chair. Seated, he said, "We have to face some unpleasantness, Miss Carson."

"I'm sorry. Please tell me." Her calm face had clouded, not, he thought, with suspicion.

"It's about you."

"About me? What have I done now?"

"I'm not accusing you. Please understand that. I don't believe what I've heard."

She answered, "Go on."

"The source of the report is highly questionable. It's Merc Marsh's boy, that Wallace, that lout of his. I don't trust him."

Again she said, "Go on."

He couldn't help fidgeting. "The subject is one I would not choose to bring up, please believe me. You are an excellent teacher. Your outside life, to my knowledge, is impeccable."

"Yes?" There seemed to be now the note of thin alarm in her voice, though her expression stayed calm.

He came to his feet and walked to the rear window, and there was Elephant Ear Butte with silent peace lying on it. Without turning back he said, "It's about you and Marie Wolf. The boy says he saw you in a compromising position, in what would be called an unnatural act."

197

He made himself wheel around. She sat straighter than ever. What color she had had left her. Muscles played at the points of her jaw. But her gaze was direct. The windows of her soul were open, he thought, if one cared to look in.

"You have only to deny it," he told her.

"I deny nothing." The unwelcome words were steady. "I love her, Mr. Collingsworth."

So there was the truth, the truth that set you free but didn't, the truth that brought two unwinked tears to the ridged face.

"You wouldn't understand," she said.

"I understand one thing." He had let his tone be harsh.

"I know," she answered before he could go on. With her fingers she wiped the tears from her eyes. "You will have my resignation before the day is over." She rose abruptly. "You're the best and fairest man I ever knew. Good-bye, Mr. Collingsworth."

He watched her walking off, saw her falter once and go on, walking straight and stiff, walking resolute, walking — was it? — mannishly.

He didn't speak his mind: God damn it! God damn it all to hell!

20

Dear Diary,

Today was a bad day. It was Father again. I wish I knew what bothers him because Mother and I might be able to help. We could be more careful but I don't know how. But he never tells me but Mother says he always tells her later and she never tells me.

He was so cross at dinner that I could not eat and then he told me I had to. Which made me throw up.

He didn't say anything after dinner but sat in the living room looking at the wall. Mother was only darning one of his socks, using a china egg, but all of a sudden he got up and kicked a chair. It went over and kind of skated off, and he hurt his foot and had to hop around. I was extra scared when Mother asked if he felt better now, but he didn't say yes or no.

Mother says I must remember how good and kind Father is underneath. I know he is. I love him. Dear Diary, in my prayers now I will pray he will be that way all the time. And I will go to sleep hoping for smiles tomorrow.

The diary was a small red book that Mary Jess kept in the bottom drawer of her dresser, sometimes not covering it with blouses or underthings. Perhaps, May Collingsworth thought, she believed no one would intrude on her privacy. Perhaps she didn't mind if Mother did. May put the book back and fumbled for garments to hide it. She let herself down then in the small rocker by the bedside and swallowed. That was what she always advised Mary Jess — to swallow her cry.

The child looked misty, fair-haired and misty, through tears misty, innocence sleeping, not dreaming troubles. May put her hand out and barely touched the blond head. She had left the lamp lighted, for Mary Jess was terrified of the dark, and now she turned the wick lower and sat back. She brushed at her eyes. Tears were too easy.

How explain to this small one? How explain to herself? How make Benton see? How temper his temper? He sat alone in the living room now, fighting some fury, which in time he would tell her about. Even so?

When the time came, she would talk to him, and he would be truly sorry — and never change. He would remain sweet and tender and moderate in righteousness and, in relaxed moments, rich with antic humor. But the demons that possessed him in spite of himself would remain, too, ready with thunderclap.

Mary Jess stirred and said, "Mother," and May stroked her hand, and Mary Jess went back to deep sleep.

Benton had never changed really, not since their first meetings at Earlham College and later at her home in Fortville, where he had proposed. She saw him as of then, though the years had altered him little, a determined, classic-featured young man, who had courted her with stiff propriety.

"May," he said, and bent his head, "I have my love to offer and not much besides. For my wife I want you above all women. Will you marry me?"

She wanted then to give herself to him. The crickets were singing all around, and the katydids, too, and the leaves of the big poplar sang, and she could see a star. She had wanted to give herself to him, no matter the sin of it, and had checked herself, sensing or knowing she would have cheapened herself in his eyes and possibly lost him. A man like Benton demanded virgin for wife.

She said, "Thank you, Benton. Yes, I'll be happy to marry you."

He kissed her, close mouthed, and went on his way. From the dark path she heard his whistling.

Now through the opened window came the remembered, good-bye smell of burning leaves. Someone was too quick with his autumn bonfire, someone too ready to lay the weakening season away. Outside, a dog howled, and another answered far off, and then they reported, one to the other, speaking challenge, wisdom or woe in curs' talk at long distance.

As a bride she had not been prepared for his fits of temper or, of course, for his driving virility. It had taken a young man of strong character to curb such desire. His sexuality she had come to welcome. His dark moods she couldn't understand altogether or influence much. More was the pity.

But there were reasons. Now, as she sat in the low light beside Mary Jess sleeping, they swam in her head as so often before. He had been a change-of-life baby, the last of a brood, and late babies were said to have aberrations.

More than that, he could have heired his quick passions. His God-loving mother had been known for bad temper, now buried but likely resurgent in Benton.

She had sat rocking that day — the mother had — a woman already old, her face square like Benton's but lined by time and unknown torment, her hair white and untended. A half a dozen callers had gathered in the little living room, people of close kin or loose connection, and someone from afar had said, "Aunt Martha, you've been blessed with quite a family. Just how many?"

Somehow the question set her jaw and lined her face the deeper. "None of your infernal business. More than enough.

That's how many." To the embarrassment of all she asked, "Who keeps tab when she's in a family way all the time? Ask my husband. He sired two others by his first wife." Then, with the quick change of mood that marks age, she had gone on, "Ten. I believe that's the way they counted 'em. Several not worth a hoot."

From such a mother had come Benton. But from her or his father, or from deeps traceable to neither, he had inherited resolution. They had no money for his higher schooling, though they endorsed it, and twice or maybe three times he had quit the university and taught country school so as to be able to return.

Mary Jess, she thought, if only I could bring you to a true appreciation. See your father trudging home from teaching school, and he is tired, and the way is dark and lonely, and in lower Indiana there are violent, vicious men ready to abuse and beat and rob a traveler, to have their sport with a man who teaches school. And here comes a covered bridge, where good people have been set upon, and your father reaches down and picks two rocks and, whistling, goes ahead. So here we are, sweetheart, loved, protected and shielded by his courage.

It was hard to believe, she wouldn't believe, that such courage failed in the face of greater opportunity. Benton was sure of himself. He feared nothing. He just loved the country he lived in. Or was that it?

Chill had crept in the window, and she drew the sheet up around the young throat, and the words of "The Lost Doll" began to hum in her head. Even now, even at her age, Mary Jess liked that too-sad, little song sung to her.

> But for old time's sake
> She is still, dears,
> The prettiest doll in the world.

202

She heard voices, men's voices, in the living room but decided not to go in. It was bedtime for her. Bed and sleep were a comfort, more so these days than they had right to be. Benton would join her later, maybe to tell her what ate at him.

Lightly she kissed Mary Jess.

21

Ewing was coming to think he might as well, or better, have gone back to the ranch except for the few chores left to do. The town drowsed. If there was scandal about, he didn't hear it. If any pot was close to the boiling point, it was heating in secret. Later there'd be talk, but talk about him and Julie and the marriage license the clerk of the court had made out. Already he had taken some courthouse joshing, from people who counted his wrinkles and noted there was gray in his hair. Let it lie.

For once the telephone had been in commission, and he had got hold of Julie to say he'd be late for reasons he'd explain on arrival, and she had answered in that clear voice of hers, "Of course, Mort. I'll be waiting." That was Julie for you.

Being close, he had dropped into the sheriff's office, which Hank Howie, through sufferance, still occupied. Was anything borne by the wind, Howie would be likely to know.

Howie said, "Good to see you, Mort. Rest your seat."

The years had made Howie fatter. They might also have made him a better sheriff. And, always affable, he had learned to be more so than ever. But it was lack of competition rather than competence or courtesy that had kept him in office. Still, he had got rid of Sarge Kraker, if by the device of recommending him for a better job as a private policeman in Butte.

"What goes?" Ewing asked.

Howie rolled a fat cigar in fat fingers. "Quiet. Not even a whisper. That's how I like it."

"Sure. That's what you're paid for — to keep things so tidy people don't need you. Huh?"

Howie had to consider. He smiled his amiable smile and said, "Oh, I keep busy enough. Yesterday, for instance, a man up on the bench tried to slip some mortgaged cows out. I put the kibosh on that."

"Good. Me, I got to see Prof Collingsworth. School business."

He watched for reaction and saw none. "He was uptown a while ago," Howie said. "Went into Marsh's."

If Collingsworth was bracing Merc Marsh, if he was still in the store in grim face-to-face, now was no time for third parties, Ewing reflected as he came out on the street. Nor, for that matter, did he see how his presence, welcome or not, could serve any purpose.

He put up his horse at McCabe's livery stable and strolled down the dead street. It was past noon now, well past, and he hadn't eaten and didn't want to. That was the way of it: delay a meal, and the belly balked.

Doctor Crabtree, a gawky sawbones with the trenched lines of life — or death — in his face, was about to enter his office. Some people complained about Doc and Doc's bedside manner, not thinking that maybe the suffering he'd ministered to had grooved their marks on him. He held up when he saw Ewing.

"How, Doc?" Ewing said. "It's not healers this cow camp needs. It's more undertakers."

"No. It's already buried and needs resurrection."

205

"That's a long wait."

"Is it? Let something happen, and the dead will shake off the dust."

"Like what?"

"Anything fresh for fresh talk. A sudden death, a bad accident, the veil off an unfaithful wife. People like us, people isolated like us, get inbred, culturally inbred. They sit and fester, watching the days go by, until someone they know gets his tit in the wringer. That's resurrection."

"Maybe so," Ewing said. For the answer he'd get he went on. "Still, for winter we have the lyceum course and for summer chautauqua."

"That's a reach for something all right, thanks mostly to Collingsworth. But the bird in the hand is a bunch of cheap performers. They only ripple the graveyard grass and blow on away. It's the immediate that brings us to life. A fart in Arfive is more important than a cyclone in Kansas."

"You're just down on your luck, Doc. Lost a patient?"

"Plenty," Doc answered, and entered his office.

An interesting mind and a tongue to match it, that was Doc Crabtree, Ewing thought, gazing after him. He had entered the town almost unknown, almost from nowhere, though the degree that hung on his wall came from Iowa. Some people imagined a cloud hung over his past, but it was more likely he had drifted, restless, until his spizzerinctum had lowered from flood tide and washed him up in Arfive. Regardless, he was an able physician.

Ewing lazed on. He passed the Gold Leaf Bar, a new one financed, it was likely, by Brudd. He passed Adlam's. He would visit it later. Now he'd pay his respects to Merc Marsh.

Marsh was strolling his store, alone, probably wondering how best to push his inventory or punish professors. He looked up as Ewing entered and said a bare, "Hi."

"Fit enough," Ewing answered. "And you?"

Marsh's gesture took in the empty store. "Not a thing."

"No sales, no news, no nothing, huh?"

Marsh adjusted his shade, so's to bring it lower over his eyes.

"Doc Crabtree says," Ewing went on, "that what the town needs is something to chew on, something more than old cuds."

"Yes. He would."

Trying to tease out a rat, a man could hardly go farther, not without using a stick. Somehow Collingsworth must have tied Marsh's tongue. But different bait might turn the trick. "Your friend Brudd's coming to spend a lot of time in Arfive," Ewing said.

"Why shouldn't he?"

"No reason. But it's a small pond for a big frog."

"He has interests here."

"Sure. Financial and political. The ladies against liquor are gaining ground, and Collingsworth stands for temperance, and it seems like more and more people are siding him."

"Not temperance!" Now Marsh's words had some heat in them. "Not temperance. Total abstinence. And it's none of his business. We hire him to superintend school."

"Did you say 'we'?"

An uncommon flush stained Marsh's cheeks. Two glints pierced the green of his eyeshade. "So what if I oppose him? He's against me. Always has been. Thinks it a sin if I sell an honest rancher a jug. Routes business away from me, you know too damn well. Naturally I voted against renewing his contract. So what? What's it to you, Ewing? He won't see it out."

"And just why won't he?"

Marsh took a deep breath. He managed to collar his anger. One hand made an indifferent gesture. "It's just a hunch," he said.

"That's how men go belly up, betting hunches," Ewing answered, and walked to the door and let himself out.

It was good to be on the nigh-empty street, away from that small, sore-assed counter jumper. A man could tramp on a bug but not if it talked and paid taxes. Not if it was made in the image of God, as the true believers believed. God sure had put out a mixed bunch of images. Herd them together and hallelujah, dear Jesus.

So now he would go see the preacher and arrange for the marriage.

The parsonage was a neat, frame house painted brown and white. The preacher, a small, tidy man, as serene of face as a baby's butt, came to the door. He said good afternoon and come in.

"I'm Mort Ewing, Reverend."

"Yes. Yes. Of course."

The place smelled of cookies. A good thing for a preacher's wife, baking cookies. A good thing for any wife, for that matter.

"Please have a seat, Mr. Ewing." The man's manner suggested he hoped as much for good will as salvation. But what really was wrong with that?

Ewing sat in the first handy chair. Smiling, the preacher let himself down on a davenport, carefully, as if the devil might have planted a tack there. From the kitchen came the sound an oven door made.

"I am happy to see you," the preacher said. "Brother Collingsworth tells me you support the church, and I thank you and hope to see you there. But perhaps you belong to a different faith?"

"It's some different."

"We would welcome you nonetheless. Now, may I help you in any way?"

From the kitchen came a soft humming. Out of old camp-meeting memory, out of his random young manhood, some words rose to mind. "Stand up, stand up for Jesus . . ." In the kitchen, cookies and Christ: here in the parlor, the evangel's overture.

"I want to get hitched," Ewing said.

"Hitched?"

"Married, that is."

"Oh, to be sure. I'll be most glad to officiate if that is your wish."

"It is."

"I must apologize, but have you or your intended been married before? Are former spouses alive? We have convictions in that direction, Mr. Ewing."

The mild, the friendly eyes questioned him. It was divorce that mattered, not the chance wrestles a man might have had. Or a woman.

Ewing answered, "I was never broke to harness. Nor my bride, either."

"I assume you mean there's been no divorce on one side or the other?"

"None."

"Fine. Marriage is and must remain a sacrament." The man's smile assumed total agreement. "When do you want to take vows?"

"Tomorrow, if it suits you."

The preacher fiddled with his fingers. "That's Saturday. I must officiate at a funeral. Old Mrs. Hyde, you know. A good, fine woman. And I have an afternoon meeting with Brother Collingsworth to go over the church budget. He has consented again to lead the finance campaign. So would four o'clock be convenient?"

"It suits."

"At the church then?"

"Good enough." Ewing came to his feet. "Thank you, Reverend. We'll see you then and there."

The sun had sunk low. It rested on the ridge of the Rockies, reluctant to give up the high plains it had seen and had warmed. Where its last rays struck, the land looked gentle and the wood of Arfive's buildings as mellow as butter. And it entered Ewing's head that he had been unkind in his thinking, unkind to that wet-eared and well-meaning preacher and ungrateful in general. For every reason, save one, today should have been of day of bright expectation. Only a jackass would have let that one reason cloud it so much.

He shook his head and brought Julie into it and went on.

This was a day when only store-tenders could be found in the stores, he thought as he entered Adlam's saloon. But Saturday would bring in the boys, for haircuts and shaves and barbershop baths and liquid talk at the bars while wives and staid husbands shopped for yard goods and groceries.

"Good places for a grog shop, Fatty," he said, approaching the bar.

"How are you, Mort? Yep. Might as well put out a no trespassing sign. Slow all week. Beer, wine, whiskey. Name it. It's on the house, seeing as I can't sell anything."

"A beer." Adlam drew it and set it out. Ewing drank. "Heard anything new?"

"About what from who? Just old Mrs. Hyde died, and to me she was just a sack dress and rheumatism."

"Well, about me?"

The eyes widened in the fat face. "Should I have?"

"Not necessarily. I want you to do me a favor."

"Anything short of horse stealing."

"I want you to stand up for me."

"Trouble, Mort? Sure. I'll stand up to be counted."

"To count me as married."

Adlam thrust his little hands forward and rested his heavy arms on the bar. The action was a question itself, but still he asked, "Married?"

"Julie and I. Tomorrow at four at the Methodist church. We want you and your missus."

After an instant Adlam came around the bar, moving light as a bubble. One small hand grabbed Ewing's. The other touched his shoulder and moved across, and the fat arm squeezed his back. He didn't speak at once. His eyes spoke for him, and somehow the whole hulk of him. "Mort, you old bachelor bastard! You and our little Julie. You bet your life we'll be there. I'll lock up this dive if I have to. Dinner at my house afterward, with champagne. The best."

"Now whoa up."

"No, sir. It's settled."

"There'll be others, like Jay Ross and old Mr. McLaine, if they can make it."

"Why, sure." A sudden shadow of doubt, of maybe regret, came on the fat face. "I don't guess Mr. and Mrs. Collingsworth would come to my house."

"It figures they couldn't attend anyway." To the still doubtful face Ewing explained, "I know Prof is up to his ears in school and church work. Course, I'd like to have him, but I don't aim to take up more of his time."

It was the truth, but not quite, not the whole truth that would have included Miss Margaret Carson, not to remention other items like unlikely companions at dinner.

Adlam didn't appear wholly satisfied. He said, "Too bad."

"Yeah, but don't go imagining things. Prof's my friend and all right with me. Take my word."

Now Adlam smiled off his doubts. "Always have. So it's all arranged, or will be soon as I get the word out. Now, me, I got some old whiskey too good for the trade. We'll have a drink to tomorrow."

It was dark when Ewing left Adlam's. It was past supper-time. Rather than go home hungry and put out Julie or Mrs. McDonald, he would eat a bite before he left town.

Eva Fox had a few tardy customers, all men save for a strange woman who sat at a table across from what might be her husband. Eva had removed the curtain that separated good people from bad and ripped out the booths where her whores used to feed. A bright place she had, cheerful and proper and antiseptic as hell. A stranger to her wouldn't have thought she had ever counted wet towels.

Ewing nodded toward the people he knew. While a girl waited table, Eva stood behind the counter, joshing easily with the men ranged along it. Her eye caught his, and she said, "Evening, Morton."

He answered, "How, Eva?" and waited until the waitress came to him. She asked, "Counter or table, sir?" Her language showed Eva's training. Somehow a table suited him better. It had an unsoiled cloth on it, a fresh napkin and bright silverware. The waitress laid down a menu.

The menu was as clean as new money and listed choices double the number old Soo Son used to offer. Old Soo Son, a good, honest Chinaman and by cow-country standards a fair-enough cook who had gone back to Canton to die, leaving the tatters of his livelihood to be assembled and cleaned and made to operate by one who knew more than he did. It wouldn't have occurred to him to dress himself as a waitress in starched, all-over white. Out of a cathouse, cultivation.

While he was eating, Eva came by. Stopping, she said quietly, "Good for you, Mort. Be kind to her." She was gone before he could answer.

He was about to ask for more coffee when Doc Crabtree entered. "Ewing!" Crabtree said. His voice was low but in-sistent. He jerked his thumb toward the door.

Outside he grasped Ewing by one arm and told him,

"Plenty talk now. The teacher, Miss Carson, is dead."

"Dead! How?"

"Poison. Laudanum by the smell of it. Maybe some drug that acts quicker. Or a combination. Hell, anyone can buy death, pill or liquid."

"Dosed herself?"

"Probable but unconfirmed."

"It fits," Ewing said.

"What fits?"

"Never mind. Nothing." But, suffering Jesus, it fitted all right. "Who found her? When? Where?"

"At home. That breed girl that lives with her banged into my office to tell me and was off like a shot. So fast it makes a man wonder."

"I wouldn't."

"No. Not my job really. But it's up to me, if I can, to determine the manner of death. Suicide or foul play. After examination I notified the sheriff and undertaker. Howie's there now."

"With a glad hand out to all callers."

"Damn it! He had to be told."

"I reckon. But why tail me up?"

"For Collingsworth. He must know her background and the names of her relatives, if anyone does. Besides, he might shed some light on the case."

"Then tell him and ask him."

Crabtree's hand went back to Ewing's sleeve. "No. You're a friend of his. You're the chairman of the school board. It may be I'll need your say-so. Please come along."

"Say-so to what?"

Crabtree hitched up a shoulder and dropped it. "She left a letter for him." He poked in his pocket. "I have it here. Will you come?"

Ewing let out a long breath. He said, "Twice in one day."

"What?"

"Elected rain crow."

"What?"

"Never mind," Ewing said again. "Let's go."

Collingsworth let them in. His pale, strong-jawed face showed no astonishment at this late visit by an unlikely pair. He said in a voice without welcome in it, "Come in. The rest of the household's asleep."

Ushered into the living room, Ewing reckoned that Collingsworth had been sitting alone, without a book, looking into space that might give him answers to what he couldn't comprehend or accept.

After they were seated, Collingsworth asked in that same close-kept tone, "What is it?"

It was Crabtree's show, and Ewing was silent. "We bring bad tidings, Professor," Crabtree answered.

Collingsworth didn't ask what, not even by manner.

It flashed on Ewing that the two were much alike and much different. Strong, stern men both, but Crabtree a cynic and Collingsworth a stoic who yet had the belief in mankind that Crabtree had lost in his practice. Scalpel and pills were for Crabtree, elevation for Collingsworth.

"Miss Margaret Carson is dead," Crabtree said. "The first but not final assumption is suicide." Ewing had seen shot brutes stay upright, numb to the bullets that had entered their bowels, unbelieving or indomitable seemingly. Crabtree reached in his pocket. "She left a letter for you."

Collingsworth took the envelope. He opened it slow. He read what was in it, refolded the letter and put it back, his eyes unspeaking.

Crabtree asked, "May we see it?"

"It's private."

"It will remain so."

"I can assure you she did away with herself."

"Privately, I take your word, Professor. I can't do it professionally. I must certify the cause of death, both as a doctor and Arfive's unwilling coroner. Suicide, if that's it, can't be left up to hearsay. Surely you understand?"

"It won't go on the record?"

"Hardly a chance. I might say never a chance. But in conscience I must see what it says. As things stand, the breed girl is suspect."

It was the reference to conscience, Ewing thought, that made Collingsworth hand over the letter.

Crabtree said, "Here, Mort. Read over my shoulder."

The letter read:

DEAR MR. COLLINGSWORTH:

When you receive this message, you will know that I have resigned. My way to me seems the only and right way.

I leave no one of close kin to be notified.

I have arranged — God pity her! — that little Marie Wolf find me, notify Doctor Crabtree and be gone at once to the reservation, where she can be reached through the agency. She will follow my written instructions.

What little I have, I leave to her, as the accompanying handwritten will specifies. If any question arises, I pray you to see to her interests.

She is a good girl, Mr. Collingsworth, and not by nature strange at all. Despite me, who has corrupted her in your eyes, she will make some man a good and intelligent and natural wife.

I thank you for all your kindnesses, recognizing that your faith was misplaced.

You will never understand, Mr. Collingsworth. I don't myself. I pray that the God who made me will do so and forgive.

Yours with esteem,
MARGARET CARSON

215

22

"To the bride and groom," Fatty Adlam said, holding up his glass.

"And for years of happiness ahead for these, our friends," old Mr. McLaine added. His veined hand spilled just a drop or two.

In this close company that toasted him and Julie, Ewing felt himself somehow aside. It was as if, changed by years or fortune, he saw old and unchanged friends again and knew they didn't know him. Marriage gave a man new slants and different shape and aim. For him it had. It made him think, not of himself alone, not as a free and single self, but as custodian of trust. Imagine it, that Julie put her life, her whole damn life, in trust to him! No guarantee, no bond on his part. Just his word. His willing word and, by God, no discount. Faith put a man on guard against the least infraction, against unthinking speech and foolish act. Against betrayal, that was it. And none could know but him.

Julie's hand sought his beneath the tablecloth, and he held it while the others drank. Some part of what he felt, he knew, was self-pride — and it was solid in its way — his male and aging pride at having her for his. It wasn't every outcast stag, or any other, that could pasture with a heifer like this one. Salute to Ewing. Inside himself, with what he knew, he could smile at the salute.

Mrs. Adlam had outdone herself — and on short notice, too. Somewhere, not in the town's market, she had corralled a young turkey. Somewhere she had found fresh tomatoes to go with the lettuce grown in the garden. She had fixed mashed potatoes and sweet potatoes and squaw corn on the cob. It was the only corn that would mature in this country and then only if the season was kind, and, though small-eared and tortured by a hard life, it had a flavor that lusher corn did not. Which made a man wonder about hardship and quality. The day wasn't done, but Mrs. Adlam had lighted two candles for show.

"Scalloped oysters!" Jay Ross said, helping himself to some. "Oysters this early."

"First of the season," Adlam answered, sounding pleased. "From Great Falls. That long-distance line works hunky-dory. Time it did, too."

At the end of a sigh Mr. McLaine said, "Makes the world smaller, for better or worse."

For better or worse, the preacher had said, not aware that it would be for the better and best, barring some deviltry from above or below. Preachers had to hedge, else how answer to unanswered prayers? The man had been dead serious and the formal vows solemn as last words; and the amusement felt because God or man couldn't tie the knot tighter had vanished. Beside him, Julie had trembled, and he was put in mind for a flash of virgins destined for blood sacrifice. He had steadied her with his hand. Now, smiling a smile meant for him alone, Julie took her hand from his and went to eating.

"It was a crackerjack of a wedding," Mrs. Adlam said, looking around to see that no one lacked for anything. She had

217

been up and down and now had taken off her apron. Last one at the trough. "We don't go to church, of course you know, but —"

Adlam cut her off. "No mix. Not Methodists and barley-corn."

"But the preacher seemed so good and earnest."

"Good and earnest," Mr. McLaine said to his plate.

Ewing knew his thoughts, for the old man had told him once in words he mostly could remember, "The trouble is, the high illusion is, that man's course is always up. Goodness will increase and at last prevail. That's Mr. Collingsworth. That's the Protestant church of any stripe. But change is order, and change can be reversion. It is alteration in taste and attitude, worse or better. No telling which from the mixed history of man. But without that high illusion, that aspiration, what? That's why I go to church."

Into his recollections Julie said, "Why so quiet, Mort?"

"Don't want to tell about my luck. It's a private cache."

"Our luck," she said, low-voiced. On his thigh he felt the quick touch of her hand.

But who wouldn't, within his secret self, taste the wish to brag, to tell the world, to lay bare the whole of it to friends who might surmise but not surmise enough. Even to Collingsworth, who might unbend, and, ahead of him, to Dunc McDonald?

He should have invited the McDonalds to the wedding, but Mrs. Adlam and her Fatty, whose board was strained enough now, would have insisted on including them. One of those things. It was Dunc who'd brushed the team into a gloss, washed the rig and saddle-soaped the harness so's the bride- and groom-to-be could go to town in style. He had stood by, holding to a bridle, while they mounted to the seat.

"Happy ride and happy days," he said. His eyes went to the fretting horses. "Team's frisky, but later on I'll saddle up and come along and watch if there's been a runaway." He smiled, knowing what the chances were. "In town I'll lift a glass to you."

"Home early, that's us," Ewing told him. "We aim to dodge a shivaree."

"And if there's a wedding cake," Julie said in parting, "we'll bring some back."

And so they'd rolled to town.

Mrs. Adlam, helped by Julie, was clearing off the dishes when a knock came at the door.

"Well?" Adlam said, and pushed back and came lightly to his feet. At the opened door he asked, "What's up, Rank? Come on in."

Rank McCabe moved far enough inside to get Ewing in his sight. He looked like the stable keeper that he was, except he had an ancient cartridge belt around him and wore a holstered pistol. It didn't take an expert to see he and a jug had mothered up. His mouth worked for words, and the words fanned his straggly mustache. "I swear, Mort, it weren't my fault. Just a little snooze I took, and they was gone."

Although he felt sure of the rest, Ewing said, "Well, tell it."

"Just a little snooze. A man gets tired. Your team, I mean. The rig and all, the whole caboodle. Stolen, by God." His hand felt for his pistol and, finding it, gave it a pat. "I been lookin'. Horse thieves can't fool with me."

"Rank, you're drunk." Ross spoke as Ewing was about to. "Horse thieves, hell! It was jokers playing pranks."

"Drunk, am I?" McCabe said as all drunks said when told. "I guess I don't know I tied 'em good? I guess I don't know they was Mort's and he'd come back by tonight?"

Ross made a noise in his throat.

"Like as not it's pranksters," Adlam said to Ewing. "With you held up, they'll shivaree you later."

"Not if I can help it," Ewing answered, and shied a glance at Julie's turned and questioning face.

No, he didn't want her put through it, not her, his wife, who had been plagued enough, and not themselves together. Hell, he didn't mind that he would have to treat the crowd. There was time yet to make ready to buy booze and something for whatever wives and small fry. What he minded was the only half-sly banter, the rude and bruising humor, the eyeful speculation as men looked at Julie and related her to him. All none of their goddam business, no matter what his grounds to brag. Eh, Collingsworth?

"We just can't stay," he said in easy explanation. "It's early home tonight and on the way to California in the morning."

"And all that packing still to do," Julie was quick to add. She blushed then, no doubt thinking.

Ewing turned. McCabe and his alcohol stood slumped and sleepy. "You got a team for hire, Rank?"

It took a second for McCabe to know his name. "Me? No. Used to, but no money in it. Just two old saddle pelters is all now."

"Take my outfit," Ross said. "Won't be the first time that I've stayed in town."

"No," Ewing answered, and got up. "Thanks, Jay, but I'll tell you what. I'll go up town and set 'em up and take the gaff and promise plenty more to come. That way I calculate they'll tell me where the team is, if any had a hand in it."

"Oh, Mort, must you?" Julie asked. With thumb and finger she plucked at his sleeve.

"I'll trail along," Adlam said.

"Me, too," Ross chimed in. He nodded to the ladies. "Just for the fun of it."

Mrs. Adlam made a despairing gesture. "We haven't even cut the wedding cake."

"Later," Adlam said, and smiled at her.

Ewing went to McCabe and guided him outside. Ross and Adlam followed. They all paused in the yard. "Hell, men," Ewing said. "No need to mount a posse."

"You don't know," Adlam told him. "Maybe they'll spill to you and maybe not. More sport for them if they kept mum. We'll just nose around on the off chance, but don't you keep us from the play."

"Sure," Ross said. He bit the end off a cigar, his eyes amused and speculative. "Our game is find the team. The odds are bad but better with three of us on scout. Fun, Mort, either way."

McCabe asked, "Anybody got a bottle?"

They separated at the first corner. Ross would go to the livery stable with McCabe, then pry around. Adlam would enter the back of his saloon, summon the barman to the rear and find what he had learned, if anything. Ewing would take the main street, go in from the front, set 'em up and see then if the boys would spill. It was just possible, if McDonald had arrived, that he had picked up something. McCabe, provided that he had a bottle, would have another drink.

The town was coming to life all right, Ewing thought, walking in the soft September dusk. Here was a buckboard and a buggy and there a wagon and now and then a saddle horse, tied up at the hitch racks or coming in to tie, and, down the street a piece, an eight-yoke freight string moving slow. Later there'd be more, the day being Saturday. And there'd be new things to talk about — Miss Carson and his marriage, first and second. Doc Crabtree's resurrection.

Already the marriage was becoming common knowledge. Friends kept stopping him, friends and acquaintances, to shake his hand and speak congratulations. Gabby, most of them, saying this and asking that, mixing marriage with the weather and that poor Miss Carson and the cattle market. By now Ross was likely at the stable and Adlam in the bar; but a man couldn't brush aside good wishes.

It was foolish, he reflected, somehow gay and foolish both, this ready entry of Ross and Adlam into a case of mere high jinks important just to him and then perhaps for reasons overblown. Gay and foolish and understandable. A pitting of side against side, wits against wits, luck against luck against the odds and, whatever the upshot, friendly frolic. Fun for fun's sake in a town that hadn't much. More resurrection, Doc.

Free for a moment of well-wishers, Ewing quickened his pace. Concern or not, he had to smile.

Through the swinging doors one voice played first fiddle from inside Adlam's bar. It sounded like Nick Brudd's, but sober-sided. Ewing pushed on in.

The customers, seated and standing, curved out from the bar. McDonald was just sitting down. Brudd had the stage, his back to Adlam. He was gesturing with one arm. The other was bent behind him, between him and the bar, as if to conceal what his hand held.

"So, my friends," he was saying, his tone and manner soapy, "I been promising you the like of what you haven't seen before." He was too caught up in his act to spot Ewing at the door. "You ought to know first that our good sheriff can vouch for what you are about to see. Junk, he called it, as who wouldn't but some rare sparrow like yours truly?"

A voice interrupted, calling, "Nick, get on with it."

Brudd lifted his free hand. "In just a minute. Let's keep in mind it's educational. It ought to be. It belonged to that poor teacher, rest her soul. Here since the first class met, she was, and rehired and raised from year to year. Yep, a favorite of one Professor Collingsworth and the board that backed him. And all along —" Brudd shook his head slowly. "It makes a man wonder. It would make any man wonder."

Ewing saw men glancing at him, their eyes curious, but not yet had Brudd discovered him. He didn't move or speak and couldn't guess what Brudd was up to. No good, that was for sure. Beneath that put-on, oily spiel was the true, eternal bastard.

"Like I said," Brudd went on, "the sheriff, being a good man and clean-minded, though it was junk. Though it was maybe a queer-like truss and no good to anyone but her. On the queer part he was right."

Now, with a flourish, Brudd brought out his hidden hand. It waved a belt. Midway of the belt, straight out from it, angled something like the handle of a file. And all at once Ewing knew. There was a name for it — a dingus, no, a dildo, an artificial shaft for women wanting and pretending to be male. The sorry shes.

"I could give a kind of demonstration," Brudd was saying.

Ewing's feet moved of themselves. His shoulder knocked a man aside. His eyes met Brudd's and saw them narrow.

"The chairman of the —" Brudd had time to say before Ewing snatched the belt. He lashed Brudd across the face and flung the belt beyond the bar where Adlam stood, wide-eyed in his fat. "Lose it!"

In that instant he felt Brudd's fist, hard against his jaw, and he gave to it and sidestepped, turning, and took another blow and drove a punch deep in the well-fed belly. Brudd folded forward, unfolded to an uppercut and went over on his back.

He wasn't out but lay unmoving, his eyes alive beside their bridge of beak, as unforgiving as a captive hawk's. The beak began to breathe out blood.

Ewing looked down at him, thinking words but having none to say. Nor did he have many when he raised his gaze and took in the half-circled, watching men. "Jesus Christ!" he threw at them. "How rank can you stand it?"

Some of the heads went down, and some of the eyes lowered as he looked; and it struck him that here was bottom decency, decency tardy in assertion and slow to comprehend but bottom decency offended. There was Brudd's mistake — to think that others were as low-down as himself.

A few spoke to him, and some gestured little signals, and Fatty called out something as he made for the door. He ignored them all.

The door swung open when he reached it. Rank McCabe lurched in. He grabbed Ewing's arm, "Found, by God!" he slobbered out. "Close, too. Ross, he had the idea."

"All right." Ewing tried to push him off.

"Fine and dandy, everything, except Ross gimped his ankle, but he'll ease along."

"All right. I said all right."

Ewing crowded past him and went out. At the edge of the boardwalk he held up. He'd get a breath and wait for Ross. Poor thanks to old McCabe, he thought, and how Brudd came by the bogus belt might stand some looking into. Unlikely, more or less, that the sheriff was so goddam innocent. Poor doings inside when it came to that. No trick to knock Brudd over, and no way out of it if a man stood for what he believed. But it was so useless. Knocked on his ass, a leper stayed a leper. What Brudd was he was. What he was he would be.

A sudden rise of voices from inside brought his gaze back to the door. Brudd stepped out backward, one hand outthrust as if to hold off followers, and wheeled around and sidled from the exit. His eyes found Ewing. Not until he brought it up did Ewing see the pistol.

Brudd said, "Now Ewing!" He was taking care to draw a bead.

"You're too smart for that." Was he? One beat of heart between trigger and discretion. One beat and then another, for men came bursting out of Adlam's. Brudd's gun hand swung to warn them. His voice cut through their protests. "Keep back!"

"No, Dunc!" Ewing cried out, and saw McDonald halt and take a backward step. And at the very tail end of his eye, before he turned to face the turning pistol, he thought he saw another figure.

"You there! You with the gun!" The voice came harsh, and it was Collingsworth's. "Down with it! Right now!"

Again Brudd shifted with the pistol. Again he ordered, "Keep back!"

"Don't Prof!" Ewing called out, and knew it was no use. Past the lined-up men, past the doorway, straight to object, Collingsworth would come. And he was coming. Nothing but a bullet would ever stay that march. Brudd was taking aim.

Ewing leaped and dived. He felt his arms clinch legs. He heard a gun go off. He was in a scramble, and all at once he wasn't. He raised himself and saw Brudd on his back, his face slack and unseeing.

He got up. Close by, Collingsworth stood silent, the pistol in his hand. "Hurt, Prof?"

Collingsworth gave a bare shake of his head. "Wild shot."

"You're a — well, by God, Prof, I don't know. But thanks."

"Here," Collingsworth held out the pistol. "I tapped him with it."

With a downward glance at Brudd, Ewing said, "Yes, I do reckon so." Then he added, "It's old Rank McCabe's revolver."

Men were clustering around them now, their voices noisy, their eyes busy. Among them Ewing saw McDonald. "When Brudd comes to," he told him, "he might enjoy a ride."

"Aye, on a rail."

Eyes consulted eyes then, and heads nodded in assent.

"Not too rough. Just something to remember."

Ewing had had enough, enough of scrapes and anger and plain mouthiness. Enough of resurrection. He touched Collingsworth's elbow. "Let's get away from here."

Up the street a ways Collingsworth brought them to a halt. A little further up, Jay Ross came limping toward them.

Collingsworth reached into his pocket and took out an envelope. "Here," he said. "For you. I was on the way to mail it."

Ross joined them, favoring his ankle. "What's the ruckus?"

Ewing didn't answer. He asked Collingsworth, "What's in it?"

"My resignation."

It took an instant for the words to percolate. "Resignation, hell!"

Ross broke in. "You signed up for two years."

"That was before. Before Miss Carson."

"And she was your fault, huh? Good Lord! Nope on your resignation. We got the votes, and we vote no. Eh, Ross?"

"No."

"That's it then."

Ewing thought perhaps he saw a fracture in the tight, controlled face as he tore up the envelope.

Part Three

23

SHE HOPED IT would be a boy. Not that a girl baby would be unwelcome, heaven knew. Mary Jess had always been a delight, a gentle, thoughtful child, perhaps a shade too devoted to home and mother — an uneasy thought — but always a delight. Biddable, her grandmother would have said. Yet at her age girls gave thought to boys, had one beau and another and giggled on the high-school steps. And here was Mary Jess today, out walking in the fields alone, field glasses in her hand. Hers was a healthy interest, Benton said. He liked to study birds.

May rolled the dough out for a pie. Of all pies Benton most liked chocolate. Tonight she'd feed him cherry. Later she would dust and still later do the churning if Mary Jess did not return in time. This week she had slow-poked on her darning and her ironing.

For an instant she had to hold tight to the rolling pin and lean against the table. It was only vertigo, and it would pass. But, steadied, she thought of other times and prayed that this time she could hold the new life in her, boy or girl, to his or her full term. And afterward, perhaps, she might expect an end to pregnancies.

She heard the gravel-grind and sputter of an automobile out on the road and heard its squawk of horn, and she hurried to the window, fearful for Mary Jess, who could lose herself somewhere inside her quiet head. But it was only a traveler, trailing dust, who squawked for squawking's sake.

Just in a few years, she thought as she went back to the kitchen, automobiles, unless of strange make, had ceased being oddities, though they still scared country horses and sometimes caused runaways. Even she and Benton had one, a Ford bought second-hand, and Benton had gone roving in it, an hour or so ago, taking the dog along for company. It looked unimpressive beside Mort Ewing's Reo and Jay Ross's Hupmobile. But it ran. Count your blessings. A car. Electric lights. A telephone. No running water yet and so no indoor toilet, not here beyond the limits of the town, not on these premises they'd contrived to buy and moved to — how long ago? — in part because they'd have their own pasture for the cow and room for the dog to run. But count your blessings. A bigger house. More privacy. A view of the western mountains beyond the art of paint or camera. A barn and chickens. A spring down in the meadow. Wild ducks on its pool, and now and then a rabbit or a gopher inside the lines of fence. How a boy would love it all!

Every place had its disadvantages, she supposed, not thinking so much of the pump and outdoor privy as of their nearest neighbors. Not neighbors, really, anyhow not close, for they lived beyond the road, across the railway tracks, down in the shallow trench along the creek. A vulgar man and woman, by name Pike, to whose shaky house birds of a feather came. She had seen the woman on occasion and somehow felt sorry for her, a thin and dowdy figure with nothing in her eyes but bloodshot. Not neighbors but near enough that their night voices too often carried over, raised in silly jubilation or argument or drunken anger. Hearing them, Benton would scowl and think, "That bunch of boozers!" And once he had called the sheriff, who came by later to explain he wasn't justified by law in arresting all or even one.

When he had gone, Benton said, "Since the law is an ass, what can we expect of its minions?"

The telephone rang. She dusted off her hands and went to answer it. The caller was Jay Ross, asking if he could stop by. She said of course.

Back in the kitchen she fixed the pie crust in a pan, dumped in the filling, covered it, saw to the range and slipped the pie into the oven. She'd have time, by hurrying, to curl her hair a bit.

She lit the kerosene lamp in the bedroom, replaced the chimney and in it set the curling iron. Next thing she'd buy would be an electric curling iron. Next thing she'd buy would be a new rug for the living room. Next thing she'd buy would be a water system. Next thing she'd buy would be an open staircase with a gentle curve. Next thing she'd buy . . . Hair was such a nuisance.

She had just finished when she heard Jay at the porch.

He said, "Howdy, Mrs. Collingsworth," and came inside. With the years he had gained weight and lost more hair. Take away that slash of mouth and those probes of eyes, and he looked something like an onion. Almost always his eyes and manner remained assertive. There was reason, she had time to think as she showed him into the living room. By drawing on every possible source of credit, by mortgaging all his property and entire financial future, he had built miles of irrigation canal and sold water rights to homesteaders on the flatlands far from town. With water they could file on twice the acreage that drylanders could and be more hopeful of return. So Jay again had money and a crossroads, Rossville, named for him.

After she had motioned to a chair and sat down on the

davenport, she said, "You've heard from Mrs. Ross again?"

"From the missus," he answered, and passed her an envelope.

Only at these times to her knowledge did Jay seem at all abashed. Perhaps he couldn't read well, much less read Mrs. Ross's puzzling hand. Ever since Mrs. Ross's absence he had brought the letters to her.

She read the letter aloud, hesitating now and then to make certain of the words. The letter was short. Though frequent, they were always short. It said she was all right as were the girls. Jane seemed awfully happy in her marriage. Beth seemed quite interested in a man perhaps too old for her, though Beth herself, as Jay knew, was somewhat past the usual age for girls to marry. Nowhere in the letter was a word of sentiment, not even an unmeaning "Love" above her name.

"She writes regular," Ross said, perhaps to cover or deny the lack of warmth. "You know that."

"Every week or two, at least."

"Anyhow the family's fine." Ross sighed and took a cigar from his pocket. "You don't mind?" At the shake of her head he lighted up and drew a long puff in and blew it out. His eyes studied the smoke. "You know, I was cut out for this country. Frances wasn't. That's the size of it."

He spoke the truth, May reflected, seeing again the woman she had thought of as the woman of the wind. The wind and loneliness and the long, sequestered days. The lady in the ranch house keeping up appearances until half her wits had blown away. He spoke the truth but not the whole of it, if what she'd heard of Jay was truth. Even now he looked ungentled by the years, a lusty, seeking male who knew where to find his pleasures, but, say it in his favor, where not to look for them.

"Prof's all right?" he asked.

"Just fine. He went for a drive."

"How's the new school board and him?"

"All right. Not as close, of course, as in old days."

"Tight-fisted bunch," he said. She caught his gaze making a quick inventory of the worn furnishings. "But any board would have to keep him on. He's that admired. Keep him on, that is, as long as he will stay."

"That means, I guess, forever." She hadn't intended to sound dreary, much less querulous.

Ross seemed to pay no heed. "I bet he keeps missing old Mr. McLaine. Too bad he died. They liked to talk. Most of it over my head, though."

"Yes. Of course. Don't laugh. Not that it was over your head but too bad he died. But since they moved here, we're getting quite well acquainted with the Stuart Alexanders. He loves to read and discuss reading. They're fine folks."

"That's what I hear." Ross tipped cigar ashes in a saucer, just in time. He reached then for the letter, which she had put back in its envelope. He waggled it. "She could live in town," he said. "I would build a good house for her. But I can't change the weather. There's the catch."

Like confirmation a wind began to shrill in the cottonwoods outside. It sang at the corners of the house and made loose shingles slap. "I've adjusted to it," she told him.

He said, without inflection, "Is that so?"

His eyes, it occurred to her as it had before, saw everything, saw the superficial everything, movements, appearances, the little changes of expression. Benton had said he was a splendid hunter, alert to color, shape and slightest action. And sometimes, appropriately or disconcertingly, he saw deeper.

It would happen then, with his gaze fixed on her, that her head began to whirl again. She put a hand to it and tried to smile. "Just a little dizziness."

He came forward in his chair. "Water? Wet cloth? Anything?"

"No. No. It's almost gone."

He looked down and spoke as if to the envelope he held. "Maybe Montana is too tough for shes, for some shes. For all of them but squaws."

She answered, "Pshaw, Jay, I can stand it."

He didn't reply. His silence seemed a question. When he did speak, it was to say, "Frances had help around the house, all the help she needed."

"When I need help I have it." The words snapped out of her and brought his eyes back up. "I don't need much. I'm healthy as a horse."

He said, "Sure. Sure." He put the envelope away and lifted from his chair. "Thanks for reading to me."

He followed her to the door. There he paused and with his bold eyes searched her face; and she knew again that often he had sight through surfaces, an unexpected knowingness from outward observation. And here, through images, a conclusion that invaded privacy. But he couldn't know she was pregnant. It was far too soon.

He said, "Take good care of yourself."

She watched him to his automobile, saw the wind flatten and balloon the garments on his sturdy figure and heard the keener shrill and whine of it and closed the door against its voice.

Then she went to the bedroom and the mirror. The pie could wait.

24

When seen from only one direction did Breast Butte support its name. Viewed from the west, it identified itself as a broken headland of large sandstone toadstools, weathered spires and dwarf plateaus that staggered to the peak. It had been thrust up, deposited and left by glaciers of the ice age, or perhaps it had stood stout, if breached, against the grinding flow while surrounding country wore away. Collingsworth told himself he should learn more about geology.

From his seat on one of the high flats, on this clear and sunlit day, he could see north to the Sweet Grass hills, which floated like dreamed shapes ninety miles away. He could see west to the broken blue of the mountains and east to flatlands that seemed at last to saucer up to sky. Down in the valley Arfive lay untroubled.

It was all his, he thought while he reached for his pipe. It was all his, and none of it was save for the little acreage he and May had bought and in time would relinquish necessarily. As it had been other men's before him, so it was his — the shimmered distance, the hills afloat across the miles, the Rockies and the crowning height that did not look like the ear of any elephant.

It was a worn but right reflection that man alone in the midst of immensities felt close to God. Here was the work of

God. Call Him the First Cause or Force or incomprehensible Power and Purpose or think of Him, as so many did, as the whiskered and watchful Creator. No matter. There was God. Even as the whispering silence whispered His presence and mystery. And here was the earth, expressly made for man.

Collingsworth pulled on his pipe and looked down and afar to the far-scattered patches of land torn by the plow, to the farm sites staked out by the hopeful. The homesteaders had been slower coming to this general area than to regions more promising, promoted earlier and closer to transport. But they had come, if not in droves excited by speculators, then in modest but noticeable numbers alike in faith. They had sifted in as richer-seeming soil was preempted, as the highway from Great Falls was improved by degrees, as a railway spur tapped and opened Arfive. They had come in the face of occasional and mostly unfortunate experience by forerunners. Land was their loadstone and home, land to till and to tame, to force to give yield.

Below him Collingsworth could see, in the yellowed-grass hide of the valley, the scratch scar of the spur. Here and there he saw a few buildings, the make-do and alien shelters and outhouses of homesteaders and the turned-over fields lying stark. And he had now to think of them as impertinences, as violations of the first and true purpose, no matter the Christian ethic that the earth was created for man. Man would put it to his use, never fear. Let fellow creatures go hang. The land was there to tear up, as elsewhere were forests to fell and minerals to gouge out and streams to force out of true for wheels, pastures and crops. Leave it to man. Leave to man what was his. To the devil, then, with men like that heretical former president, Theodore Roosevelt, and his colleague Gifford Pinchot, who had acted to conserve the forests of the public domain.

Collingsworth knocked out his pipe and shifted position, feeling undirected and at odds with himself. Nothing made a man more nearly a eunuch than to be undecided, to allow himself to be pulled in opposing directions. Much could be said for breadth of mind, but, indulged in too much, it ended in impotence. In human numbers and enterprises this western country was growing and should be. Growth was health. Growth was foredained, from seed to flower, from fetus to child to adult. And so it was with communities, from opportunity to exploitation, from cabin to village to city, from virgin soil to soil productive. And the result of this natural growth depended on man. Hope for him, beyond the shaky assurance of a hereafter, lay in himself. That was where education came in.

Behind and below him, out of sight, the two schoolboys he'd brought along raised their voices occasionally, voices young and strong yet here remindful of echoes. The two were bright youngsters, hound-keen on the trail of this country's history. Arrowheads and like artifacts, paths first worn by game or perhaps hunting parties, the curiosities of nature, earthen or animal — these were the interests he himself had awakened in them. By and by they would come to him and tell and show what they'd found and ask question on question. By and by. Now they were occupied and safe enough. Rattlesnakes were denned up by October.

Though he couldn't hear them, the dog and Smoky Moreau would be near the boys. He had come to enjoy Smoky's occasional company. That old, gentle Indian, or breed, was a sort of entry into the past. Through experience, through recitals by elders at lodge fires during his boyhood, he had gathered a great store of knowledge. He knew the perished ways of his race, the plants used for food and restoratives, the sites of camps and skirmishes and medicine-makings. He knew the tribal myths and seemed somewhat to believe in them still. It took patience and sympathy to draw on this store. Pressed or doubted, Smoky kept quiet.

Theirs had been a gradual but growing relationship, Collingsworth reflected. There had been that first meeting, high on the ridge of the river, where old Charlie Blackman, now dead, had made them acquainted. Then had come chance encounters, longer conversations and an expedition or two made together. A funeral had brought them still closer, one he didn't like much to remember.

One spring morning — five or seven years ago, time went so fast — Smoky had appeared at the back door. It was the month when reservation Indians with their rattletraps, teepees, curs, cayuses and tramp followers went to Shaw Academy to pick up their children and, to and fro, broke the journey on the campsite at Arfive. Their number had grown fewer with the years, but still they came and went and came. Now they were here.

Smoky had taken off his hat and turned the brim in his hands. He always came to the back door, for no reason. There seemed even less reason for an air almost of apology, of embarrassed, still-unspoken appeal.

Collingsworth had invited him in, but he stood there with his hat and apology, and his eyes put a question that he followed with words. Would the professor please speak at a funeral? For a breed baby? Would he conduct it?

"Why, Smoky," he answered, "surely you know I'm not the man for it. They'll want a priest."

Smoky shook his head slowly. "Anyhow, no priest around."

"The Methodist minister then. I'll be glad to make arrangements."

Smoky's head again said no. "They ask for you."

"Who asked? I don't understand. Did you suggest me?"

"They sent me to ask."

"But who are they, Smoky? What's their name?"

Smoky looked toward the ground and appeared to try to remember. "On the reservation they go by Beaver, I think. Not full bloods."

"I can't say yes, Smoky, without knowing more. All I know is that a baby is dead and that you've come to me. What are the circumstances? Tell me."

It had come out then, or a part of it had, though in pieces, in meek if reluctant answers to questions. Last night there had been a breed dance. No, not for old full bloods. They mostly held to old customs. The place was the small, empty freight house just south of town, the one breeds usually used. Mrs. Beaver had laid her baby on a bench. She had danced. By accident someone sat on the baby. Later the baby was found to be dead. Who knew how much later?

"Drunk!" Collingsworth didn't try to hold back his outrage. "Everybody drunk!"

"Too many." Smoky looked unhappy. He was known to the town as one sober Indian.

The word was in Collingsworth's mouth. Give Smoky no and have done with it. But before the answer came out Smoky went on. "My people are no good with whiskey."

"Nobody is."

"Worse for Injuns. No good with whiskey. No good with other presents from white men."

By heavens he was right. No good with whiskey. No good with introduced pestilences. No good, much, with an imposed religion. Mistreated and cheated, Injuns no good with the agents and suppliers of reservations, themselves the presents of the superior race. And whoever's sin, the sin of its death was not the sin of the baby. Yet Collingsworth wanted the answer to one other question.

"Just who sat on this baby?"

"It was an accident."

"But someone was guilty."

Smoky barely lifted one shoulder. "What good to know him?"

Here, Collingsworth thought, was a jelly in attitude, a soft and silly forgiveness. The culprit should be nailed and held to account, drunk or sober, remorseful, forgetful or callous, breed or full blood or what. To forgive was to beget. Accident on accident, by people's weak leave. And yet — eunuch asking — and yet?

"All right, Smoky, I'll do it," he said.

The funeral had taken place that very day in the very same freight house where the child met its death. Entering, Collingsworth felt a shrink in his nostrils and halted to ask himself if he had become so nice, so persnickety, as to imagine an atmosphere. The place smelled, or seemed to smell, of stale spirits, grease, bodies and smoke from dead campfires.

Someone, probably Smoky, had scrounged a few folding chairs that went mostly unoccupied. The fifteen or so mourners, if they were that, stood toward the back or along the side walls. Among them he saw as he made his way forward two blanketed, hair-braided full bloods. The rest wore castoffs and makeshifts and shoddy if showy gear that might have been agency issued. The old buckskin garments had almost disappeared. A few bits of fine beadwork, in which the squaws had excelled, served as reminders of what once had been.

He paused at the coffin. It was a box, no more than that, which rested on two planks supported by carpenters' trestles. A striped blanket covered all but the head of the baby. The face looked shriveled and woebegone, forever fretful for the bosom of mother.

Beyond it Collingsworth turned and for a silent moment surveyed the small crowd. There was no style to the women, he thought, hardly a suggestion of shape, unless it was the shapeless, squat shape of decline. In the eyes was a wonderless waiting. Only one woman appeared untouched by the general fate, and she was a youngster. Another, the mother probably, stood bowed and kept a cloth over most of her face.

Under the circumstances, it had seemed to Collingsworth before he arrived, there was a right and immediate theme for his few minutes' talk. It was the assurance of Jesus, made in reproof of the disciples who had sought to shield him from children. "Suffer the little children to come unto me, and forbid them not: for of such is the kingdom of God." He enlarged briefly on the words and read three Psalms. Then, since it seemed especially fitting to circumstance, he asked the congregation to join in the Lord's Prayer. Some of them knew it, or parts of it, though theirs was the Catholic version.

The burial was not his affair, and he walked slow to the door, past Smoky who gave thanks with his eyes and past the silent men and women until, toward the rear, there came a pluck at his sleeve. Turning, he saw the woman who had kept a cloth to her face. In a voice he strained to hear she said, "It was good of you, Professor." She let the cloth down and stood as if both stoic and meek. Oh no! he thought before full recognition came to him. Oh, good Lord, no! Not this dumpy creature with the swollen face and eyes reddened by drink and by grief. Not this subject of ravage. Not Marie. Not Marie Wolf, so soon changed from student to squaw, so brutally changed.

He nodded and started to go on but paused and let himself say, "I'm sorry, Marie."

There were conclusions to draw and a question, unanswered, to ask. She had feared, and no doubt informed Smoky, that he wouldn't appear if he knew her identity. Rather than preacher or priest, she had wanted him at the services. But why? There was the question. Why?

He was still fiddling around for an answer when Smoky came from the back of the butte and sat down and lighted his own pipe while his eyes traveled.

"Boys all right?" Collingsworth asked.

"Sure." Smoky blew out a mouthful of smoke and, reaching in the loose pocket of his old jacket, went on. "They be surprised." He brought forth a horned toad, so torpid as to be almost beyond movement.

Collingsworth examined the frilled and spiked monster, the harmless miniature that, magnified by a million or so, might be the reptilian horror of ages ago.

"Asleep," Smoky said, gently fingering it. "In the sand. Under a rock." After a silence he asked, "They were here before anybody? Before our fathers, maybe?"

"At least something resembling it was."

"Injuns come later and die off, buffalo go, but toad stays."

There was brooding in the dark eyes. He turned them then to the valley and plains, and his arm made a sweep. "Man, he is not so much as he thinks. Not by-damn homesteaders for sure. They say 'mine' for land not their own. They turn over the good grass. They plant seed this earth does not know. But no medicine big enough. Snow, cold, no rain. They will freeze up and dry up and go, those homesteaders."

It was seldom Smoky spoke at such length. Collingsworth answered, "They have been told that rain follows the plow."

Smoky spat. "Weeds follow. Dust. They make desert."

"We'll have to see."

Smoky gave his attention again to the toad, which, warmed by his hand, was moving more though not much. "We all die," he said. "I die. You die. Toad stays."

"I suppose so, if not that very one."

Smoky fell silent as if he might not have heard. Watching him, seeing him stroke it, Collingsworth thought it was as if the toad, or the sure generations of toads, secured his place in

242

the flow of time or, rather, that it gave him some assurance that something endured. Old friends fell away, old times faded back, known places grew strange, dear ones died. *Tempora mutantur, et nos mutamur in illis.* Was the toad, to Moreau, so different from Elephant Ear Butte to himself?

Tempora mutantur, and May had been young and blithe and not pregnant then and the home-talent play at the school just about as wretched as could be. Except for her, who liked drama and had had some college roles. Except for her, who was the light in the twilight, the grace in the graceless, with spirit and youth in her and such loveliness as to humble the heart.

Mutamur, and the years that the locust hath eaten, and she could not play that part again. But despite time, despite or because of her growing independence of attitude, he loved her the more. Without her?

The sun was lowering. In its long beams the tans and blues, the browns and blacks and purples of the land came out, clear, merged, divided and all complementary, all part and parcel of eternal distance; and it was as if a man could take the sum within his dwarfed and bursting self and with his loves fly forever free.

An October breeze began to blow, chill with portent. Collingsworth said, "Smoky, it's about time to pick up the boys and go down to the car. Think so?"

Moreau nodded and got up. He studied the horned toad in his hand and slowly shook his head. Then he turned over a slab of stone, pawed a hole in the sand, put the toad in and covered it and brought the slab back over.

All he said was, "Better so."

25

IT WAS A good gathering, small, congenial and brightened by the kind of talk that Benton enjoyed. The Stuart Alexanders, May reflected, were always pleasant to be with. And here were Mort Ewing and his Julie and Doctor Crabtree, who for once could spare time from his practice.

She felt good herself, awkward and unwieldy of course, but good. Gone were the mornings of nausea, the days of uncertainty, the fears of another miscarriage. The life inside of her lived. It kicked and moved about like restlessness seeking greater comfort in bed. Vigorous restlessness. She changed position to accommodate it.

The conversation had moved from topic to topic. Weather had been one of them, naturally, but it had elicited more than common comments like "Nice day" and "Cold out" because it was colder than cold. Over the almost snowless, bleak valley the arctic had settled. Things snapped in the still grip of it, inanimate things with the voices of protest. It had been a chore to get the car started — rear wheel jacked up, blowtorch on the manifold, and crank and crank and crank.

"Don't look for a break," Mort had just said. "Sun dogs by day, moon rings by night — that means bad medicine and still more to come."

But here was warmth, here in this great, new country house before a fire in one of the two home fireplaces May had seen in Montana. Here were warmth and full stomachs and her cozy assurance of things to come.

Mr. Alexander rose from his chair and put another log in the fireplace. A blaze began to flare up. The logs popped comfortably.

The conversation flowed around her. For the most part women kept quiet when menfolk engaged in men's talk. It gave them an advantage unrecognized: they could think and observe and remember outside the subjects. Yet all was not gain. Somewhat uncomfortably she had come to feel, as she felt now, that women's silence and deference were wrong and demeaning. What was men's talk, indeed, that partners of equal interest shouldn't share in it? She dismissed the question.

Let the men agree on the tariff. They were all Republicans, though earlier Mort had joined the Bull Moosers in support of Theodore Roosevelt and Benton had rather a liking for President Wilson, in part because of his rhetoric. His shame was that once he had voted for William Jennings Bryan.

May let her eyes and thoughts drift. Mrs. Alexander was doing fancywork. Her bosom was almost big and bold enough for a bench. Julie sat on a sofa by Mort. The years — they weren't so many in fact — might have been just months in her life. They had brought her only from the promise of spring to the effulgence of summer, the lovely, almost hurting effulgence. And Mort would never change, unless it was to grow backward. If anything, he looked younger now than when she first met him. An unlikely match, and good for them both. And the house? What a house, and such a kitchen, with fixed cabinets and counters and drawers and a sink and ready hot water!

Mary Jess, seated under a lamp beyond the group, had

found a book. They weren't hard to find here. She wouldn't have had much to say anyway. She never did, not in company. Well-mannered, politely responsive, restrained — that was Mary Jess. Perhaps there had been too many and too strict admonitions, earlier in her little life, about being seen and not heard. May found herself looking at Benton.

Benton ran a hand over his hair. There was a good deal of gray in it now, but his face, though fretted a little or fretted more than time's slow work let her realize, hadn't sagged into that weary acceptance evident in so many men of his age. It still showed decision and strength. Which made strange his increasing withdrawal from former pursuits and enjoyments, from public concerns like good roads and chautauqua and from personal interests like going afield with shotgun or rod. More and more home was his haven. School and church, yes, but home first of all. It was there he brought or found reason for and shortly cooled his instant vexations. More than the men here, who were among the few he enjoyed, he enjoyed the distant company of writers like William James or Robert Frost, that new poet. Except for them and what close communion she could provide, he was lonely, lonely by his own cranky choice.

They went on, the men did, while the women listened or didn't or spoke in asides. Inside the baby squirmed. Her baby. His baby. Their baby. She shifted to give ease to it and herself. No one noticed. They had gone from the tariff to the big war in Europe.

"Until recently," Benton was saying, "I thought war impossible ever again. It was beyond civilized comprehension. And it's here I'll concede Woodrow Wilson his due. He has kept us apart from that European insanity." He put his hand to his head again. "It's unfortunate but incidental to the issue that what's good for us is a help to the Kaiser."

Mrs. Alexander put down her fancywork. "If it were left to the women there'd be no war ever."

Doctor Crabtree held up his big physician's hand. "Now. Now." His tone was rough, as always, and his face as deep-lined as old age.

"And also," Mrs. Alexander went on, "if you give us the vote, there'll be no more alcohol, no saloons." It must have been with an effort that she had kept quiet so far. She was known as an outspoken woman, one with convictions. So many bold-fronted women were bold.

Benton broke in, "Prohibition is sure to come anyway."

"Sure as bad booze," Mort said, his tone light.

Mrs. Alexander was still looking at Doctor Crabtree. "Do you mean you're against women's suffrage?" The words came out more as accusation than question.

"Now did I say that?" Doctor Crabtree softened his voice. It was as if, when discussion with a woman neared dispute, moderation was seemly. A half smile deepened the lines in his face. "Shall we forget Prohibition, which is somewhat beside the point. Suffrage? Of course. Let women vote. I don't mean to deprecate them. It's only that I won't entertain myth. Let them vote, but don't expect magical changes. Faced with choices, women will act as men do in politics, social issues, international affairs, business, professions, whatever. They aren't angels. Women know that. Men won't admit it, for to admit it would be to destroy their creations."

"Go on," Mrs. Alexander said. "Their creations?"

"All right." Doctor Crabtree ceased to smile. His voice seemed edged. "Their creations, of course. Home and motherhood and hair the crowning glory. Nobility, purity, a higher, heavenly order of being; but don't forget long-suffering, and so, woman, wipe the brats' noses, scrub floors, keep house, cook meals and say amen to the lords and masters."

So faintly that May barely heard him, Ewing said, "Say amen to the master."

"Amen," Julie answered. Her hand made a little slap as it met his palm.

"You're asking for a change in biology," Benton said to Doctor Crabtree.

"I'm not asking for anything." Doctor Crabtree clipped off the words. "I'm just contending that women will react to choice like men. If to say that is to diminish them, it is at the same time to give them equality."

Mort seemed about to speak but deferred to Mr. Alexander. "The emphasis now is on the vote, as if that were the all," Mr. Alexander said. "It wasn't always so. During the Civil War years and before, women worked for the emancipation of Negroes, equating their lot with that of slaves."

Now Mort did speak. "And nothin' came of that but disappointment because the freed bucks, when it came down to their women, acted just like white men."

"To be expected," Doctor Crabtree put in. "Biology, as Mr. Collingsworth would have it."

"Not as I would have it." Benton's voice was sharp. "Not as I would have it, but as it is."

"So," Doctor Crabtree answered without emphasis.

Mrs. Alexander was quick to speak. "We can agree, I think, on one thing. What women want is simple acknowledgment of their full capacities."

"True, so far as it goes," Doctor Crabtree answered. "Please forgive me, Mrs. Alexander, but nutshell statements leave good parts of the kernel out." He paused as if brooding and went on with a sort of slow severity. "We can't escape biology, as Mr. Collingsworth contends. It has placed a burden on the women. But men have done more than accept that inequality of nature. They've endorsed and added to it, if not gladly then witlessly. Women are subordinates. The curse on Eve, yeah, and fiddle-de-dee. It need not and should not exist — the felt superiority of men and, along with it, the added and onerous expectations, the burdens that men pile on top of a burden already and inescapably there. Ah-h." He blew out a breath. "All of which has nothing much to do with women's suffrage."

"Not much." Benton, smiling now, broke the little silence. "But what you said about suffrage is right. Don't expect miracles if women vote. Most women would vote as their husbands do. Let them go to the polls. We'll double the electorate without changing the outcomes."

"You might be surprised." The words burst out of her, urgent but unpremeditated. Uttered, they seemed to keep sounding, their mere prickle grown to a pronouncement demanding reinforcement. "You're being smug, Benton."

He turned to her, his smile shortened. "Why, May, don't we always agree?"

"You mean, don't I always agree with you?"

The question went unanswered. She had made, she knew, all the company uncomfortable. Mary Jess had lifted her gaze from the book. Benton looked not so angry as bewildered, and for him she felt an instant sympathy she wouldn't speak.

As if to put an end to the disquiet, the telephone rang. Mr. Alexander excused himself and went into the hall to answer it. Returning, he said, "For you, Doctor Crabtree."

The doctor came back to announce, "Deliverance can wait: deliveries can't." He hustled into his overshoes and heavy coat, put on his ear-flapped cap and bulky gloves. He said thanks to his hosts and good-bye to the others. The door thudded shut after him.

It was the hour, not his going, that broke up the evening. Mr. Alexander helped the ladies on with their wraps. Everybody said what good food and what a fine evening. Benton adjusted earmuffs that fitted under his hat. He didn't like caps on himself.

They filed out the door against clouds of vapor. The Ewings and the Collingsworths bade one another good night, their words fogged in a cold that nipped at the lungs. Benton removed two blankets that he'd spread over the hood of the Ford to keep in the heat. There wasn't, May supposed, much chance of its having frozen up, not with kerosene in the radiator in place of water. She took the blankets and insisted that Mary Jess, in the back seat, snug them around her legs and feet. For herself it was as well to remain outside. The car, even with all curtains buttoned or all buttoned that could be, was as cold as the world.

Benton, reaching inside, adjusted what he called gadgets and returned to the front to crank up. She watched the hard wrench of his shoulders and the puff and increased puff of his breath. He straightened a minute to ease his lungs, looking set and grim even in night light. Then he bent again to the crank.

Someone — Mort — was approaching. He asked, "Trouble, Prof?"

"These infernal machines!"

"Let me look." Mort went to the car door, opened it and leaned in to examine the gadgets. Then he said, "Hop in, you two. I'll give her a whirl. Trouble was, Prof, the switch wasn't switched on to magneto."

Benton stood, unmoving and silent. Mort made two fast turns with the crank. The engine started, uneven at first, then even as ever. Mort raised one hand in a salute that was also good-bye. May moved past Benton to call, "Thank you, Mort." Benton was tardy in seconding her.

Benton drove silently, hands hard and abrupt on the wheel. The Ford might have been a horse, an ornery one to be made

250

obedient only by a tight rein. Machinery always thwarted and balked him and raised his gorge. And on top of all that, to be helped from his helplessness, and on top of that, to be caught in a stupid oversight.

Not until they neared home did he speak. It was to say then, "Smug, huh, and I might be surprised?"

"I won't say I'm sorry, even if I a little bit am. All right, I am a woman, your wife, but first of all I am myself. Don't you know that's what the conversation concerned?"

The car shuddered to the home stop, and the three of them got out. Before they entered the house, he turned his face to her, said, "Spitfire," and grinned.

26

It was autumn that day and night in Indianapolis, sad, soft, rich September, Benton had thought as the Monon–Vandalia clanked on from Bloomington through fields fruited and reaped. A haze touched them, he saw through the train window, a drowsy haze that seemed to say not yet but sleep soon.

Not yet. Not yet had he seen the big city. Much of what he knew of it, and it wasn't much, he knew from his Uncle Alf, who took cattle to market there and returned with pockets of money and tales of things done and seen. So he would see for himself and do for himself and come back to college less coun-trified. He could say, sure, he had been there.

And now he was with Joe Bair, of his university class and his home neighborhood if not of his unreserved liking; and dark had fallen, and a degenerate saloon rose beside them. From inside issued a sweet-sour emanation.

Joe said, "Now, and at last, let's have a drink."

"Not for me. Thanks."

"God sake, Bent! Always no. You and that family of yours. Rather spit shit than say it. You're too old to suck and old enough, then, to act like a man."

"I don't like it, that's all."

"How do you know? You never tried."

He wouldn't reveal that his knowledge of whiskey was limited to the teaspoonful that his parents had added to castor oil for administration when he felt puny. It was supposed to make the oil less offensive. It made both of them loathsome. He looked at his feet.

"We didn't come just to gawk," Joe went on. "Hell, build them up to the sky, and buildings are buildings, and people are people no matter how many. You're just spoiling the fun."

"I don't mean to."

"You're supposed to have brains, but here you are finding fault without proof. Q.E.D. but no demonstration ahead of it." Joe pulled at his arm and let go. "Come on or we split up right here."

They went in.

The place was dingy and odorous, as uninviting as the hell that it led to. Two older customers stood toward the end of the bar. They wore rough dress, like men of the country or railroads or shops. One was oversize, with shoulders and arm muscles that bulged his shirt. A woman, by the looks of her a young woman, sat alone at a table. She eyed them as they came in.

Joe pushed him up to the bar. The bartender came opposite. He had a red mustache. "Two whiskies," Joe said as if practiced.

"Beer or water to go along with it?"

"Beer."

From down the bar the big man said, "College dandies, or my name is bull nuts." He had a smile on his face. The other man studied them through reddened eyes. The woman looked at them, too. She didn't seem bothered.

They were out of place in this workingman's bar, out of place with their suits, white shirts, stiff collars and ties, trapped in a hole they shouldn't have entered.

Joe elbowed him in the ribs. "Drink up!" he said from the side of his mouth. "Damn it, drink up!"

The whiskey scalded his throat. It tasted of old castor oil. He kept it down with a swallow of beer.

Joe had faced down the bar. "What else but bull nuts?" he said to the big man.

The big man smiled out an "Ah-h."

It didn't do any good to tell Joe to shut up; he went on, "Now that that's settled, maybe we can have a quiet drink. Maybe not. Your choice."

"That sounds like man's talk," the big man answered, still smiling. "I say not. But I'm thinkin' to warm up on your friend afore he runs out on you."

Under his red mustache the bartender said, "Not here, boys. Not here."

Joe spoke to the big man, "I wouldn't advise it."

"No real ruckus, Red," the big man said to the bartender. "Small doin's to clean out the young fry."

The half swallow of whiskey in the small glass blazed down his throat. Beer cooled it.

The big man was saying, "How about it there, you that hasn't give tongue? Game or turntail?" He had pushed back from the bar and was coming ahead, walking easily while his mouth grinned.

"Not here. Not here," the bartender kept pleading.

Joe asked, "How about me?"

"Later. That's a promise. Yours truly."

The man's large hand wrenched him around. "Put 'em up or skedaddle." Past the heavy shoulder he could see that the woman had drawn her chair back to the wall. Then through the red he saw nothing, nothing but the mouth that had grinned and the jaw and the belly. He knew he was down and up and down and up and down again, and then there were hands on him, tearing him loose, and a voice saying, "Good

God! You'll kill him!" And he stood up, held tight, and saw the big man on the floor, his face lax and bleeding.

"Calm down now, man," someone said. He looked to his right and his left and saw that his holders were strangers.

"He started it," he said, fearing the law, and the men answered, "Sure. Sure. We know. Long time he's had it coming." They dropped their hands.

"Some dandy, my partner is," Joe said to all. He had a grip on the red-eyed man.

Shrinking, the red-eyed man said, "I'm not huntin' trouble. He's my cousin. Leave me take him away. Thing is, with a few in him, he likes to fight. He don't get mad. He just thinks fightin' is fun." The red eyes turned accusing. "But Jesuss, not murder."

The bartender came over with a pitcher of water and doused the face of the big man. He and the cousin got the man to his feet and helped him to the door. His legs were beginning to work. At the door the cousin said, "I can cut 'er now," and struggled away.

"Good riddance, no damage, and drinks on the house," the bartender announced.

There were half a dozen customers in the place now. They talked in low tones while they looked, and a couple of them came over to shake hands and speak congratulations and thanks. The woman had moved back to the table.

"I'll take the drink to the lady," Joe said, picking it up from the bar. "Come along, Bent."

The woman was a girl, really, no older than he was, maybe younger. She had paint on her cheeks and paint on her mouth. She said, "Make yourself comfortable."

"Nice to see you here," Joe told her, his tone lightly questioning. "Some places, I hear, the police don't abide girls in saloons."

"Sit down. They owe me a few favors."

"Meet the gladiator," Joe said. "He feeds Christians to lions." He put the drink in front of her.

"I never looked for to see it," the girl answered. "That's Big Dud you whopped."

Joe replied for him. "Down in Tunnelton, which you never heard of, we eat Caesar's meat. Here's to Shakespeare."

The girl didn't look at Joe. She looked at him and said, "Shakespeare, then," and lifted her glass and drank. Her knee moved up and down against his. "Got the teetotals, fightin' man?"

He moved his leg and looked at the glass and then at the door and said, "I've had some already."

"He likes to keep in trim," Joe told the girl. "In trim for the last trumpet." Joe's smile wasn't nice.

The whiskey swallowed smoother this time.

They might have been an island, he thought, a tabled island that heard the jumbled echoes from the bar and received an occasional glance. Slowly inside of him he began to feel a warm loosening.

"Any time now," the girl said, "I look for a friend to show up."

Joe asked, "Gender?"

"Gender?"

"Male or female? He or she?"

"Another girl."

"Good," Joe said. "Even number, divided right." He got up and put out his hand. "Your turn to buy, Bent."

While Joe was gone, the girl moved closer. "I'm real nice," she said. Her knee stroked his again. He let it stroke.

After that drink the second girl entered and swayed to the table. She seemed breasted like a bobwhite. Joe put on his manners for her. There was another drink, no more biting than water.

The whole of him began aching. What didn't ache throbbed. He adjusted his trousers, feeling confessional and exposed under the gaze of the girl. But what sense in the denial of nature? What wisdom in taught abnegation? Under the swimming paint, the swimming girl, surely willing. He pressed his knee against hers. Another drink had appeared.

He was climbing a stairway. He was handing out money. He was taking off his clothes in a room with a bed. He was watching Eve standing naked, serene in her possession of parts.

The room billowed and turned, the whole earth revolved, but there was a center, a sure center with fond places along the way to it; and he thrust himself at it, hearing beneath him, "God alive! Easy! You'd think it was your first time." But now he was home in it, thrust-and-thrust home; and he burst in close and far dazzles sooner than wished. Then he slept.

He roused to the incessant cheep of some bird outside. He sat up in bed and looked down at the woman's uncovered body. All that seemed clean of it was one nipple and the blood-darkened circle around it. The fool bird was still chirping.

His clothes were tangled and obstinate. He put them on quietly and quietly made for the door. The woman opened one eye. "Going so soon, honey?" she asked, wetting her lips with her tongue. "Not once more?"

He opened the door and walked out into the clean sunlight.

❦

He awakened with the realization that he was wet. He wiped his abdomen with the tail of his nightshirt and made a damp ball of the cloth and let it lie. He cleared his nose of the whiff of musk that seeped from under the covers.

May slept by his side, now and then softly complaining, he

supposed as the child moved inside her. He brought the blankets closer around her throat and lay motionless, reluctant to get up in the cold.

From restlessness and unwelcome remembrance, he thought, and then on into the dream that in detail repeated the fact. What it didn't repeat was the aftermath. Brother Charlie had been spared death by syphilis. He hadn't. It had claimed him shamefully, remorselessly, a thousand times, it and gonorrhea, before he could dare to think that, by the grace of God, he was clean. Praise God, clean — and by all that was holy never another transgression. No more dirty flirting with the wages of sin. And no more whiskey brawls and no whiskey, ever.

At his age to suffer erotic dreams, to be plagued still by nocturnal emissions! But soon now May would give birth, soon they wouldn't have to give thought to the baby unborn. He moved enough to see her head on the pillow. What devil, inciting dreams, made a man dream of undesired and abhorrent partners in sex?

He would get up now and cleanse himself with warm water from the coal range's reservoir, and then he would dress and fire the stoves and put on coffee for May. He squirmed out of bed into the clean bite of the cold.

27

THOSE DAYS, to see outside the house, May had had to open a
door, for a half inch of ice coated the windows that earlier had
been patterned with bright Jack Frost tracery. Through the
swung door the cold would billow inside, white clouds of it
that damped the fires and drove through her clothes and
reached for the center flutter of life. On field and rooftop and
road the snow lay deep, deformed where the wind had at-
tacked it and frozen dead everywhere. The mountains to
westward rose white, fixed under the still oppression of sky.
When the sun shone, it shone without heart, part and parcel
of winter's conspiracy. She had to keep stoking the stoves.
Montana.

Benton had given up on the Ford, though once he had tried
to arouse it with hot water and blowtorch and the jacking up
of a wheel and returned to the house winded and out of sorts.
And once, though it was doubtful that, started, it would get
him to town, he had had a truck tow it as far as the gate,
thinking the turn of the wheels would bring the engine to life.
The wheels wouldn't turn. They slid like sled runners.

Twice a day the outside pump had to be thawed, for the
needs of the household and chickens and cow. The cow
stayed in the barn, feeding on the hay that Benton pitched
down from the loft. Now and then she poked her head

through the half door and gazed dolefully out. Benton feared her udder would freeze. The combs of the chickens did freeze and later turned black. The whole flock would have perished, it was likely, but for an old, coal-oil heater she had thought about tardily and Benton had put in the henhouse. If a hen laid an egg, it cracked in mere minutes. Benton had said, if a man wanted one, he had to catch it fresh-laid and run for the house.

In large part he kept cheerful. "The days are growing longer," he would say. "Who says the winter solstice is the beginning of winter? It's getting over the hump. We're on the way to the vernal equinox."

But the still cold continued. It squeezed life into solitary confinement in the prison of indoors and wraps. When the wind blew, as it could, it blew below zero. "In town it's forty-eight on the minus side," Benton reported one day, after coming home with the tip of his nose frosted white.

Yet in hardship he seemed to find some satisfaction. He would return from school cold, his face pinched, his breath blowing, and remark on the cold as if it were an honorable but conquerable enemy. With grim but good nature he would thaw out the pump, carry water to the chickens and cow, feed them, milk the cow, fill the woodbox and coal scuttles, take out the ashes, dump the waste-water bucket, go with the slop jars out to the privy and, all tasks attended to, take off his wraps with an air of success. It was as if it were good to have something solid and defined to oppose.

After morning chores and breakfast he would pull on his overshoes, don his heavy coat, clap on his ear protectors and hat, fit a scarf around his neck and arrange it to cover nostrils and mouth, push his hands into gloves inside mittens and go forth, ready for the mile-long battle to school. Only once had he been really ill-natured, and then out of concern. Mary Jess, thinking to pump a quick bucket of water, had put a moist hand on the pump handle, where the skin froze. Warm water released it without any great hurt.

Mary Jess accompanied Benton to school, bundled as he was, her slim, her exquisite, body lumpy with wraps. Oftener than not she came back before he did. They had good and dear moments then, moments of open, self-to-self talk while Mary Jess toasted her stocking feet in the oven.

She moved about the house heavily or sat idly, waiting the weather out, waiting her time, waiting the hurt she knew she could stand and the first, the dear, helpless squall of life expelled. Two weeks, more or less, Doctor Crabtree had estimated. These days she didn't read much, for the printed words wandered and didn't relate one to another in patterns of meaning. And she didn't do enough. Pshaw, she would tell herself, she was letting pregnancy amount to paralysis, against nature and reason and right. Squaws on the trail were known to retreat to a thicket and catch up with the column bearing the newborn. She would get up and do some little something and then sit.

How blessed to have a husband like Benton, she would think day by day. He was ever solicitous. He kept cautioning her against lifting or overdoing in whatever manner. He told her to get plenty of rest. As best he could he helped Mary Jess keep the house. In other days she would have laughed at his awkwardness and shooed him out of the kitchen. But a draggy woman, clumsy and puffy with weight, welcomed even inexperienced aid. Above all, she welcomed loving concern, a concern that watched for the least signs of discomfort and labor.

For all his cheer, true or pretended, Benton slept restlessly. He kept twitching and turning in bed, and his hands went from face to shoulder to head. Lay his fitfulness to his concern. Lay it to her female presence and the kicks and shifts of her baby. In decency a pregnant woman was not available nor, far pregnant, was she easy to sleep with. There was no easing him even. There he tossed, beyond help, removed from the manual relief she could have given and would have but for his scruples. Come down to it, women took nature for what it was; by word, if not steady deed, men tried to make it unworldly.

Then, it came to mind as she sat resting, had come a break in the weather, a chinook blowing from over the high, inverted icicles of mountains, a warm breath from the dark mother cloud that hung beyond the main range. Eaves dripped, snow shriveled, and puddles formed in barnyard and path. Almost, a person could see trees taking heart, almost feel the covered life of grass and flowers stirring. "Not at least one day in any month in Montana that a man won't be warm enough in his shirt sleeves," Benton had said as he kicked off his muddy overshoes at the doorway. "Old-timers will bet you on that." So — a night and a day of renewal, of pinched expectation let loose.

And then again the still cold. Though not so severe as before, it was far below freezing. Ice burdened or slicked everything — trees, bushes, barnyard, walks, roadway and snowdrifts. Against the risk of slips and falls Benton wound strips of gunny sacks over his overshoes. Mary Jess skated to school, complaining only that the skate blades cut through the crusted drifts.

"Some snow would make better footing," Benton said, after reporting that old Mrs. Emerson had fallen that day and probably fractured her hip. They sat by the stove in the living room, having these moments alone now that Mary Jess had kissed them good night and gone on to bed. He had a book in his hand, some philosophical work by a writer named Bergson which seemed not to engage him. She was darning. Cold-weather trampings were hard on socks. "But, as they say," he went on, "the backbone of winter seems to be broken.

Twenty-six above today and likely to go . . . Now what in the devil?"

Over his words had sounded a screaming. While they listened, it drew closer, went past the side of the house and joined with a banging at the back door.

Benton got up, darkly frowning, and made for the kitchen, pulling light cords as he went. She followed.

The door opened on a woman. "Help! Help!" she cried. "He's going to kill me."

Benton stood silent and stolid.

The woman, May could tell now, was Mrs. Pike, their creek-bottom neighbor. She wore a torn, man's mackinaw and a tam-o'-shanter, pulled down. From underneath it her hair straggled wild.

"He'll be comin'. Please help me." Her face looked all mouth, all mouth under rolling, red marbles of eyes.

Benton asked in his hard voice, "Who is coming?"

"My husband. He's drunk and he'll kill me."

On this forlorn and derelict woman, May had time to think, on this mean, born-to-be castoff had been loosed the blind furies, had been directed the visitations of gods angered with her for their original sin. She said, "Come in, Mrs. Pike."

Benton moved to block the door. "You're drunk yourself," he said.

"Let her come in, Benton."

"No. You can see she's drunk. She stinks of it. No."

Mrs. Pike's mouth opened and closed. Her eyes steadied and widened. They said good-bye to help. They wondered why. She wheeled around and started away.

May pushed Benton aside. "You — you — " she said and wrenched free from his grasping hand.

Outside, she hurried after the woman, calling, "Come back, Mrs. Pike. Please come back."

For an instant, before she slipped and fell, she thought Mrs. Pike hesitated.

She felt Benton's hands and arms on her. She could hear him saying, "Good God, Maysie! Merciful God!"

From behind her came, "Mother! Oh, Mother!"

28

DOCTOR CRABTREE waited just outside the bedroom, knowing he would be called soon enough. He had done all he could, all he knew how to do, but where was the consolation when his best was not good enough? What comfort was it that he had saved the boy baby? It was the new life that counted, the pulpit wiseacres said, voting in favor of unproven life against proven. It was a good bet that the baby, grown up, would not be the equal of May Collingsworth. So much for doctrine.

Through the open door came small sounds of movement and murmurings of lost hope still clung to. Hope when all hope was done. A city hospital might have been able to save her. Probably not, but the possibility couldn't be dodged. Neither could the fact be erased that he was what he was — a cow-country sawbones, a defensive bush doctor who kept telling himself that what she had needed was not new methods or medicines but a new body.

A thin cry sounded from another bedroom; but the baby was as healthy as any pup and attended by a wet nurse he himself had found finally. No trouble there.

He sat down and, waiting, took idle notice of the worn furnishings, the carpet with paths trodden in it, the despairing wallpaper, the sofa molded by rumps. A teacher's salary didn't allow luxuries, unless books were indulgences.

The bedroom voices grew into words, grew, as he had expected they would, into a last conversation that deceived hearts. So often some final energy, some terminal assertion of life came to the dying. He sat without moving. He had better stay within hearing, but these moments were for the family alone.

Now Mrs. Collingsworth's voice came to him, thin but clear. "Is the baby all right?"

"Fine. Just fine." The answer was Collingsworth's, charged with meant cheer.

"Let's name him Benton. Now."

"Well, sure, but later you can think about that."

"No. Not later, Benton." For an instant she was silent. "I'm not afraid, Benton."

"Mother, you mustn't!" Mary Jess couldn't make her voice hearty.

"You take good care of your father, dear. He will of you. And the baby. Baby Benton."

"Mother! Don't say good-bye!"

"Don't grieve. I'm not afraid." The voice was failing now. It ended with a little cry. "Oh, Benton, whatever will you do?"

"Don't worry yourself. You're going —"

The words were shut off, shut off by a silence that Crabtree comprehended before Collingsworth called out, "Doctor! Doctor!"

He went in and made sure and nodded the small, professional nod he disliked. "I'm sorry."

Mary Jess kissed her mother's brow, leaving tears there, and fled from the room as if from the pervading evil of death. Collingsworth's face was bleak, without blood, set forever against the final adversity. He sat down dumbly and reached for the dead hand of his wife.

"Excuse me," Crabtree said, and pulled up the sheet. Collingsworth held to the hand outside it. "I'd best call the undertaker, I think."

Collingsworth let go the hand and lurched from his chair. He seized Crabtree's lapels. "What of?" he demanded. "What of?"

"I hear you. The fall didn't help, I can tell you. It hurt and hastened delivery, but alone it wasn't the cause."

"Then what of?"

"Not any one thing. At last her heart just gave out."

Collingsworth shook him. It was as if he could shake out an acceptable diagnosis, as if, having got it, he could repair the irreparable. "That's no answer!"

Crabtree wrenched the hands from his coat. The goddam man wanted a goddam answer, an impossible definitive answer, and he wouldn't like what he got.

For an instant Crabtree debated. Was it angers in him, old and new, was it some wish to hurt that made him want to go on? Or was it a fierce reaching for truth, for disclosure of the unwelcome truth?

He asked, "How many children has your wife borne?"

"Four. Two died."

"How many miscarriages?"

"Three, if you must know."

"I see. Now how many wives has your father had?"

"The devil with this!"

"You wanted an answer. How many?"

"Three. No divorces. Two died."

"That's all." Crabtree turned and walked toward the door.

"That's all?" There seemed to be some wonderment, some little discernment in Collingsworth's tone.

"If that isn't enough, I'll tell you more." He hated to say it but had to somehow. He hated to remember but did. He said, "I wore out one wife myself."

Without watching or waiting for reaction he went through the door. Mary Jess, forlorn as a sick and lost pullet, stood near the entrance. He hoped she hadn't heard.

29

Dunc McDonald drove a Hudson. It was a better-than-fair machine, Ewing thought as they rolled toward Arfive. And Dunc could afford it, being by nature a prudent man with a part interest, rightfully earned, in the ranch.

The chains kept banging the fenders, making talk difficult, supposing a man wanted to talk. The headlights poked at the dark, finding the track if not much besides. The night closed them in, the windy night that huffed drafts of chill inside the car.

No complaint, though. They'd be there soon, sooner than a buggy could make it on an untroubled day. Whatever could be said for horse travel, it was winking out and the horse along with it — which was bad or good or both, depending on a man's years and how were his bowels at the moment. Sure, horses were in demand now, but for English and French cavalry and the requirements of war. Those foreigners would settle down after a while, recall their commission men, and bang would go bangtails. If a person could see far enough, he might see a day when ranch work would be mechanized — hay cut and put up and crops harvested all by machine — and horses used just for handling cattle. Saddle horses. So long, old Rex and old Babe, you're bound for the canners. But not his old

Rexes and Babes. Long service deserved more than a shooting gallery.

McDonald came to a stop in front of Eva Fox's cafe. "Sure you won't have a bite?" Ewing asked before he got out.

"And have my wife fussing? When a late supper will be waiting?" McDonald quit shaking his head. "I'll go pay my respects. A good woman. A good mon."

"All right. Then you'll take me out to pay mine? Half-hour or so. I'll wait in front of the Arfive House. Tell Julie I'll be along."

For a moment, after McDonald had gone, Ewing stood on the sidewalk. The town was dark save for a scattering of lights that seemed to wave in the wind. The damn wind, chill and unkind to grief. The bare cottonwoods clacked in it under a sky of no promise. If heaven was up there, it was one hell of a ways, one hell of a ways from a dead and fine lady who would be taken to a screaming slope of graveyard day after tomorrow.

Bless Julie and the spirit that shone in her no matter what. She had driven in early to the Collingsworth house. Tomorrow she would be there again, kind and competent, as soothing to grief as grief allowed. To the house she had taken a beef stew and two roast chickens, honest food as against the cakes and pies and frills that too many women seemed to consider appropriate to sorrow. Cookies for consolation!

He shook the wind off, or tried to, and went into the restaurant. It was warm and smelled of good food. And it was fairly busy. It was always fairly or very busy, depending. Eva had made herself a new reputation that shaded or superseded the old.

She met him just inside the door, saying, "Good evening, Mort. Let me take your wraps." He remembered her as the unabashed queen of a whorehouse. Now age and feminine art had given her the air and appearance of queenly propriety. She led him to a table. "I'll send you a waitress."

"No, Eva," he answered. "Just burn me a quick steak, if you got one that wouldn't smooth-mouth a coyote."

"A coyote would howl thanks for the one I'll pick out." As she turned, she asked, "And, Mort, don't leave without seeing me."

The steak was good enough. It was better than good, he supposed, though things on a man's mind dulled his taste, just as they made him indifferent to the words said around him and the greetings of people he knew. What say to the grief-stricken? What comfort give them? Not God knows best, that easy oil of persons themselves uneasy about coming exercises of heavenly wisdom. There was one best epitaph, fitting to old, young and in-between, the good and no-good and run of the herd. It was: Shit out of luck.

Eva took his money and made change. Then she handed him a package, saying, "You'll be going to the Collingsworths. Take this. Two poor loaves of bread but mine own."

"But, Eva —"

"You don't have to tell where it's from. Good night, Mort."

He hesitated out in the wind and then fought it across the street to the Arfive House and what had been Adlam's saloon. Adlam had heired money from an uncle somewhere, sold out and gone south, saying he was glad to be shut of his place. And he had made a special call on Collingsworth to tell him saloonkeeping was "the cursedest business on earth."

Cursedest or not, Adlam hadn't improved it by getting out. The place had no style anymore, Ewing thought as he entered. It was all noisy bullshit and dirt, and let a man go in for a quiet drink and some loving, blabbering drunk would drool spit down his neck.

"Hi-yu, Mort," a voice called from the crowd. The voice belonged to Les Carver, a here-and-there ranch hand he had hired and fired and maybe would hire again. No hard feelings.

As Ewing paused and sized up the customers, the voice sounded closer. "You know P. A. Pike." Les was pushing and pulling Pike along with him.

"Sure. How are you, Pike?"

Pike smiled for an answer. He appeared amiable and half-drunk. He had the slow look of a pet beef that on occasion might take a notion to butt.

Ewing started for the bar, but Les said, "Hold it, Mort. Pike has a story to tell. P. A. Pike has. Tell it, Pike."

"Aw, no, Les. Cut it out." Pike's tone seemed to speak some hazy amusement, some enjoyment of the story he shied off from telling.

"Too good to skip, so here goes," Les announced. He liked to spin yarns and did so with the flourishes and exaggerations that made some older cowpunchers famous. "Pike, you bust in if I don't get 'er right. Mort, it's like this. Pike, he got a case of the jimmies a couple nights or so ago, and what he decided was he'd slice up his wife."

"Naw. Naw," Pike put in. "It wasn't a real butcherin' I had in my head. Just a little brand, like. But I was loco, all right."

"But that wife of his," Les went on, "she didn't aim to be carved on, and she's half-fox and all she-wolf."

"You got it right there," Pike said.

Three other men had gathered around to hear, Ewing supposed, what to them was a told story already.

Les went on, using gestures as befitted the increase in audience. "So that missus of Pike's, after he had chased her awhile and got winded, she snuck around and somewhere got hold of a hayfork. Meanwhile, Pike, here, had decided to sleep on his slicin', thinkin' a little nap never hurt nobody. But it sure God hurt him."

"Show me someone as can stand up to a pitchfork," Pike said, his face serious.

"First jab," Les continued, "and Pike was out of the window and her after him, fleet of foot, as they say, anyhow fleet enough that old Pike, when he lagged in the collar, got encouraged to step right along. They tell me hell heard him holler."

Pike nodded. "She's fast."

Someone said, "Go on."

"It don't matter now," Pike answered, smiling again. "Me and the wife, we done made up."

"We got to tie it up," Les said, proceeding no doubt to a suitable finish. "Pike, can you sit down?"

"On one cheek, kind of." The grin was still amiable.

"So, gents," Les said, swinging his hands out, "you can savvy why he's now P. A. Pike. The P is for Polka Dot, the A is for Ass. Polka Dot Ass Pike. If that ain't a tasty mouthful. Shake hands, Pike."

They were still laughing, Pike loud as any, when Ewing went to the bar and bought half a pint of Old Crow.

Outside, McDonald was waiting for him. He got in the Hudson and asked, "Well, Dunc?"

McDonald waited to answer until he had the car moving. "What a mon would expect. Friends coming and going. Food enough to founder the town. Mr. Collingsworth doesn't say much or mix much. The girl, either."

"He wouldn't."

"Julie smooths things. Without her?" McDonald fell silent.

The Collingsworth house was lit up. Three automobiles were ranked in front of it and more at one side. A man and a woman were emerging, their condolences said. Probably they had taken sweets in and were bringing self-esteem out. Nothing like a death to prove the good in people.

"Thanks, Dunc," Ewing said. "I'll sneak around to the back."

"Here. You're forgetting your parcel."

Ewing took it and watched McDonald roll away, bound for the ranch and late supper.

He let himself through the kitchen door without knocking. Collingsworth was there, so was Mary Jess and so was Julie, all on their feet. Except for Julie, he thought, it was as if they were in retreat, as if they were forted up for a last stand. He said, "Evening to you all."

"Hello, Mort," Julie answered. She didn't come to embrace him, maybe thinking an embrace out of place in the light of Collingsworth's loss. But in the instant before more was said, it recurred to him that his sour thoughts disappeared or were put where they belonged in the presence of Julie. He laid the parcel on a counter.

Collingsworth looked as if he saw, without flinching, the end of the world. "Stoic" was the right word. He took Ewing's hand. Sometimes the hand could say more than the mouth. The mouth said, "Yes, Mort."

Mary Jess was silent. For the time being, at least, her tears had dried up, leaving swollen the banks of her eyes.

"The wind bites you tonight," Ewing said, and wished that he hadn't. For bad times even the weather wasn't a safe enough subject if it was bad.

One of the ladies — Mrs. Tyler from the Methodist church — bustled in from the dining room. "Can't I fix you a plate, Mr. Collingsworth?" she asked. "You've hardly eaten a thing, and the table's just loaded with the best food."

"Thank you. No."

"What about you, Mary Jess?"

Mary Jess shook her head.

Mrs. Tyler went out, shaking hers.

Collingsworth moved over and closed the door she'd left open, closed it against the voices that came in and the sympathizers who might.

Julie's gaze went to the wrapped bread, but she didn't ask about it, no doubt thinking that in good time it would be explained. "I think I had better go in," she said then. She went to the door, opened it and carefully closed it after her.

She was back in a few minutes, back before Ewing could single out a subject for talk. They had just stood there while she was gone, dumb as dust to dust, except that Collingsworth had suggested he sit himself down.

"The women are seeing to things," Julie said now with a nod. "But, Mr. Collingsworth, some people you haven't seen would like to see you. Would you care to go in?"

"No. I wouldn't care to." Collingsworth turned his back on Julie and stepped to the west window and stared at the pane. It couldn't be that he saw into the night, across the blown fields, beyond the fringed river to the starched rock of the mountains.

Julie threw a quick look at Ewing and said, "I'll explain."

"Wait," Ewing asked. "Prof, not my business, but I'd give another thought to it. You and Mary Jess both. You see, well —" Only lame words came to him and he limped out with them. "They're friends and well meanin'."

"So many people mean well," Collingsworth answered, his eyes still fixed on the window. His voice seemed to come from far off, or down deep under his throat. He made a slow swing around to face Ewing. "It isn't worth it," he said in the same tone. "Wasn't and isn't and won't be."

"Now how's that? What isn't, Prof?"

"Nothing."

Ewing pulled in a long breath. "Prof," he said, trying for the right tone, trying for the truth that sounded bogus so often, "now's no time for a tally. You'll count better later. You don't realize it, you can't realize it in this sorry time, but there's many a man and a woman in debt to you, those as have graduated under you, those as have seen their own graduate, those as are counting on sending their young ones to you. They own up to it, and glad to, all over the county. It's big thanks you've earned, yes, you and your May, who wouldn't want you talking discouraged."

He might have been speaking to a damn cliff face, a shaped rock, a deaf-dummy. He might have been listening for echoes that no yelling could raise.

"Try seeing it true, Prof. You've done more'n a heap of good for the county and town, and you got more to do. And it's not just students and parents that side you. I couldn't name 'em all, Lord knows, but count just a few that come quick to mind. Count the Stuart Alexanders, count old Mr. McLaine though he's gone now. Count Jay Ross and Doc Crabtree —"

The deaf-dummy could say in a dead voice, "Doctor Crabtree?"

"Sure thing. And count me and Julie, even if she did graduate under you. Count Smoky Moreau, who can't read, I guess, but is plenty savvy. And didn't Fatty Adlam come see you just to allow you were right?"

An audience without ears, without interest, without life! Ewing slapped his hand on the parcel. "Why, damn it, man, even Eva Fox, she made this bread for you."

"Throw it out!" And old, hard force had come into Collingsworth's voice. Beyond grief, Ewing thought, lived the entrail conviction. "Throw it out!"

"No, Father, no!" The cry came from Mary Jess. "Can't you ever see? Won't you ever know?" While Ewing watched, hate came on the young face, such a torn, grieving hate as unsteadied a man. "You're small and you're mean," the girl cried on. "Plain, simple mean. Poor Mother!"

Collingsworth stepped back as if physically battered. His eyes went to the floor and lifted slowly to Mary Jess. They looked blank with hurt. He said, "Yes, sweetheart," and stood without moving.

Now, in the young face, along with the hate, there appeared such a flooding of love, of tortured love, that Ewing had to turn his gaze down. He heard Mary Jess cry, "Father! Father!" When he looked up, they were in each other's arms, held tight in their grief. He had never expected to hear Collingsworth sob.

He left the bread on the counter. After a second's thought, he added the half pint. If there was a time for everything, now was Collingsworth's time for a drink. He motioned to Julie.

❧

"Don't see any antelopes along the road anymore," Ewing said as he steered the Reo toward home. "Nor anywheres else. The homesteaders poached 'em. Had to or croak."

"That's not what you're thinking about," Julie answered. He could see her profile, a fine, lovely line in the dark.

"Just part of it," he said. "Another is if a man lives long enough, he sees a lot of sons of bitches go down. Merc Marsh squeezed his heart dead squeezing for profits. Nick Brudd, I hear, has softening of the brain, which is short for paresis, which is short for long syphilis. There's more. So I count the good against the bad and come out maybe even."

"You're an unconscious genius, Mort. It was a sure stroke, that mentioning where the bread came from."

"Even fools can have luck."

"Subject closed then, you genius. I wonder what poor Mr. Collingsworth will do. You know, with the baby and all."

"I been thinking on it. I even been thinking there's nothing to keep us from taking care of it, if that's right with you."

"For a while?"

"Long as need be, I reckon."

She moved closer to him. Her gloved hand stroked his on the steering wheel. "Of course, Mort," she said, "but can you stand it?" She paused and added in the softest of tones, "The Collingsworth baby, in time, would make two."

The words milled around in his head and lined out.

"Well, I'll be —" The voice wasn't his. A high leap of blood strangled it. "Crucified Jesus!"